When a Man's a Man

Harold Bell Wright

ÆGYPAN PRESS

1916

Text from the Grosset & Dunlap (New York) edition.

When a Man's a Man
A publication of
ÆGYPAN PRESS
www.aegypan.com

When a Man's a Man

Other books by Harold Bell Wright:

Helen of the Old House
That Printer of Udell's
The Calling of Dan Matthews
The Re-Creation of Brian Kent
The Shepherd of the Hills
The Winning of Barbara Worth
Their Yesterdays
When a Man's a Man

What though on hamely fare we dine,
   Wear hoddin grey, an' a' that?
Gie fools their silks, and knaves their wine —
   A man's a man for a' that.
For a' that, an' a' that,
   Their tinsel show, an' a' that,
The honest man, tho' e'er sae poor,
   Is king o' men for a' that.

Ye see yon birkie ca'd 'a lord,'
   Wha struts, an' stares, an' a' that?
Tho' hundreds worship at his word,
   He's but a cuif for a' that.
For a' that, an' a' that,
   His ribband, star, an' a' that,
The man o' independent mind,
   He looks an' laughs at a' that.

— Robert Burns, from "Is There for Honest Poverty"

To my sons
GILBERT AND PAUL NORMAN
THIS STORY OF MANHOOD
IS AFFECTIONATELY DEDICATED
BY THEIR FATHER.

Acknowledgment

*I*t is fitting that I should here express my indebtedness to those Williamson Valley friends who in the kindness of their hearts made this story possible.

To Mr. George A. Carter, who so generously introduced me to the scenes described in these pages, and who, on the Pot-Hook-S ranch, gave to my family one of the most delightful summers we have ever enjoyed; to Mr. J.H. Stephens and his family, who so cordially welcomed me at rodeo time; to Mr. and Mrs. Joe Contreras, for their kindly hospitality; to Mr. and Mrs. J.W. Stewart, who, while this story was first in the making, made me so much at home in the Cross-Triangle home-ranch; to Mr. J.W. Cook, my constant companion, helpful guide, patient teacher and tactful sponsor, who, with his charming wife, made his home mine; to Mr. and Mrs. Herbert N. Cook, and to the many other cattlemen and cowboys, with whom, on the range, in the rodeos, in the wild horse chase about Toohey, after outlaw cattle in Granite Basin, in the corrals and pastures, I rode and worked and lived, my gratitude is more than I can put in words. Truer friends or better companions than these great-hearted, outspoken, hardy riders, no man could have. If my story in any degree wins the approval of these, my comrades of ranch and range. I shall be proud and happy.

— H.B.W.
"Camp Hole-in-the-Mountain"
Near Tucson, Arizona
April 29, 1916

Chapter I
AFTER THE CELEBRATION

There is a land where a man, to live, must be a man. It is a land of granite and marble and porphyry and gold — and a man's strength must be as the strength of the primeval hills. It is a land of oaks and cedars and pines — and a man's mental grace must be as the grace of the untamed trees. It is a land of far-arched and unstained skies, where the wind sweeps free and untainted, and the atmosphere is the atmosphere of those places that remain as God made them — and a man's soul must be as the unstained skies, the unburdened wind, and the untainted atmosphere. It is a land of wide mesas, of wild, rolling pastures and broad, untilled, valley meadows — and a man's freedom must be that freedom which is not bounded by the fences of a too weak and timid conventionalism.

In this land every man is — by divine right — his own king; he is his own jury, his own counsel, his own judge, and — if it must be — his own executioner. And in this land where a man, to live, must be a man, a woman, if she be not a woman, must surely perish.

This is the story of a man who regained that which in his youth had been lost to him; and of how, even when he had recovered that which had been taken from him, he still paid the price of his loss. It is the story of a woman who was saved from herself; and of how she was led to hold fast to those things, the loss of which cost the man so great a price.

The story, as I have put it down here, begins at Prescott, Arizona, on the day following the annual Fourth-of-July celebration in one of those far-western years that saw the passing of the Indian and the coming of the automobile.

The man was walking along one of the few roads that lead out from the little city, through the mountain gaps and passes, to the wide, unfenced ranges, and to the lonely scattered ranches on the creeks and flats and valleys of the great open country that lies beyond.

From the fact that he was walking in that land where the distances are such that men most commonly ride, and from the many marks that environment and training leave upon us all, it was evident that the pedestrian was a stranger. He was a man in the prime of young manhood – tall and exceedingly well proportioned – and as he went forward along the dusty road he bore himself with the unconscious air of one more accustomed to crowded streets than to that rude and unpaved highway. His clothing bore the unmistakable stamp of a tailor of rank. His person was groomed with that nicety of detail that is permitted only to those who possess both means and leisure, as well as taste. It was evident, too, from his movement and bearing, that he had not sought the mile-high atmosphere of Prescott with the hope that it holds out to those in need of health. But, still, there was a something about him that suggested a lack of the manly vigor and strength that should have been his.

A student of men would have said that Nature made this man to be in physical strength and spiritual prowess, a comrade and leader of men – a man's man – a man among men. The same student, looking more closely, might have added that in some way – through some cruel trick of fortune – this man had been cheated of his birthright.

The day was still young when the stranger gained the top of the first hill where the road turns to make its steep and winding way down through scattered pines and scrub oak to the Burnt Ranch.

Behind him the little city – so picturesque in its mountain basin, with the wild, unfenced land coming down to its very dooryards – was slowly awakening after the last mad night of its celebration. The tents of the tawdry shows that had tempted the crowds with vulgar indecencies, and the booths that had sheltered the petty games of chance where loud-voiced criers had persuaded the multitude with the hope of winning a worthless bauble or a tinsel toy, were being cleared away from the borders of the plaza, the beauty of which their presence had marred. In the plaza itself – which is the heart of the town, and is usually kept with much pride and care – the bronze statue of the vigorous Rough Rider Bucky O'Neil and his spirited charger seemed pathetically out of place among the litter of colored confetti and exploded fireworks, and the refuse from various "treats" and lunches left by the celebrating citizens and their guests. The flags and bunting that from window and roof and pole and doorway had given the day its gay note of color hung faded and listless, as though, spent with their gaiety, and mutely conscious that the spirit and purpose of their gladness was past, they waited the hand that would remove them to the ash barrel and the rubbish heap.

Pausing, the man turned to look back.

For some minutes he stood as one who, while determined upon a certain course, yet hesitates — reluctant and regretful — at the beginning of his venture. Then he went on; walking with a certain reckless swing, as though, in ignorance of that land toward which he had set his face, he still resolutely turned his back upon that which lay behind. It was as though, for this man, too, the gala day, with its tinseled bravery and its confetti spirit, was of the past.

A short way down the hill the man stopped again. This time to stand half turned, with his head in a listening attitude. The sound of a vehicle approaching from the way whence he had come had reached his ear.

As the noise of wheels and hoofs grew louder a strange expression of mingled uncertainty, determination, and something very like fear came over his face. He started forward, hesitated, looked back, then turned doubtfully toward the thinly wooded mountain side. Then, with tardy decision he left the road and disappeared behind a clump of oak bushes, an instant before a team and buckboard rounded the turn and appeared in full view.

An unmistakable cattleman — grizzly-haired, square-shouldered and substantial — was driving the wild looking team. Beside him sat a motherly woman and a little boy.

As they passed the clump of bushes the near horse of the half-broken pair gave a catlike bound to the right against his tracemate. A second jump followed the first with flashlike quickness; and this time the frightened animal was accompanied by his companion, who, not knowing what it was all about, jumped on general principles. But, quick as they were, the strength of the driver's skillful arms met their weight on the reins and forced them to keep the road.

"You blamed fools" — the driver chided good-naturedly, as they plunged ahead — "been raised on a cow ranch to get scared at a calf in the brush!"

Very slowly the stranger came from behind the bushes. Cautiously he returned to the road. His fine lips curled in a curious mocking smile. But it was himself that he mocked, for there was a look in his dark eyes that gave to his naturally strong face an almost pathetic expression of self-depreciation and shame.

As the pedestrian crossed the creek at the Burnt Ranch, Joe Conley, leading a horse by a riata which was looped as it had fallen about the animal's neck, came through the big corral gate across the road from the house. At the barn Joe disappeared through the small door of the saddle room, the coil of the riata still in his hand, thus compelling his mount to await his return.

At sight of the cowboy the stranger again paused and stood hesitating in indecision. But as Joe reappeared from the barn with bridle, saddle blanket and saddle in hand, the man went reluctantly forward as though prompted by some necessity.

"Good morning!" said the stranger, courteously, and his voice was the voice that fitted his dress and bearing, while his face was now the carefully schooled countenance of a man world-trained and well-poised.

With a quick estimating glance Joe returned the stranger's greeting and, dropping the saddle and blanket on the ground, approached his horse's head. Instantly the animal sprang back, with head high and eyes defiant; but there was no escape, for the rawhide riata was still securely held by his master. There was a short, sharp scuffle that sent the gravel by the roadside flying – the controlling bit was between the reluctant teeth – and the cowboy, who had silently taken the horse's objection as a matter of course, adjusted the blanket, and with the easy skill of long practice swung the heavy saddle to its place.

As the cowboy caught the dangling cinch, and with a deft hand tucked the latigo strap through the ring and drew it tight, there was a look of almost pathetic wistfulness on the watching stranger's face – a look of wistfulness and admiration and envy.

Dropping the stirrup, Joe again faced the stranger, this time inquiringly, with that bold, straightforward look so characteristic of his kind.

And now, when the man spoke, his voice had a curious note, as if the speaker had lost a little of his poise. It was almost a note of apology, and again in his eyes there was that pitiful look of self-depreciation and shame.

"Pardon me," he said, "but will you tell me, please, am I right that this is the road to the Williamson Valley?"

The stranger's manner and voice were in such contrast to his general appearance that the cowboy frankly looked his wonder as he answered courteously, "Yes, sir."

"And it will take me direct to the Cross-Triangle Ranch?"

"If you keep straight ahead across the valley, it will. If you take the right-hand fork on the ridge above the goat ranch, it will take you to Simmons. There's a road from Simmons to the Cross-Triangle on the far side of the valley, though. You can see the valley and the Cross-Triangle home ranch from the top of the Divide."

"Thank you."

The stranger was turning to go when the man in the blue jumper and fringed leather chaps spoke again, curiously.

"The Dean with Stella and Little Billy passed in the buckboard less than an hour ago, on their way home from the celebration. Funny they didn't pick you up, if you're goin' there!"

The other paused questioningly. "The Dean?"

The cowboy smiled. "Mr. Baldwin, the owner of the Cross-Triangle, you know."

"Oh!" The stranger was clearly embarrassed. Perhaps he was thinking of that clump of bushes on the mountain side.

Joe, loosing his riata from the horse's neck, and coiling it carefully, considered a moment. Then: "You ain't goin' to walk to the Cross-Triangle, be you?"

That self-mocking smile touched the man's lips; but there was a hint of decisive purpose in his voice as he answered, "Oh, yes."

Again the cowboy frankly measured the stranger. Then he moved toward the corral gate, the coiled riata in one hand, the bridle rein in the other. "I'll catch up a horse for you," he said in a matter-of-fact tone, as if reaching a decision.

The other spoke hastily. "No, no, please don't trouble."

Joe paused curiously. "Any friend of Mr. Baldwin's is welcome to anything on the Burnt Ranch, Stranger."

"But I — ah — I — have never met Mr. Baldwin," explained the other lamely.

"Oh, that's all right," returned the cowboy heartily. "You're a-goin' to, an' that's the same thing." Again he started toward the gate.

"But I — pardon me — you are very kind — but I — I prefer to walk."

Once more Joe halted, a puzzled expression on his tanned and weather-beaten face. "I suppose you know it's some walk," he suggested doubtfully, as if the man's ignorance were the only possible solution of his unheard-of assertion.

"So I understand. But it will be good for me. Really, I prefer to walk."

Without a word the cowboy turned back to his horse, and proceeded methodically to tie the coiled riata in its place on the saddle. Then, without a glance toward the stranger who stood watching him in embarrassed silence, he threw the bridle reins over his horse's head, gripped the saddle horn and swung to his seat, reining his horse away from the man beside the road.

The stranger, thus abruptly dismissed, moved hurriedly away.

Halfway to the creek the cowboy checked his horse and looked back at the pedestrian as the latter was making his way under the pines and up the hill. When the man had disappeared over the crest of the hill, the cowboy muttered a bewildered something, and, touching his horse with the spurs, loped away, as if dismissing a problem too complex for his simple mind.

All that day the stranger followed the dusty, unfenced road. Over his head the wide, bright sky was without a cloud to break its vast expanse. On the great, open range of mountain, flat and valley the cattle lay quietly in the shade of oak or walnut or cedar, or, with slow, listless movement, sought the watering places to slake their thirst. The wild things retreated to their secret hiding places in rocky den and leafy thicket to await the cool of the evening hunting hour. The very air was motionless, as if the never-tired wind itself drowsed indolently.

And alone in the hushed bigness of that land the man walked with his thoughts — brooding, perhaps, over whatever it was that had so strangely placed him there — dreaming, it may be, over that which might have been, or that which yet might be — viewing with questioning, wondering, half-fearful eyes the mighty, untamed scenes that met his eye on every hand. Nor did anyone see him, for at every sound of approaching horse or vehicle he went aside from the highway to hide in the bushes or behind convenient rocks. And always when he came from his hiding place to resume his journey that odd smile of self-mockery was on his face.

At noon he rested for a little beside the road while he ate a meager sandwich that he took from the pocket of his coat. Then he pushed on again, with grim determination, deeper and deeper into the heart and life of that world which was, to him, so evidently new and strange. The afternoon was well spent when he made his way — wearily now, with drooping shoulders and dragging step — up the long slope of the Divide that marks the eastern boundary of the range about Williamson Valley.

At the summit, where the road turns sharply around a shoulder of the mountain and begins the steep descent on the other side of the ridge, he stopped. His tired form straightened. His face lighted with a look of wondering awe, and an involuntary exclamation came from his lips as his unaccustomed eyes swept the wide view that lay from his feet unrolled before him.

Under that sky, so unmatched in its clearness and depth of color, the land lay in all its variety of valley and forest and mesa and mountain — a scene unrivaled in the magnificence and grandeur of its beauty. Miles upon miles in the distance, across those primeval reaches, the faint blue peaks and domes and ridges of the mountains ranked — an uncounted sentinel host. The darker masses of the timbered hillsides, with the varying shades of pine and cedar, the lighter tints of oak brush and chaparral, the dun tones of the open grass lands, and the brighter note of the valley meadows' green were defined, blended and harmonized by the overlying haze with a delicacy exquisite beyond all human power to picture. And in the nearer distances, chief of that army of mountain peaks, and master of the many miles that lie within their circle, Granite Mountain, grey and grim, reared its mighty bulk of cliff and crag as if in supreme defiance of the changing years or the hand of humankind.

In the heart of that beautiful land upon which, from the summit of the Divide, the stranger looked with such rapt appreciation, lies Williamson Valley, a natural meadow of lush, dark green, native grass. And, had the man's eyes been trained to such distances, he might have distinguished in the blue haze the red roofs of the buildings of the Cross-Triangle Ranch.

For some time the man stood there, a lonely figure against the sky, peculiarly out of place in his careful garb of the cities. The schooled indifference of his face was broken. His self-depreciation and mockery were forgotten. His dark eyes glowed with the fire of excited anticipation – with hope and determined purpose. Then, with a quick movement, as though some ghost of the past had touched him on the shoulder, he looked back on the way he had come. And the light in his eyes went out in the gloom of painful memories. His countenance, unguarded because of his day of loneliness, grew dark with sadness and shame. It was as though he looked beyond the town he had left that morning, with its litter and refuse of yesterday's pleasure, to a life and a world of tawdry shams, wherein men give themselves to win by means fair or foul the tinsel baubles that are offered in the world's petty games of chance.

And yet, even as he looked back, there was in the man's face as much of longing as of regret. He seemed as one who, realizing that he had reached a point in his life journey – a divide, as it were – from which he could see two ways, was resolved to turn from the path he longed to follow and to take the road that appealed to him the least. As one enlisting to fight in a just and worthy cause might pause a moment, before taking the oath of service, to regret the ease and freedom he was about to surrender, so this man paused on the summit of the Divide.

Slowly, at last, in weariness of body and spirit, he stumbled a few feet aside from the road, and, sinking down upon a convenient rock, gave himself again to the contemplation of that scene which lay before him. And there was that in his movement now that seemed to tell of one who, in the grip of some bitter and disappointing experience, was yet being forced by something deep in his being to reach out in the strength of his manhood to take that which he had been denied.

Again the man's untrained eyes had failed to note that which would have first attracted the attention of one schooled in the land that lay about him. He had not seen a tiny moving speck on the road over which he had passed. A horseman was riding toward him.

Chapter II

ON THE DIVIDE

*H*ad the man on the Divide noticed the approaching horseman it would have been evident, even to one so unacquainted with the country as the stranger, that the rider belonged to that land of riders. While still at a distance too great for the eye to distinguish the details of fringed leather chaps, soft shirt, short jumper, sombrero, spurs and riata, no one could have mistaken the ease and grace of the cowboy who seemed so literally a part of his horse. His seat in the saddle was so secure, so easy, and his bearing so unaffected and natural, that every movement of the powerful animal he rode expressed itself rhythmically in his own lithe and sinewy body.

While the stranger sat wrapped in meditative thought, unheeding the approach of the rider, the horseman, coming on with a long, swinging lope, watched the motionless figure on the summit of the Divide with careful interest. As he drew nearer the cowboy pulled his horse down to a walk, and from under his broad hat brim regarded the stranger intently. He was within a few yards of the point where the man sat when the latter caught the sound of the horse's feet, and, with a quick, startled look over his shoulder, sprang up and started as if to escape. But it was too late, and, as though on second thought, he whirled about with a half defiant air to face the intruder.

The horseman stopped. He had not missed the significance of that hurried movement, and his right hand rested carelessly on his leather clad thigh, while his grey eyes were fixed boldly, inquiringly, almost challengingly, on the man he had so unintentionally surprised.

As he sat there on his horse, so alert, so ready, in his cowboy garb and trappings, against the background of Granite Mountain, with all its rugged, primeval strength, the rider made a striking picture of virile manhood. Of some years less than thirty, he was, perhaps, neither as tall nor as heavy as the stranger; but in spite of a certain boyish look on his smooth-shaven, deeply-bronzed face, he bore himself with the unmistakable air of a matured and self-reliant man. Every nerve and fiber of him seemed alive with that vital energy which is the true beauty and the glory of life.

The two men presented a striking contrast. Without question one was the proud and finished product of our most advanced civilization. It was as evident that the splendid manhood of the other had never been dwarfed by the weakening atmosphere of an overcultured, too conventional and too complex environment. The stranger with his carefully tailored clothing and his man-of-the-world face and bearing was as unlike this rider of the unfenced lands as a daintily groomed thoroughbred from the sheltered and guarded stables of fashion is unlike a wild, untamed stallion from the hills and ranges about Granite Mountain. Yet, unlike as they were, there was a something that marked them as kin. The man of the ranges and the man of the cities were, deep beneath the surface of their beings, as like as the spirited thoroughbred and the unbroken wild horse. The cowboy was all that the stranger might have been. The stranger was all that the cowboy, under like conditions, would have been.

As they silently faced each other it seemed for a moment that each instinctively recognized this kinship. Then into the dark eyes of the stranger — as when he had watched the cowboy at the Burnt Ranch — there came that look of wistful admiration and envy.

And at this, as if the man had somehow made himself known, the horseman relaxed his attitude of tense readiness. The hand that had held the bridle rein to command instant action of his horse, and the hand that had rested so near the rider's hip, came together on the saddle horn in careless ease, while a boyish smile of amusement broke over the young man's face.

That smile brought a flash of resentment into the eyes of the other and a flush of red darkened his untanned cheeks. A moment he stood; then with an air of haughty rebuke he deliberately turned his back, and, seating himself again, looked away over the landscape.

But the smiling cowboy did not move. For a moment as he regarded the stranger his shoulders shook with silent, contemptuous laughter;

then his face became grave, and he looked a little ashamed. The minutes passed, and still he sat there, quietly waiting.

Presently, as if yielding to the persistent, silent presence of the horseman, and submitting reluctantly to the intrusion, the other turned, and again the two who were so like and yet so unlike faced each other.

It was the stranger now who smiled. But it was a smile that caused the cowboy to become on the instant kindly considerate. Perhaps he remembered one of the Dean's favorite sayings: "Keep your eye on the man who laughs when he's hurt."

"Good evening!" said the stranger doubtfully, but with a hint of conscious superiority in his manner.

"Howdy!" returned the cowboy heartily, and in his deep voice was the kindliness that made him so loved by all who knew him. "Been having some trouble?"

"If I have, it is my own, sir," retorted the other coldly.

"Sure," returned the horseman gently, "and you're welcome to it. Every man has all he needs of his own, I reckon. But I didn't mean it that way; I meant your horse."

The stranger looked at him questioningly. "Beg pardon?" he said. "What?"

"I do not understand."

"Your horse — where is your horse?"

"Oh, yes! Certainly — of course — my horse — how stupid of me!" The tone of the man's answer was one of half apology, and he was smiling whimsically now as if at his own predicament, as he continued. "I have no horse. Really, you know, I wouldn't know what to do with one if I had it."

"You don't mean to say that you drifted all the way out here from Prescott on foot!" exclaimed the astonished cowboy.

The man on the ground looked up at the horseman, and in a droll tone that made the rider his friend, said, while he stretched his long legs painfully: "I like to walk. You see I — ah — fancied it would be good for me, don't you know."

The cowboy laughingly considered — trying, as he said afterward, to figure it out. It was clear that this tall stranger was not in search of health, nor did he show any of the distinguishing marks of the tourist. He certainly appeared to be a man of means. He could not be looking for work. He did not seem a suspicious character — quite the contrary — and yet — there was that significant hurried movement as if to escape when the horseman had surprised him. The etiquette of the country forbade a direct question, but —

"Yes," he agreed thoughtfully, "walking comes in handy sometimes. I don't take to it much myself, though." Then he added shrewdly, "You were at the celebration, I reckon."

The stranger's voice betrayed quick enthusiasm, but that odd wistfulness crept into his eyes again and he seemed to lose a little of his poise.

"Indeed I was," he said. "I never saw anything to compare with it. I've seen all kinds of athletic sports and contests and exhibitions, with circus performances and riding, and that sort of thing, you know, and I've read about such things, of course, but" — and his voice grew thoughtful — "that men ever actually did them — and all in the day's work, as you may say — I — I never dreamed that there *were* men like that in these days."

The cowboy shifted his weight uneasily in the saddle, while he regarded the man on the ground curiously. "She was sure a humdinger of a celebration," he admitted, "but as for the show part I've seen things happen when nobody was thinking anything about it that would make those stunts at Prescott look funny. The horse racing was pretty good, though," he finished, with suggestive emphasis.

The other did not miss the point of the suggestion. "I didn't bet on anything," he laughed.

"It's funny nobody picked you up on the road out here," the cowboy next offered pointedly. "The folks started home early this morning — and Jim Reid and his family passed me about an hour ago — they were in an automobile. The Simmons stage must have caught up with you somewhere."

The stranger's face flushed, and he seemed trying to find some answer.

The cowboy watched him curiously; then in a musing tone added the suggestion, "Some lonesome up here on foot."

"But there are times, you know," returned the other desperately, "when a man prefers to be alone."

The cowboy straightened in his saddle and lifted his reins. "Thanks," he said dryly, "I reckon I'd better be moving."

But the other spoke quickly. "I beg your pardon, Mr. Acton, I did not mean that for you."

The horseman dropped his hands again to the saddle horn, and resumed his lounging posture, thus tacitly accepting the apology. "You have the advantage of me," he said.

The stranger laughed. "Everyone knows that 'Wild Horse Phil' of the Cross-Triangle Ranch won the bronco-riding championship yesterday. I saw you ride."

Philip Acton's face showed boyish embarrassment.

The other continued, with his strange enthusiasm. "It was great work — wonderful! I never saw anything like it."

There was no mistaking the genuineness of his admiration, nor could he hide that wistful look in his eyes.

"Shucks!" said the cowboy uneasily. "I could pick a dozen of the boys in that outfit who can ride all around me. It was just my luck, that's all — I happened to draw an easy one."

"Easy!" ejaculated the stranger, seeing again in his mind the fighting, plunging, maddened, outlawed brute that this boy-faced man had mastered. "And I suppose catching and throwing those steers was easy, too?"

The cowboy was plainly wondering at the man's peculiar enthusiasm for these most commonplace things. "The roping? Why, that was no more than we're doing all the time."

"I don't mean the roping," returned the other, "I mean when you rode up beside one of those steers that was running at full speed, and caught him by the horns with your bare hands, and jumped from your saddle, and threw the beast over you, and then lay there with his horns pinning you down! You aren't doing that all the time, are you? You don't mean to tell me that such things as that are a part of your everyday work!"

"Oh, the bulldoggin'! Why, no," admitted Phil, with an embarrassed laugh, "that was just fun, you know."

The stranger stared at him, speechless. Fun! In the name of all that is most modern in civilization, what manner of men were these who did such things in fun! If this was their recreation, what must their work be!

"Do you mind my asking," he said wistfully, "how you learned to do such things?"

"Why, I don't know — we just do them, I reckon."

"And could anyone learn to ride as you ride, do you think?" The question came with marked eagerness.

"I don't see why not," answered the cowboy honestly.

The stranger shook his head doubtfully and looked away over the wild land where the shadows of the late afternoon were lengthening.

"Where are you going to stop tonight?" Phil Acton asked suddenly.

The stranger did not take his eyes from the view that seemed to hold for him such peculiar interest. "Really," he answered indifferently, "I had not thought of that."

"I should think you'd be thinking of it along about supper time, if you've walked from town since morning."

The stranger looked up with sudden interest; but the cowboy fancied that there was a touch of bitterness under the droll tone of his reply.

"Do you know, Mr. Acton, I have never been really hungry in my life. It might be interesting to try it once, don't you think?"

Phil Acton laughed, as he returned, "It might be interesting, all right, but I think I better tell you, just the same, that there's a ranch down yonder in the timber. It's nothing but a goat ranch, but I reckon they would take you in. It's too far to the Cross-Triangle for me to ask you there. You can see the buildings, though, from here."

The stranger sprang up in quick interest. "You can? The Cross-Triangle Ranch?"

"Sure," the cowboy smiled and pointed into the distance. "Those red spots over there are the roofs. Jim Reid's place — the Pot-Hook-S — is just this side of the meadows, and a little to the south. The old Acton homestead — where I was born — is in that bunch of cottonwoods, across the wash from the Cross-Triangle."

But strive as he might the stranger's eyes could discern no sign of human habitation in those vast reaches that lay before him.

"If you are ever over that way, drop in," said Phil cordially. "Mr. Baldwin will be glad to meet you."

"Do you really mean that?" questioned the other doubtfully.

"We don't say such things in this country if we don't mean them, Stranger," was the cool retort.

"Of course, I beg your pardon, Mr. Acton," came the confused reply. "I should like to see the ranch. I may — I will — That is, if I —" He stopped as if not knowing how to finish, and with a gesture of hopelessness turned away to stand silently looking back toward the town, while his face was dark with painful memories, and his lips curved in that mirthless, self-mocking smile.

And Philip Acton, seeing, felt suddenly that he had rudely intruded upon the privacy of one who had sought the solitude of that lonely place to hide the hurt of some bitter experience. A certain native gentleness made the man of the ranges understand that this stranger was face to face with some crisis in his life — that he was passing through one of those trials through which a man must pass alone. Had it been possible the cowboy would have apologized. But that would have been an added unkindness. Lifting the reins and sitting erect in the saddle, he said indifferently, "Well, I must be moving. I take a short cut here. So long! Better make it on down to the goat ranch — it's not far."

He touched his horse with the spur and the animal sprang away.

"Good-bye!" called the stranger, and that wistful look was in his eyes as the rider swung his horse aside from the road, plunged down the mountain side, and dashed away through the brush and over the rocks with reckless speed. With a low exclamation of wondering admiration, the man climbed hastily to a higher point, and from there watched until horse and rider, taking a steeper declivity without checking their break-neck course, dropped from sight in a cloud of dust. The faint sound of the sliding rocks and gravel dislodged by the flying feet died away; the cloud of dust dissolved in the thin air. The stranger looked away into the blue distance in another vain attempt to see the red spots that marked the Cross-Triangle Ranch.

Slowly the man returned to his seat on the rock. The long shadows of Granite Mountain crept out from the base of the cliffs farther and farther over the country below. The blue of the distant hills changed to mauve with deeper masses of purple in the shadows where the canyons are. The lonely figure on the summit of the Divide did not move.

The sun hid itself behind the line of mountains, and the blue of the sky in the west changed slowly to gold against which the peaks and domes and points were silhouetted as if cut by a graver's tool, and the bold cliffs and battlements of old Granite grew coldly grey in the gloom. As the night came on and the details of its structure were lost, the mountain, to the watching man on the Divide, assumed the appearance of a mighty fortress — a fortress, he thought, to which a generation of men might retreat from a civilization that threatened them with destruction; and once more the man faced back the way he had come.

The faraway cities were already in the blaze of their own artificial lights — lights valued not for their power to make men see, but for their power to dazzle, attract and intoxicate — lights that permitted no kindly dusk at eventide wherein a man might rest from his day's work — a quiet hour; lights that revealed squalid shame and tinsel show — lights that hid the stars. The man on the Divide lifted his face to the stars that now in the wide-arched sky were gathering in such unnumbered multitudes to keep their sentinel watch over the world below.

The cool evening wind came whispering over the lonely land, and all the furred and winged creatures of the night stole from their dark hiding places into the gloom which is the beginning of their day. A coyote crept stealthily past in the dark and from the mountain side below came the weird, ghostly call of its mate. An owl drifted by on silent wings. Night birds chirped in the chaparral. A fox barked on the ridge above. The shadowy form of a bat flitted here and there. From somewhere in the distance a bull bellowed his deep-voiced challenge.

Suddenly the man on the summit of the Divide sprang to his feet and, with a gesture that had he not been so alone might have seemed affectedly dramatic, stretched out his arms in an attitude of wistful longing while his lips moved as if, again and again, he whispered a name.

Chapter III

IN THE BIG PASTURE

*I*n the Williamson Valley country the spring round-up, or "rodeo," as it is called in Arizona, and the shipping are well over by the last of June. During the long summer weeks, until the beginning of the fall rodeo in September, there is little for the riders to do. The cattle roam free on the open ranges, while calves grow into yearlings, yearlings become two-year-olds, and two-year-olds mature for the market. On the Cross-Triangle and similar ranches, three or four of the steadier year-round hands only are held. These repair and build fences, visit the watering places, brand an occasional calf that somehow has managed to escape the dragnet of the rodeo, and with "dope bottle" ever at hand doctor such animals as are afflicted with screwworms. It is during these weeks, too, that the horses are broken; for, with the hard and dangerous work of the fall and spring months, there is always need for fresh mounts.

The horses of the Cross-Triangle were never permitted to run on the open range. Because the leaders of the numerous bands of wild horses that roamed over the country about Granite Mountain were always ambitious to gain recruits for their harems from their civilized neighbors, the freedom of the ranch horses was limited by the fences of a four-thousand-acre pasture. But within these miles of barbed wire boundaries the brood mares with their growing progeny lived as free and untamed as their wild cousins on the unfenced lands about them. The colts, except for one painful experience, when they were roped and branded, from the day of their birth until they were ready to be broken were never handled.

On the morning following his meeting with the stranger on the Divide Phil Acton, with two of his cowboy helpers, rode out to the big pasture to bring in the band.

The owner of the Cross-Triangle always declared that Phil was intimately acquainted with every individual horse and head of stock between the Divide and Camp Wood Mountain, and from Skull Valley to the Big Chino. In moments of enthusiasm the Dean even maintained stoutly that his young foreman knew as well every coyote, fox, badger, deer, antelope, mountain lion, bobcat and wild horse that had home or hunting ground in the country over which the lad had ridden since his babyhood. Certain it is that "Wild Horse Phil," as he was called by admiring friends — for reasons which you shall hear — loved this work and life to which he was born. Every feature of that wild land, from lonely mountain peak to hidden canyon spring, was as familiar to him as the streets and buildings of a man's home city are well known to the one reared among them. And as he rode that morning with his comrades to the day's work the young man felt keenly the call of the primitive, unspoiled life that throbbed with such vital strength about him. He could not have put that which he felt into words; he was not even conscious of the forces that so moved him; he only knew that he was glad.

The days of the celebration at Prescott had been enjoyable days. To meet old friends and comrades; to ride with them in the contests that all true men of his kind love; to compare experiences and exchange news and gossip with widely separated neighbors — had been a pleasure. But the curious crowds of strangers; the throngs of sightseers from the, to him, unknown world of cities, who had regarded him as they might have viewed some rare and little-known creature in a menagerie, and the brazen presence of those unclean parasites and harpies that prey always upon such occasions had oppressed and disgusted him until he was glad to escape again to the clean freedom, the pure vitality and the unspoiled spirit of his everyday life and environment. In an overflow of sheer physical and spiritual energy he lifted his horse into a run and with a shrill cowboy yell challenged his companions to a wild race to the pasture gate.

It was some time after noon when Phil checked his horse near the ruins of an old Indian lookout on the top of Black Hill. Below, in the open land above Deep Wash, he could see his cowboy companions working the band of horses that had been gathered slowly toward the narrow pass that at the eastern end of Black Hill leads through to the flats at the upper end of the big meadows, and so to the gate and to the way they would follow to the corral. It was Phil's purpose to ride across Black Hill down the western and northern slope, through the cedar timber, and, picking up any horses that might be ranging there, join the others at the gate. In the meanwhile there was time for a few minutes rest. Dismounting, he loosed the girths and lifted saddle and blanket from Hobson's steaming back. Then, while the good horse, wearied with the hard riding and the steep climb up the mountain side, stood quietly in the shade of a cedar his master, stretched on the ground near by, idly scanned the world that lay below and about them.

Very clearly in that light atmosphere Phil could see the trees and buildings of the home ranch, and, just across the sandy wash from the Cross-Triangle, the grove of cottonwoods and walnuts that hid the little old house where he was born. A mile away, on the eastern side of the great valley meadows, he could see the home buildings of the Reid ranch — the Pot-Hook-S — where Kitty Reid had lived all the days of her life except those three years which she had spent at school in the East.

The young man on the top of Black Hill looked long at the Reid home. In his mind he could see Kitty dressed in some cool, simple gown, fresh and dainty after the morning's housework, sitting with book or sewing on the front porch. The porch was on the other side of the house, it is true, and the distance was too great for him to distinguish a person in any case, but all that made no difference to Phil's vision — he could see her just the same.

Kitty had been very kind to Phil at the celebration. But Kitty was always kind — nearly always. But in spite of her kindness the cowboy felt that she had not, somehow, seemed to place a very high valuation upon the medal he had won in the bronco-riding contest. Phil himself did not greatly value the medal; but he had wanted greatly to win that championship because of the very substantial money prize that went with it. That money, in Phil's mind, was to play a very important part in a long cherished dream that was one of the things that Phil Acton did not talk about. He had not, in fact, ridden for the championship at all, but for his dream, and that was why it mattered so much when Kitty seemed so to lack interest in his success.

As though his subconscious mind directed the movement, the young man looked away from Kitty's home to the distant mountain ridge where the night before on the summit of the Divide he had met the stranger. All the way home the cowboy had wondered about the man; evolving many theories, inventing many things to account for his presence, alone and on foot, so far from the surroundings to which he was so clearly accustomed. Of one thing Phil was sure — the man was in trouble — deep trouble. The more that the clean-minded, gentle-hearted lad of the great out-of-doors thought about it, the more strongly he felt that he had unwittingly intruded at a moment that was sacred to the stranger — sacred because the man was fighting one of those battles that every man must fight — and fight alone. It was this feeling that had kept the young man from speaking of the incident to anyone — even to the Dean, or to "Mother," as he called Mrs. Baldwin. Perhaps, too, this feeling was the real reason for Phil's sense of kinship with the stranger, for the cowboy himself had moments in his life that he could permit no man to look upon. But in his thinking of the man whose personality had so impressed him one thing stood out above all the rest — the stranger clearly belonged to that world of which, from experience, the young foreman of the Cross-Triangle knew nothing. Phil Acton had no desire for the world to which the stranger belonged, but in his heart there was a troublesome question. If — if he himself were more like the man whom he had met on the Divide; if — if he knew more of that other world; if he, in some degree, belonged to that other world, as Kitty, because of her three years in school belonged, would it make any difference?

From the distant mountain ridge that marks the eastern limits of the Williamson Valley country, and thus, in a degree, marked the limit of Phil's world, the lad's gaze turned again to the scene immediately before him.

The band of horses, followed by the cowboys, were trotting from the narrow pass out into the open flats. Some of the band — the mothers — went quietly, knowing from past experience that they would in a few hours be returned to their freedom. Others — the colts and yearlings — bewildered, curious and fearful, followed their mothers without protest. But those who in many a friendly race or primitive battle had proved their growing years seemed to sense a coming crisis in their lives, hitherto peaceful. And these, as though warned by that strange instinct which guards all wild things, and realizing that the open ground between the pass and the gate presented their last opportunity, made final desperate efforts to escape. With sudden dashes, dodging and doubling, they tried again and again for freedom. But always between them and the haunts they loved there was a persistent horseman. Running, leaping, whirling, in their efforts to be everywhere at once, the riders worked their charges toward the gate.

The man on the hilltop sprang to his feet. Hobson threw up his head, and with sharp ears forward eagerly watched the game he knew so well. With a quickness incredible to the uninitiated, Phil threw blanket and saddle to place. As he drew the cinch tight, a shrill cowboy yell came up from the flat below.

One of the band, a powerful bay, had broken past the guarding horsemen, and was running with every ounce of his strength for the timber on the western slope of Black Hill. For a hundred yards one of the riders had tried to overtake and turn the fugitive; but as he saw how the stride of the free horse was widening the distance between them, the cowboy turned back lest others follow the successful runaway's example. The yell was to inform Phil of the situation.

Before the echoes of the signal could die away Phil was in the saddle, and with an answering shout sent Hobson down the rough mountain side in a wild, reckless, plunging run to head the, for the moment, victorious bay. An hour later the foreman rejoined his companions who were holding the band of horses at the gate. The big bay, reluctant, protesting, twisting and turning in vain attempts to outmaneuver Hobson, was a captive in the loop of "Wild Horse Phil's" riata.

In the big corral that afternoon Phil and his helpers with the Dean and Little Billy looking on, cut out from the herd the horses selected to be broken. These, one by one, were forced through the gate into the adjoining corral, from which they watched with uneasy wonder and many excited and ineffectual attempts to follow, when their more fortunate companions were driven again to the big pasture. Then Phil opened another gate, and the little band dashed wildly through, to find themselves in the small meadow pasture where they would pass the last night before the one great battle of their lives — a battle that would be for them a dividing point between those years of ease and freedom which had been theirs from birth and the years of hard and useful service that were to come.

Phil sat on his horse at the gate watching with critical eye as the unbroken animals raced away. "Some good ones in the bunch this year, Uncle Will," he commented to his employer, who, standing on the watering trough in the other corral, was looking over the fence.

"There's bound to be some good ones in every bunch," returned Mr. Baldwin. "And some no account ones, too," he added, as his foreman dismounted beside him.

Then, while the young man slipped the bridle from his horse and stood waiting for the animal to drink, the older man regarded him silently, as though in his own mind the Dean's observation bore somewhat upon Phil himself. That was always the way with the Dean. As Sheriff Fellows once remarked to Judge Powell in the old days of the cattle rustlers' glory, "Whatever Bill Baldwin says is mighty nigh always double-barreled."

There are also two sides to the Dean. Or, rather, to be accurate, there is a front and a back. The back — flat and straight and broad — indicates one side of his character — the side that belongs with the square chin and the blue eyes that always look at you with such frank directness. It was this side of the man that brought him barefooted and penniless to Arizona in those days long gone when he was only a boy and Arizona a strong man's country. It was this side of him that brought him triumphantly through those hard years of the Indian troubles, and in those wild and lawless times made him respected and feared by the evildoers and trusted and followed by those of his kind who, out of the hardships and dangers of those turbulent days, made the Arizona of today. It was this side, too, that finally made the barefoot, penniless boy the owner of the Cross-Triangle Ranch.

I do not know the exact number of the Dean's years — I only know that his hair is grey, and that he does not ride as much as he once did. I have heard him say, though, that for thirty-five years he lived in the saddle, and that the Cross-Triangle brand is one of the oldest irons in the State. And I know, too, that his back is still flat and broad and straight.

The Dean's front, so well-rounded and hearty, indicates as clearly the other side of his character. And it is this side that belongs to the full red cheeks, the ever-ready chuckle or laugh; that puts the twinkle in the blue eyes, and the kindly tones in his deep voice. It is this side of the Dean's character that adds so large a measure of love to the respect and confidence accorded him by neighbors and friends, business associates and employees. It is this side of the Dean, too, that, in these days, sits in the shade of the big walnut trees — planted by his own hand — and talks to the youngsters of the days that are gone, and that makes the young riders of this generation seek him out for counsel and sympathy and help.

Three things the Dean knows — cattle and horses and men. One thing the Dean will not, cannot tolerate — weakness in one who should be strong. Even bad men he admires, if they are strong — not for their badness, but for their strength. Mistaken men he loves in spite of their mistakes — if only they be not weaklings. There is no place anywhere in the Dean's philosophy of life for a weakling. I heard him tell a man once — nor shall I ever forget it — "You had better die like a man, sir, than live like a sneaking coyote."

The Dean's sons, men grown, were gone from the home ranch to the fields and work of their choosing. Little Billy, a nephew of seven years, was — as Mr. and Mrs. Baldwin said laughingly — their second crop.

When Phil's horse — satisfied — lifted his dripping muzzle from the watering trough, the Dean walked with his young foreman to the saddle shed. Neither of the men spoke, for between them there was that companionship which does not require a constant flow of talk to keep it alive. Not until the cowboy had turned his horse loose, and was hanging saddle and bridle on their accustomed peg did the older man speak.

"Jim Reid's goin' to begin breakin' horses next week."

"So I heard," returned Phil, carefully spreading his saddle blanket to dry.

The Dean spoke again in a tone of indifference. "He wants you to help him."

"Me! What's the matter with Jack?"

"He's goin' to the D.1 tomorrow."

Phil was examining the wrapping on his saddle horn with – the Dean noted – quite unnecessary care.

"Kitty was over this mornin'," said the Dean gently.

The young man turned, and, taking off his spurs, hung them on the saddle horn. Then as he kicked off his leather chaps he said shortly, "I'm not looking for a job as a professional bronco-buster."

The Dean's eyes twinkled. "Thought you might like to help a neighbor out; just to be neighborly, you know."

"Do you want me to ride for Reid?" demanded Phil.

"Well, I suppose as long as there's broncs to bust somebody's got to bust 'em," the Dean returned, without committing himself. And then, when Phil made no reply, he added laughing, "I told Kitty to tell him, though, that I reckoned you had as big a string as you could handle here."

As they moved away toward the house, Phil returned with significant emphasis, "When I have to ride for anybody besides you it won't be Kitty Reid's father."

And the Dean commented in his reflective tone, "It does sometimes seem to make a difference who a man rides for, don't it?"

In the pasture by the corrals, the horses that awaited the approaching trial that would mark for them the beginning of a new life passed a restless night. Some in meekness of spirit or, perhaps, with deeper wisdom fed quietly. Others wandered about aimlessly, snatching an occasional uneasy mouthful of grass, and looking about often in troubled doubt. The more rebellious ones followed the fence, searching for some place of weakness in the barbed barrier that imprisoned them. And one, who, had he not been by circumstance robbed of his birthright, would have been the strong leader of a wild band, stood often with wide nostrils and challenging eye, gazing toward the corrals and buildings as if questioning the right of those who had brought him there from the haunts he loved.

And somewhere in the night of that land which was as unknown to him as the meadow pasture was strange to the unbroken horses, a man awaited the day which, for him too, was to stand through all his remaining years as a mark between the old life and the new.

As Phil Acton lay in his bed, with doors and windows open wide to welcome the cool night air, he heard the restless horses in the near-by pasture, and smiled as he thought of the big bay and the morrow — smiled with the smile of a man who looks forward to a battle worthy of his best strength and skill.

And then, strangely enough, as he was slipping into that dreamless sleep of those who live as he lived, his mind went back again to the stranger whom he had met on the summit of the Divide. If he were more like that man, would it make any difference — the cowboy wondered.

Chapter IV

AT THE CORAL

*I*n the beginning of the morning, when Granite Mountain's fortress-like battlements and towers loomed grey and bold and grim, the big bay horse trumpeted a warning to his less watchful mates. Instantly, with heads high and eyes wide, the band stood in frightened indecision. Two horsemen — shadowy and mysterious forms in the misty light — were riding from the corral into the pasture.

As the riders approached, individuals in the band moved uneasily, starting as if to run, hesitating, turning for another look, maneuvering to put their mates between them and the enemy. But the bay went boldly a short distance toward the danger and stood still with wide nostrils and fierce eyes as though ready for the combat.

For a few moments, as the horsemen seemed about to go past, hope beat high in the hearts of the timid prisoners. Then the riders circled to put the band between themselves and the corral gate, and the frightened animals knew. But always as they whirled and dodged in their attempts to avoid that big gate toward which they were forced to move, there was a silent, persistent horseman barring the way. The big bay alone, as though realizing the futility of such efforts and so conserving his strength for whatever was to follow, trotted proudly, boldly into the corral, where he stood, his eyes never leaving the riders, as his mates crowded and jostled about him.

"There's one in that bunch that's sure aimin' to make you ride some," said Curly Elson with a grin, to Phil, as the family sat at breakfast.

On the Cross-Triangle the men who were held through the summer and winter seasons between the months of the rodeos were considered members of the family. Chosen for their character, as well as for their knowledge of the country and their skill in their work the Dean and "Stella," as Mrs. Baldwin is called throughout all that country, always spoke of them affectionately as "our boys." And this, better than anything that could be said, is an introduction to the mistress of the Cross-Triangle household.

At the challenging laugh which followed Curly's observation, Phil returned quietly with his sunny smile, "Maybe I'll quit him before he gets good and started."

"He's sure fixin' to make you back the decision of them contest judges," offered Bob Colton.

And Mrs. Baldwin, young in spirit as any of her boys, added, "Better not wear your medal, son. It might excite him to know that you are the champion buster of Arizona."

"Shucks!" piped up Little Billy excitedly, "Phil can ride anything what wears hair, can't you, Phil?"

Phil, embarrassed at the laughter which followed, said, with tactful seriousness, to his little champion, "That's right, kid. You stand up for your pardner every time, don't you? You'll be riding them yourself before long. There's a little sorrel in that bunch that I've picked out to gentle for you." He glanced at his employer meaningly, and the Dean's face glowed with appreciation of the young man's thoughtfulness. "That old horse, Sheep, of yours," continued Phil to Little Billy, "is getting too old and stiff for your work. I've noticed him stumbling a lot lately." Again he glanced inquiringly at the Dean, who answered the look with a slight nod of approval.

"You'd better make him gentle your horse first, Billy," teased Curly. "He might not be in the business when that big one gets through with him."

Little Billy's retort came in a flash. "Huh, 'Wild Horse Phil' will be a-ridin' 'em long after you've got your'n, Curly Elson."

"Look out, son," cautioned the Dean, when the laugh had gone round again. "Curly will be slippin' a burr under your saddle, if you don't."

Then to the men: "What horse is it that you boys think is goin' to be such a bad one? That big bay with the blazed face?"

The cowboys nodded.

"He's bad, all right," said Phil.

"Well," commented the Dean, leaning back in his chair and speaking generally, "he's sure got a license to be bad. His mother was the wickedest piece of horse flesh I ever knew. Remember her, Stella?"

"Indeed I do," returned Mrs. Baldwin. "She nearly ruined that Windy Jim who came from nobody knew where, and bragged that he could ride anything."

The Dean chuckled reminiscently. "She sure sent Windy back where he came from. But I tell you, boys, that kind of a horse makes the best in the world once you get 'em broke right. Horses are just like men, anyhow. If they ain't got enough in 'em to fight when they're bein' broke, they ain't generally worth breakin'."

"The man that rides that bay will sure be a-horseback," said Curly.

"He's a man's horse, all right," agreed Bob.

Breakfast over, the men left the house, not too quietly, and laughing, jesting and romping like school boys, went out to the corrals, with Little Billy tagging eagerly at their heels. The Dean and Phil remained for a few minutes at the table.

"You really oughtn't to say such things to those boys, Will," reproved Mrs. Baldwin, as she watched them from the window. "It encourages them to be wild, and land knows they don't need any encouragement."

"Shucks," returned the Dean, with that gentle note that was always in his voice when he spoke to her. "If such talk as that can hurt 'em, there ain't nothin' that could save 'em. You're always afraid somebody's goin' to go bad. Look at me and Phil here," he added, as they in turn pushed their chairs back from the table; "you've fussed enough over us to spoil a dozen men, and ain't we been a credit to you all the time?"

At this they laughed together. But as Phil was leaving the house Mrs. Baldwin stopped him at the door to say earnestly, "You will be careful today, won't you, son? You know my other Phil —" She stopped and turned away.

The young man knew that story — a story common to that land where the lives of men are not infrequently offered a sacrifice to the untamed strength of the life that in many forms they are daily called upon to meet and master.

"Never mind, mother," he said gently. "I'll be all right." Then more lightly he added, with his sunny smile, "If that big bay starts anything with me, I'll climb the corral fence pronto."

Quietly, as one who faces a hard day's work, Phil went to the saddle shed where he buckled on chaps and spurs. Then, after looking carefully to stirrup leathers, cinch and latigos, he went on to the corrals, the heavy saddle under his arm.

Curly and Bob, their horses saddled and ready, were making animated targets of themselves for Little Billy, who, mounted on Sheep, a gentle old cow-horse, was whirling a miniature riata. As the foreman appeared, the cowboys dropped their fun, and, mounting, took the coils of their own rawhide ropes in hand.

"Which one will you have first, Phil?" asked Curly, as he moved toward the gate between the big corral and the smaller enclosure that held the band of horses.

"That black one with the white star will do," directed Phil quietly. Then to Little Billy: "You'd better get back there out of the way, pardner. That black is liable to jump clear over you and Sheep."

"You better get outside, son," amended the Dean, who had come out to watch the beginning of the work.

"No, no — please, Uncle Will," begged the lad. "They can't get me as long as I'm on Sheep."

Phil and the Dean laughed.

"I'll look out for him," said the young man. "Only," he added to the boy, "you must keep out of the way."

"And see that you stick to Sheep, if you expect him to take care of you," finished the Dean, relenting.

Meanwhile the gate between the corrals had been thrown open, and with Bob to guard the opening Curly rode in among the unbroken horses to cut out the animal indicated by Phil, and from within that circular enclosure, where the earth had been ground to fine powder by hundreds of thousands of frightened feet, came the rolling thunder of quick-beating hoofs as in a swirling cloud of yellow dust the horses rushed and leaped and whirled. Again and again the frightened animals threw themselves against the barrier that hemmed them in; but that fence, built of cedar posts set close in stockade fashion and laced on the outside with wire, was made to withstand the maddened rush of the heaviest steers. And always, amid the confusion of the frenzied animals, the figure of the mounted man in their midst could be seen calmly directing their wildest movements, and soon, out from the crowding, jostling, whirling mass of flying feet and tossing manes and tails, the black with the white star shot toward the gate. Bob's horse leaped aside from the way. Curly's horse was between the black and his mates, and before the animal could gather his confused senses he was in the larger corral. The day's work had begun.

The black dodged skillfully, and the loop of Curly's riata missed the mark.

"You better let somebody put eyes in that rope, Curly," remarked Phil, laconically, as he stepped aside to avoid a wild rush.

The chagrined cowboy said something in a low tone, so that Little Billy could not hear.

The Dean chuckled.

Bob's riata whirled, shot out its snaky length, and his trained horse braced himself skillfully to the black's weight on the rope. For a few minutes the animal at the loop end of the riata struggled desperately — plunging, tugging, throwing himself this way and that; but always the experienced cow-horse turned with his victim and the rope was never slack. When his first wild efforts were over and the black stood with his wide braced feet, breathing heavily as that choking loop began to tell, the strain on the taut riata was lessened, and Phil went quietly toward the frightened captive.

No one moved or spoke. This was not an exhibition the success of which depended on the vicious wildness of the horse to be conquered. This was work, and it was not Phil's business to provoke the black to extremes in order to exhibit his own prowess as a rider for the pleasure of spectators who had paid to see the show. The rider was employed to win the confidence of the unbroken horse entrusted to him; to force obedience, if necessary; to gentle and train, and so make of the wild creature a useful and valuable servant for the Dean.

There are riders whose methods demand that they throw every un-broken horse given them to handle, and who gentle an animal by beating it about the head with loaded quirts, ripping its flanks open with sharp spurs and tearing its mouth with torturing bits and ropes. These turn over to their employers as their finished product horses that are broken, indeed — but broken only in spirit, with no heart or courage left to them, with dispositions ruined, and often with physical injuries from which they never recover. But riders of such methods have no place among the men employed by owners of the Dean's type. On the Cross-Triangle, and indeed on all ranches where conservative business principles are in force, the horses are handled with all the care and gentleness that the work and the individuality of the animal will permit.

After a little Phil's hand gently touched the black's head. Instantly the struggle was resumed. The rider dodged a vicious blow from the strong fore hoofs and with a good natured laugh softly chided the desperate animal. And so, presently, the kind hand was again stretched forth; and then a broad band of leather was deftly slipped over the black's frightened eyes. Another thicker and softer rope was knotted so that it could not slip about the now sweating neck, and fashioned into a hackamore or halter about the animal's nose. Then the riata was loosed. Working deftly, silently, gently — ever wary of those dangerous hoofs — Phil next placed blanket and saddle on the trembling black and drew the cinch tight. Then the gate leading from the corral to the open range was swung back. Easily, but quickly and surely, the rider swung to his seat. He paused a moment to be sure that all was right, and then leaning forward he reached over and raised the leather blindfold. For an instant the wild, unbroken horse stood still, then reared until it seemed he must fall, and then, as his forefeet touched the ground again, the spurs went home, and with a mighty leap forward the frenzied animal dashed, bucking, plunging, pitching, through the gate and away toward the open country, followed by Curly and Bob, with Little Billy spurring old Sheep, in hot pursuit.

For a little the Dean lingered in the suddenly emptied corral. Stepping up on the end of the long watering trough, close to the dividing fence, he studied with knowing eye the animals on the other side. Then leisurely he made his way out of the corral, visited the windmill pump, looked in on Stella from the kitchen porch, and then saddled Browny, his own particular horse that grazed always about the place at privileged ease, and rode off somewhere on some business of his own.

When the black horse had spent his strength in a vain attempt to rid himself of the dreadful burden that had attached itself so securely to his back, he was herded back to the corral, where the burden set him free. Dripping with sweat, trembling in every limb and muscle, wild-eyed, with distended nostrils and heaving flanks, the black crowded in among his mates again, his first lesson over — his years of ease and freedom past forever.

"And which will it be this time?" came Curly's question.

"I'll have that buckskin this trip," answered Phil.

And again that swirling cloud of dust raised by those thundering hoofs drifted over the stockade enclosure, and out of the mad confusion the buckskin dashed wildly through the gate to be initiated into his new life.

And so, hour after hour, the work went on, as horse after horse at Phil's word was cut out of the band and ridden; and every horse, according to disposition and temper and strength, was different. While his helpers did their part the rider caught a few moments rest. Always he was good natured, soft spoken and gentle. When a frightened animal, not understanding, tried to kill him, he accepted it as evidence of a commendable spirit, and, with that sunny, boyish smile, informed his pupil kindly that he was a good horse and must not make a fool of himself.

In so many ways, as the Dean had said at breakfast that morning, horses are just like men.

It was mid-afternoon when the master of the Cross-Triangle again strolled leisurely out to the corrals. Phil and his helpers, including Little Billy, were just disappearing over the rise of ground beyond the gate on the farther side of the enclosure as the Dean reached the gate that opens toward the barn and house. He went on through the corral, and slowly, as one having nothing else to do, climbed the little knoll from which he could watch the riders in the distance. When the horsemen had disappeared among the scattered cedars on the ridge, a mile or so to the west, the Dean still stood looking in that direction. But the owner of the Cross-Triangle was not watching for the return of his men. He was not even thinking of them. He was looking beyond the cedar ridge to where, several miles away, a long, mesa-topped mountain showed black against the blue of the more distant hills. The edge of this high table-land broke abruptly in a long series of vertical cliffs, the formation known to Arizonians as rim rocks. The deep shadows of the towering black wall of cliffs and the gloom of the pines and cedars that hid the foot of the mountain gave the place a sinister and threatening appearance.

As he looked, the Dean's kindly face grew somber and stern; his blue eyes were for the moment cold and accusing; under his grizzled mustache his mouth, usually so ready to smile or laugh, was set in lines of uncompromising firmness. In these quiet and well-earned restful years of the Dean's life the Tailholt Mountain outfit was the only disturbing element. But the Dean did not permit himself to be long annoyed by the thoughts provoked by Tailholt Mountain. Philosophically he turned his broad back to the intruding scene, and went back to the corral, and to the more pleasing occupation of looking at the horses.

If the Dean had not so abruptly turned his back upon the landscape, he would have noticed the figure of a man moving slowly along the road that skirted the valley meadow leading from Simmons to the Cross-Triangle Ranch.

Presently the riders returned, and Phil, when he had removed saddle, blanket and hackamore from his pupil, seated himself on the edge of the watering trough beside the Dean.

"I see you ain't tackled the big bay yet," remarked the older man.

"Thought if I'd let him look on for a while, he might figure it out that he'd better be good and not get himself hurt," smiled Phil. "He's sure some horse," he added admiringly. Then to his helpers: "I'll take that black with the white forefoot this time, Curly."

Just as the fresh horse dashed into the larger corral a man on foot
appeared, coming over the rise of ground to the west; and by the time
that Curly's loop was over the black's head the man stood at the gate.
One glance told Phil that it was the stranger whom he had met on the
Divide.

The man seemed to understand that it was no time for greetings and,
without offering to enter the enclosure, climbed to the top of the big
gate, where he sat, with one leg over the topmost bar, an interested
spectator.

The maneuvers of the black brought Phil to that side of the corral,
and, as he coolly dodged the fighting horse, he glanced up with his
boyish smile and a quick nod of welcome to the man perched above
him. The stranger smiled in return, but did not speak. He must have
thought, though, that this cowboy appeared quite different from the
picturesque rider he had seen at the celebration and on the summit of
the Divide. *That* Phil Acton had been — as the cowboy himself would
have said — "all togged out in his glad rags." This man wore chaps that
were old and patched from hard service; his shirt, unbuttoned at the
throat, was the color of the corral dirt, and a generous tear revealed one
muscular shoulder; his hat was greasy and battered; his face grimed and
streaked with dust and sweat, but his sunny, boyish smile would have
identified Phil in any garb.

When the rider was ready to mount, and Bob went to open the gate,
the stranger climbed down and drew a little aside. And when Phil,
passing where he stood, looked laughingly down at him from the back
of the bucking, plunging horse, he made as if to applaud, but checked
himself and went quickly to the top of the knoll to watch the riders
until they disappeared over the ridge.

"Howdy! Fine weather we're havin'." It was the Dean's hearty voice.
He had gone forward courteously to greet the stranger while the latter
was watching the riders.

The man turned impulsively, his face lighted with enthusiasm. "By
Jove!" he exclaimed, "but that man can ride!"

"Yes, Phil does pretty well," returned the Dean indifferently. "Won
the championship at Prescott the other day." Then, more heartily: "He's
a mighty good boy, too — take him any way you like."

As he spoke the cattleman looked the stranger over critically, much
as he would have looked at a steer or horse, noting the long limbs, the
well-made body, the strong face and clear, dark eyes. The man's dress
told the Dean simply that the stranger was from the city. His bearing
commanded the older man's respect. The stranger's next statement, as

he looked thoughtfully over the wide Land of valley and hill and mesa and mountain, convinced the Dean that he was a man of judgment.

"Arizona is a wonderful country, sir — wonderful!"

"Finest in the world, sir," agreed the Dean promptly. "There just naturally can't be any better. We've got the climate; we've got the land; and we've got the men."

The stranger looked at the Dean quickly when he said "men." It was worth much to hear the Dean speak that word.

"Indeed you have," he returned heartily. "I never saw such men."

"Of course you haven't," said the Dean. "I tell you, sir, they just don't make 'em outside of Arizona. It takes a country like this to produce real men. A man's got to be a man out here. Of course, though," he admitted kindly, "we don't know much except to ride, an' throw a rope, an' shoot, mebby, once in a while."

The riders were returning and the Dean and the stranger walked back down the little hill to the corral.

"You have a fine ranch here, Mr. Baldwin," again observed the stranger.

The Dean glanced at him sharply. Many men had tried to buy the Cross-Triangle. This man certainly appeared prosperous even though he was walking. But there was no accounting for the queer things that city men would do.

"It does pretty well," the cattleman admitted. "I manage to make a livin'."

The other smiled as though slightly embarrassed. Then: "Do you need any help?"

"Help!" The Dean looked at him amazed.

"I mean — I would like a position — to work for you, you know."

The Dean was speechless. Again he surveyed the stranger with his measuring, critical look. "You've never done any work," he said gently.

The man stood very straight before him and spoke almost defiantly. "No, I haven't, but is that any reason why I should not?"

The Dean's eyes twinkled, as they have a way of doing when you say something that he likes. "I'd say it's a better reason why you should," he returned quietly.

Then he said to Phil, who, having dismissed his four-footed pupil, was coming toward them:

"Phil, this man wants a job. Think we can use him?"

The young man looked at the stranger with unfeigned surprise and with a hint of amusement, but gave no sign that he had ever seen him before. The same natural delicacy of feeling that had prevented the cowboy from discussing the man upon whose privacy he felt he had intruded that evening of their meeting on the Divide led him now to ignore the incident — a consideration which could not but command the strange man's respect, and for which he looked his gratitude.

There was something about the stranger, too, that to Phil seemed different. This tall, well-built fellow who stood before them so self-possessed, and ready for anything, was not altogether like the uncertain, embarrassed, half-frightened and troubled gentleman at whom Phil had first laughed with thinly veiled contempt, and then had pitied. It was as though the man who sat that night alone on the Divide had, out of the very bitterness of his experience, called forth from within himself a strength of which, until then, he had been only dimly conscious. There was now, in his face and bearing, courage and decision and purpose, and with it all a glint of that same humor that had made him so bitterly mock himself. The Dean's philosophy touching the possibilities of the man who laughs when he is hurt seemed in this stranger about to be justified. Phil felt oddly, too, that the man was in a way experimenting with himself — testing himself as it were — and being altogether a normal human, the cowboy felt strongly inclined to help the experimenter. In this spirit he answered the Dean, while looking mischievously at the stranger.

"We can use him if he can ride."

The stranger smiled understandingly. "I don't see why I couldn't," he returned in that droll tone. "I seem to have the legs." He looked down at his long lower limbs reflectively, as though quaintly considering them quite apart from himself.

Phil laughed.

"Huh," said the Dean, slightly mystified at the apparent understanding between the young men. Then to the stranger: "What do you want to work for? You don't look as though you needed to. A sort of vacation, heh?"

There was spirit in the man's answer. "I want to work for the reason that all men want work. If you do not employ me, I must try somewhere else."

"Come from Prescott to Simmons on the stage, did you?"

"No, sir, I walked."

"Walked! Huh! Tried anywhere else for a job?"

"No, sir."

"Who sent you out here?"

The stranger smiled. "I saw Mr. Acton ride in the contest. I learned that he was foreman of the Cross-Triangle Ranch. I thought I would rather work where he worked, if I could."

The Dean looked at Phil. Phil looked at the Dean. Together they looked at the stranger. The two cowboys who were sitting on their horses near-by grinned at each other.

"And what is your name, sir?" the Dean asked courteously.

For the first time the man hesitated and seemed embarrassed. He looked uneasily about with a helpless inquiring glance, as though appealing for some suggestion.

"Oh, never mind your name, if you have forgotten it," said the Dean dryly.

The stranger's roaming eyes fell upon Phil's old chaps, that in every wrinkle and scar and rip and tear gave such eloquent testimony as to the wearer's life, and that curious, self-mocking smile touched his lips. Then, throwing up his head and looking the Dean straight in the eye, he said boldly, but with that note of droll humor in his voice, "My name is Patches, sir, Honorable Patches."

The Dean's eyes twinkled, but his face was grave. Phil's face flushed; he had not failed to identify the source of the stranger's inspiration. But before either the Dean or Phil could speak a shout of laughter came from Curly Elson, and the stranger had turned to face the cowboy.

"Something seems to amuse you," he said quietly to the man on the horse; and at the tone of his voice Phil and the Dean exchanged significant glances.

The grinning cowboy looked down at the stranger in evident contempt. "Patches," he drawled. "Honorable Patches! That's a hell of a name, now, ain't it?"

The man went two long steps toward the mocking rider, and spoke quietly, but with unmistakable meaning.

"I'll endeavor to make it all of that for you, if you will get off your horse."

The grinning cowboy, with a wink at his companion, dismounted cheerfully. Curly Elson was held to be the best man with his hands in Yavapai County. He could not refuse so tempting an opportunity to add to his well-earned reputation.

Five minutes later Curly lifted himself on one elbow in the corral dust, and looked up with respectful admiration to the quiet man who stood waiting for him to rise. Curly's lip was bleeding generously; the side of his face seemed to have slipped out of place, and his left eye was closing surely and rapidly.

"Get up," said the tall man calmly. "There is more where that came from, if you want it."

The cowboy grinned painfully. "I ain't hankerin' after anymore," he mumbled, feeling his face tenderly.

"It said that my name was Patches," suggested the stranger.

"Sure, Mr. Patches, I reckon nobody'll question that."

"Honorable Patches," again prompted the stranger.

"Yes, sir. You bet; Honorable Patches," agreed Curly with emphasis. Then, as he painfully regained his feet, he held out his hand with as nearly a smile as his battered features would permit. "Do you mind shaking on it, Mr. Honorable Patches? Just to show that there's no hard feelin's?"

Patches responded instantly with a manner that won Curly's heart. "Good!" he said. "I knew you would do that when you understood, or I wouldn't have bothered to show you my credentials."

"My mistake," returned Curly. "It's them there credentials of yourn, not your name, that's hell."

He gingerly mounted his horse again, and Patches turned back to the Dean as though apologizing for the interruption.

"I beg your pardon, sir, but — about work?"

The Dean never told anyone just what his thoughts were at that particular moment; probably because they were so many and so contradictory and confusing. Whether from this uncertainty of mind; from a habit of depending upon his young foreman, or because of that something, which Phil and the stranger seemed to have in common, he shifted the whole matter by saying, "It's up to Phil here. He's foreman of the Cross-Triangle. If he wants to hire you, it's all right with me."

At this the two young men faced each other; and on the face of each was a half questioning, half challenging smile. The stranger seemed to say, "I know I am at your mercy; I don't expect you to believe in me after our meeting on the Divide, but I dare you to put me to the test."

And Phil, if he had spoken, might have said, "I felt when I met you first that there was a man around somewhere. I know you are curious to see what you would do if put to the test. I am curious, too. I'll give you a chance." Aloud he reminded the stranger pointedly, "I said we might use you if you could ride."

Patches smiled his self-mocking smile, evidently appreciating his predicament. "And I said," he retorted, "that I didn't see why I couldn't."

Phil turned to his grinning but respectful helpers. "Bring out that bay with the blazed face."

"Great Snakes!" ejaculated Curly to Bob, as they reached the gate leading to the adjoining corral. "His name is Patches, all right, but he'll be pieces when that bay devil gets through with him, if he can't ride. Do you reckon he can?"

"Dunno," returned Bob, as he unlatched the gate without dismounting. "I thought he couldn't fight."

"So did I," returned Curly, grimly nursing his battered face. "You cut out the horse; I can't more'n half see."

It was no trouble to cut out the bay. The big horse seemed to understand that his time had come. All day he had seen his mates go forth to their testing, had watched them as they fought with all their strength the skill and endurance of that smiling, boy-faced man, and then had seen them as they returned, sweating, trembling, conquered and subdued. As Bob rode toward him, he stood for one defiant moment as motionless as a horse of bronze; then, with a suddenness that gave Curly at the gate barely time to dodge his rush, he leaped forward into the larger arena.

Phil was watching the stranger as the big horse came through the gate. The man did not move, but his eyes were glowing darkly, his face was flushed, and he was smiling to himself mockingly — as though amused at the thought of what was about to happen to him. The Dean also was watching Patches, and again the young foreman and his employer exchanged significant glances as Phil turned and went quickly to Little Billy. Lifting the lad from his saddle and seating him on the fence above the long watering trough, he said, "There's a grandstand seat for you, pardner; don't get down unless you have to, and then get down outside. See?"

At that moment yells of warning, with a "Look out, Phil!" came from Curly, Bob and the Dean.

A quick look over his shoulder, and Phil saw the big horse with ears wickedly flat, eyes gleaming, and teeth bared, making straight in his direction. The animal had apparently singled him out as the author of his misfortunes, and proposed to dispose of his arch-enemy at the very outset of the battle. There was only one sane thing to do, and Phil did it. A vigorous, scrambling leap placed him beside Little Billy on the top of the fence above the watering trough.

"Good thing I reserved a seat in your grandstand for myself, wasn't it, pardner?" he smiled down at the boy by his side.

Then Bob's riata fell true, and as the powerful horse plunged and fought that strangling noose Phil came leisurely down from the fence.

"Where was you goin', Phil?" chuckled the Dean.

"You sure warn't losin' any time," laughed Curly.

And Bob, without taking his eyes from the vicious animal at the end of his taut riata, and working skillfully with his trained cow-horse to foil every wicked plunge and wild leap, grinned with appreciation, as he added, "I'll bet four bits you can't do it again, Phil, without a runnin' start."

"I just thought I'd keep Little Billy company for a spell," smiled Phil. "He looked so sort of lonesome up there."

The stranger, at first amazed that they could turn into jest an incident which might so easily have been a tragedy, suddenly laughed aloud — a joyous, ringing laugh that made Phil look at him sharply.

"I beg your pardon, Mr. Acton," said Patches meekly, but with that droll voice which brought a glint of laughter into the foreman's eyes and called forth another chuckle from the Dean.

"You can take my saddle," said Phil pointedly. "It's over there at the end of the watering trough. You'll find the stirrups about right, I reckon — I ride with them rather long."

For a moment the stranger looked him straight in the eyes, then without a word started for the saddle. He was halfway to the end of the watering trough when Phil overtook him.

"I believe I'd rather saddle him myself," the cowboy explained quietly, with his sunny smile. "You see, I've got to teach these horses some cow sense before the fall rodeo, and I'm rather particular about the way they're handled at the start."

"Exactly," returned Patches, "I don't blame you. That fellow seems rather to demand careful treatment, doesn't he?"

Phil laughed. "Oh, you don't need to be too particular about his feelings once you're up in the middle of him," he retorted.

The big bay, instead of acquiring sense from his observations, as Phil had expressed to the Dean a hope that he would, seemed to have gained courage and determination. Phil's approach was the signal for a mad plunge in the young man's direction, which was checked by the skill and weight of Bob's trained cow-horse on the rope. Several times Phil went toward the bay, and every time his advance was met by one of those vicious rushes. Then Phil mounted Curly's horse, and from his hand the loop of another riata fell over the bay's head. Shortening his rope by coiling it in his rein hand, he maneuvered the trained horse closer and closer to his struggling captive, until, with Bob's cooperation on the other side of the fighting animal, he could with safety fix the leather blindfold over those wicked eyes.

When at last hackamore and saddle were in place, and the bay stood trembling and sweating, Phil wiped the perspiration from his own forehead and turned to the stranger.

"Your horse is ready, sir."

The man's face was perhaps a shade whiter than its usual color, but his eyes were glowing, and there was a grim set look about his smiling lips that made the hearts of those men go out to him. He seemed to realize so that the joke was on himself, and with it all exhibited such reckless indifference to consequences. Without an instant's hesitation he started toward the horse.

"Great Snakes!" muttered Curly to Bob, "talk about nerve!"

The Dean started forward. "Wait a minute, Mr. Patches," he said.

The stranger faced him.

"Can you ride that horse?" asked the Dean, pointedly.

"I'm going to," returned Patches. "But," he added with his droll humor, "I can't say how far."

"Don't you know that he'll kill you if he can?" questioned the Dean curiously, while his eyes twinkled approval.

"He does seem to have some such notion," admitted Patches.

"You better let him alone," said the Dean. "You don't need to kill yourself to get a job with this outfit."

"That's very kind of you, sir," returned the stranger gratefully. "I'm rather glad you said that. But I'm going to ride him just the same."

They looked at him in amazement, for it was clear to them now that the man really could not ride.

The Dean spoke kindly. "Why?"

"Because," said Patches slowly, "I am curious to see what I will do under such circumstances, and if I don't try the experiment now I'll never know whether I have the nerve to do it or not." As he finished he turned and walked deliberately toward the horse.

Phil ran to Curly's side, and the cowboy at his foreman's gesture leaped from his saddle. The young man mounted his helper's horse, and with a quick movement caught the riata from the saddle horn and flipped open a ready loop.

The stranger was close to the bay's off, or right, side.

"The other side, Patches," called Phil genially. "You want to start in right, you know."

Not a man laughed — except the stranger.

"Thanks," he said, and came around to the proper side.

"Take your time," called Phil again. "Stand by his shoulder and watch his heels. Take the stirrup with your right hand and turn it to catch your foot. Stay back by his shoulder until you are ready to swing up. Take your time."

"I won't be long," returned Patches, as he awkwardly gained his seat in the saddle.

Phil moved his horse nearer the center of the corral, and shook out his loop a little.

"When you're ready, lean over and pull up the blindfold," he called.

The man on the horse did not hesitate. With every angry nerve and muscle strained to the utmost, the powerful bay leaped into the air, coming down with legs stiff and head between his knees. For an instant the man miraculously kept his place. With another vicious plunge and a cork-screw twist the maddened brute went up again, and this time the man was flung from the saddle as from a gigantic catapult, to fall upon his shoulders and back in the corral dust, where he lay still. The horse, rid of his enemy, leaped again; then with catlike quickness and devilish cunning whirled, and with wicked teeth bared and vicious, blazing eyes, rushed for the helpless man on the ground.

With a yell Bob spurred to put himself between the bay and his victim, but had there been time the move would have been useless, for no horse could have withstood that mad charge. The vicious brute was within a bound of his victim, and had reared to crush him with the weight of heavy hoofs, when a rawhide rope tightened about those uplifted fore-feet and the bay himself crashed to earth. Leaving the cow-horse to hold the riata tight, Phil sprang from his saddle and ran to the fallen man. The Dean came with water in his felt hat from the trough, and presently the stranger opened his eyes. For a moment he lay looking up into their faces as though wondering where he was, and how he happened there.

"Are you hurt bad?" asked the Dean.

That brought him to his senses, and he got to his feet somewhat unsteadily, and began brushing the dust from his clothes. Then he looked curiously toward the horse that Curly was holding down by the simple means of sitting on the animal's head. "I certainly thought my legs were long enough to reach around him," he said reflectively. "How in the world did he manage it? I seemed to be falling for a week."

Phil yelled and the Dean laughed until the tears ran down his red cheeks, while Bob and Curly went wild.

Patches went to the horse, and gravely walked around him. Then, "Let him up," he said to Curly.

The cowboy looked at Phil, who nodded.

As the bay regained his feet, Patches started toward him.

"Here," said the Dean peremptorily. "You come away from there."

"I'm going to see if he can do it again," declared Patches grimly.

"Not today, you ain't," returned the Dean. "You're workin' for me now, an' you're too good a man to be killed tryin' anymore crazy experiments."

At the Dean's words the look of gratitude in the man's eyes was almost pathetic.

"I wonder if I am," he said, so low that only the Dean and Phil heard.

"If you are what?" asked the Dean, puzzled by his manner.

"Worth anything — as a man — you know," came the strange reply.

The Dean chuckled. "You'll be all right when you get your growth. Come on over here now, out of the way, while Phil takes some of the cussedness out of that fool horse."

Together they watched Phil ride the bay and return him to his mates a very tired and a much wiser pupil. Then, while Patches remained to watch further operations in the corral, the Dean went to the house to tell Stella all about it.

"And what do you think he really is?" she asked, as the last of a long list of questions and comments.

The Dean shook his head. "There's no tellin'. A man like that is liable to be anything." Then he added, with his usual philosophy: "He acts, though, like a genuine thoroughbred that's been badly mishandled an' has just found it out."

When the day's work was finished and supper was over Little Billy found Patches where he stood looking across the valley toward Granite Mountain that loomed so boldly against the soft light of the evening sky. The man greeted the boy awkwardly, as though unaccustomed to children. But Little Billy, very much at ease, signified his readiness to help the stranger to an intimate acquaintance with the world of which he knew so much more than this big man.

He began with no waste of time on mere preliminaries.

"See that mountain over there? That's Granite Mountain. There's wild horses live around there, an' sometimes we catch 'em. Bet you don't know that Phil's name is 'Wild Horse Phil'."

Patches smiled. "That's a good name for him, isn't it?"

"You bet." He turned and pointed eagerly to the west. "There's another mountain over there I bet you don't know the name of."

"Which one do you mean? I see several."

"That long, black lookin' one. Do you know about it?"

"I'm really afraid that I don't."

"Well, I'll tell you," said Billy, proud of his superior knowledge. "That there's Tailholt Mountain."

"Indeed!"

"Yes, and Nick Cambert and Yavapai Joe lives over there. Do you know about them?"

The tall man shook his head. "No, I don't believe that I do."

Little Billy lowered his voice to a mysterious whisper. "Well, I'll tell you. Only you mus'n't ever say anything 'bout it out loud. Nick and Yavapai is cattle thieves. They been a-brandin' our calves, an' Phil, he's goin' to catch 'em at it some day, an' then they'll wish they hadn't. Phil, he's my pardner, you know."

"And a fine pardner, too, I'll bet," returned the stranger, as if not wishing to acquire further information about the men of Tailholt Mountain.

"You bet he is," came the instant response. "Only Jim Reid, he don't like him very well."

"That's too bad, isn't it?"

"Yes. You see, Jim Reid is Kitty's daddy. They live over there." He pointed across the meadow to where, a mile away, a light twinkled in the window of the Pot-Hook-S ranch house. "Kitty Reid's a mighty nice girl, I tell you, but Jim, he says that there needn't no cow-puncher come around tryin' to get her, 'cause she's been away to school, you know, an' I think Phil —"

"Whoa! Hold on a minute, sonny," interrupted Patches hastily.

"What's the matter?" questioned Little Billy.

"Why, it strikes me that a boy with a pardner like 'Wild Horse Phil' ought to be mighty careful about how he talked over that pardner's private affairs with a stranger. Don't you think so?"

"Mebby so," agreed Billy. "But you see, I know that Phil wants Kitty 'cause —"

"Sh! What in the world is that?" whispered Patches in great fear, catching his small companion by the arm.

"That! Don't you know an owl when you hear one? Gee! but you're a tenderfoot, ain't you?" Catching sight of the Dean who was coming toward them, he shouted gleefully. "Uncle Will, Mr. Patches is scared of an owl. What do you know about that; Patches is scared of an owl!"

"Your Aunt Stella wants you," laughed the Dean.

And Billy ran off to the house to share his joke on the tenderfoot with his Aunt Stella and his "pardner," Phil.

"I've got to go to town tomorrow," said the Dean. "I expect you better go along and get your trunk, or whatever you have and some sort of an outfit. You can't work in them clothes."

Patches answered hesitatingly. "Why, I think I can get along all right, Mr. Baldwin."

"But you'll want your stuff — your trunk or grip — or whatever you've got," returned the Dean.

"But I have nothing in Prescott," said the stranger slowly.

"You haven't? Well, you'll need an outfit anyway," persisted the cattleman.

"Really, I think I can get along for a while," Patches returned diffidently.

The Dean considered for a little; then he said with straightforward bluntness, but not at all unkindly, "Look here, young man, you ain't afraid to go to Prescott, are you?"

The other laughed. "Not at all, sir. It's not that. I suppose I must tell you now, though. All the clothes I have are on my back, and I haven't a cent in the world with which to buy an outfit, as you call it."

The Dean chuckled. "So that's it? I thought mebby you was dodgin' the sheriff. If it's just plain broke that's the matter, why you'll go to town with me in the mornin', an' we'll get what you need. I'll hold it out of your wages until it's paid." As though the matter were settled, he turned back toward the house, adding, "Phil will show you where you're to sleep."

When the foreman had shown the new man to his room, the cowboy asked casually, "Found the goat ranch, all right, night before last, did you?"

The other hesitated; then he said gravely, "I didn't look for it, Mr. Acton."

"You didn't look for it?"

"No, sir."

"Do you mean to say that you spent the night up there on the Divide without blankets or anything?"

"Yes, sir, I did."

"And where did you stop last night?"

"At Simmons."

"Walked, I suppose?"

The stranger smiled. "Yes."

"But, look here," said the puzzled cowboy, "I don't mean to be asking questions about what is none of my business, but I can't figure it out. If you were coming out here to get a job on the Cross-Triangle, why didn't you go to Mr. Baldwin in town? Anybody could have pointed him out to you. Or, why didn't you say something to me, when we were talking back there on the Divide?"

"Why, you see," explained the other lamely, "I didn't exactly want to work on the Cross-Triangle, or anywhere."

"But you told Uncle Will that you wanted to work here, and you were on your way when I met you."

"Yes, I know, but you see — oh, hang it all, Mr. Acton, haven't you ever wanted to do something that you didn't want to do? Haven't you ever been caught in a corner that you were simply forced to get out of when you didn't like the only way that would get you out? I don't mean anything criminal," he added, with a short laugh.

"Yes, I have," returned the other seriously, "and if you don't mind there's no handle to my name. Around here I'm just plain Phil, Mr. Patches."

"Thanks. Neither does Patches need decorating."

"And now, one more," said Phil, with his winning smile. "Why in the name of all the obstinate fools that roam at large did you walk out here when you must have had plenty of chances to ride?"

"Well, you see," said Patches slowly, "I fear I can't explain, but it was just a part of my job."

"Your job! But you didn't have any job until this afternoon."

"Oh, yes, I did. I had the biggest kind of a job. You see, that's what I was doing on the Divide all night; trying to find some other way to do it."

"And do you mind telling me what that job is?" asked Phil curiously.

Patches laughed as though at himself. "I don't know that I can, exactly," he said. "I think, perhaps, it's just to ride that big bay horse out there."

Phil laughed aloud — a hearty laugh of good-fellowship. "You'll do that all right."

"Do you think so, really," asked Patches, eagerly.

"Sure; I know it."

"I wish I could be sure," returned the strange man doubtfully — and the cowboy, wondering, saw that wistful look in his eyes.

"That big devil is a man's horse, all right," mused Phil.

"Why, of course — and that's just it — don't you see?" cried the other impulsively. Then, as if he regretted his words, he asked quickly, "Do you name your horses?"

"Sure," answered the cowboy; "we generally find something to call them."

"And have you named the big bay yet?"

Phil laughed. "I named him yesterday, when he broke away as we were bringing the bunch in, and I had to rope him to get him back."

"And what did you name him?"

"Stranger."

"Stranger! And why Stranger?"

"Oh, I don't know. Just one of my fool notions," returned Phil. "Good-night!"

Chapter V
A BIT OF THE PAST

*T*he next morning Mr. Baldwin and Patches set out for town.

"I suppose," said the Dean, and a slightly curious tone colored the remark, "that mebby you've been used to automobiles. Buck and Prince here, an' this old buckboard will seem sort of slow to you."

Patches was stepping into the rig as the Dean spoke. As the young man took his seat by the cattleman's side, the Dean nodded to Phil who was holding the team. At the signal Phil released the horses' heads and stepped aside, whereupon Buck and Prince, of one mind, looked back over their shoulders, made a few playful attempts to twist themselves out of the harness, lunged forward their length, stood straight up on their hind feet, then sprang away as if they were fully determined to land that buckboard in Prescott within the next fifteen minutes.

"Did you say slow?" questioned Patches, as he clung to his seat.

The Dean chuckled and favored his new man with a twinkling glance of approval.

A few seconds later, on the other side of the sandy wash, the Dean skillfully checked their headlong career, with a narrow margin of safety between the team and the gate.

"I reckon we'll get through with less fuss if you'll open it," he said to Patches. Then to Buck and Prince: "Whoa! you blamed fools. Can't you stand a minute?"

"Stella's been devilin' me to get a machine ever since Jim Reid got his," he continued, while the horses were repeating their preliminary contortions, and Patches was regaining his seat. "But I told her I'd be scared to death to ride in the fool contraption."

At this Buck and Prince, in a wild riot of animal strength and spirit, leaped a slight depression in the road with such vigor that the front wheels of the buckboard left the ground. Patches glanced sidewise at his employer, with a smile of delighted appreciation, but said nothing.

The Dean liked him for that. The Dean always insists that the hardest man in the world to talk to is the one who always has something to say for himself.

"Why," he continued, with a burst of honest feeling, "if I was ever to bring one of them things home to the Cross-Triangle, I'd be ashamed to look a horse or steer in the face."

They dashed through a patch of wild sunflowers that in the bottom lands grow thick and rank; whirled past the tumble-down corner of an old fence that enclosed a long neglected garden; and dashed recklessly through a deserted and weed-grown yard. On one side of the road was the ancient barn and stable, with sagging, weather-beaten roof, leaning walls and battered doors that hung dejectedly on their rusty and broken hinges. The corral stockade was breached in many places by the years that had rotted the posts. The old-time windlass pump that, operated by a blind burro, once lifted water for the long vanished herds, was a pathetic old wreck, incapable now of offering drink to a thirsty sparrow. On their other hand, beneath the wide branches of giant sycamores and walnuts, and backed by a tangled orchard wilderness, stood an old house, empty and neglected, as if in the shadowy gloom of the untrimmed trees it awaited, lonely and forlorn, the kindly hand of oblivion.

"This is the old Acton homestead," said the Dean quietly, as one might speak beside an ancient grave.

Then as they were driving through the narrow lane that crosses the great meadow, he indicated with a nod of his head group of buildings on the other side of the green fields, and something less than a mile to the south.

"That's Jim Reid's place. His iron is the Pot-Hook-S. Jim's stock runs on the old Acton range, but the homestead belongs to Phil yet. Jim Reid's a fine man." The Dean spoke stoutly, almost as though he were making the assertion to convince himself. "Yes, sir, Jim's all right. Good neighbor; good cowman; square as they make 'em. Some folks seem to think he's a mite overbearin' an' rough-spoken sometimes, and he's kind of quick at suspicionin' everybody; but Jim and me have always got along the best kind."

Again the Dean was silent, as though he had forgotten the man beside him in his occupation with thoughts that he could not share.

When they had crossed the valley meadows and, climbing the hill on the other side, could see the road for several miles ahead, the Dean pointed to a black object on the next ridge.

"There's Jim's automobile now. They're headin' for Prescott, too. Kitty's drivin', I reckon. I tell Stella that that machine and Kitty's learnin' to run the thing is about all the returns that Jim can show for the money he's spent in educatin' her. I don't mean," he added, with a quick look at Patches, as though he feared to be misunderstood, "that Kitty's one of them good-for-nothin' butterfly girls. She ain't that by a good deal. Why, she was raised right here in this neighborhood, an' we love her the same as if she was our own. She can cook a meal or make a dress 'bout as well as her mother, an' does it, too; an' she can ride a horse or throw a rope better'n some punchers I've seen, but —" The Dean stopped, seemingly for want of words to express exactly his thought.

"It seems to me," offered Patches abstractedly, "that education, as we call it, is a benefit only when it adds to one's life. If schooling or culture, or whatever you choose to term it, is permitted to rob one of the fundamental and essential elements of life, it is most certainly an evil."

"That's the idea," exclaimed the Dean, with frank admiration for his companion's ability to say that which he himself thought. "You say it like a book. But that's it. It ain't the learnin' an' all the stuff that Kitty got while she was at school that's worryin' us. It's what she's likely to lose through gettin' 'em. This here modern, down-to-the-minute, higher livin', loftier sphere, intellectual supremacy idea is all right if folks'll just keep their feet on the ground.

"You take Stella an' me now. I know we're old fashioned an' slow an' all that, an' we've seen a lot of hardships since we was married over in Skull Valley where she was born an' raised. She was just a girl then, an' I was only a kid, punchin' steers for a livin'. I suppose we've seen about as hard times as anybody. At least that's what they would be called now. But, hell, *we* didn't think nothin' of it then; we was happy, sir, and we've been happy for over forty year. I tell you, sir, we've lived — just lived every minute, and that's a blamed sight more than a lot of these higher-cultured, top-lofty, half-dead couples that marry and separate, and separate and marry again nowadays can say.

"No, sir, 'tain't what a man gets that makes him rich; it's what he keeps. And these folks that are swoppin' the old-fashioned sort of love that builds homes and raises families and lets man and wife work together, an' meet trouble together, an' be happy together, an' grow old bein' happy together — if they're swoppin' all that for these here new, down-to-date ideas of such things, they're makin' a damned poor bargain, accordin' to my way of thinkin'. There is such a thing, sir, as educatin' a man or woman plumb out of reach of happiness.

"Look at our Phil," the Dean continued, for the man beside him was a wonderful listener. "There just naturally couldn't be a better all round man than Phil Acton. He's healthy; don't know what it is to have an hour's sickness; strong as a young bull; clean, honest, square, no bad habits, a fine worker, an' a fine thinker, too — even if he ain't had much schoolin', he's read a lot. Take him any way you like — just as a man, I mean — an' that's the way you got to take 'em — there ain't a better man that Phil livin'. Yet a lot of these folks would say he's nothin' but a cow-puncher. As for that, Jim Reid ain't much more than a cow-puncher himself. I tell you, I've seen cow-punchers that was mighty good men, an' I've seen graduates from them there universities that was plumb good for nothin' — with no more real man about 'em than there is about one of these here wax dummies that they hang clothes on in the store windows. What any self-respectin' woman can see in one of them that would make her want to marry him is more than I've ever been able to figger out."

If the Dean had not been so engrossed in his own thoughts, he would have wondered at the strange effect of his words upon his companion. The young man's face flushed scarlet, then paled as though with sudden illness, and he looked sidewise at the older man with an expression of shame and humiliation, while his eyes, wistful and pleading, were filled with pain. Honorable Patches who had won the admiration of those men in the Cross-Triangle corrals was again the troubled, shamefaced, half-frightened creature whom Phil met on the Divide.

But the good Dean did not see, and so, encouraged by the other's silence, he continued his dissertation. "Of course, I don't mean to say that education and that sort of thing spoils every man. Now, there's young Stanford Manning —"

If the Dean had suddenly fired a gun at Patches, the young man could not have shown greater surprise and consternation. "Stanford Manning!" he gasped.

At his tone the Dean turned to look at him curiously. "I mean Stanford Manning, the mining engineer," he explained. "Do you know him?"

"I have heard of him," Patches managed to reply.

"Well," continued the Dean, "he came out to this country about three years ago — straight from college — and he has sure made good. He's got the education an' culture an' polish an' all that, an' with it he can hold his own among any kind or sort of men livin'. There ain't a man — cow-puncher, miner or anything else — in Yavapai County that don't take off his hat to Stanford Manning."

"Is he in this country now?" asked Patches, with an effort at self-control that the Dean did not notice.

"No, I understand his Company called him back East about a month ago. Goin' to send him to some of their properties up in Montana, I heard."

When his companion made no comment, the Dean said reflectively, as Buck and Prince climbed slowly up the grade to the summit of the Divide, "I'll tell you, son, I've seen a good many changes in this country. I can remember when there wasn't a fence in all Yavapai County — hardly in the Territory. And now — why the last time I drove over to Skull Valley I got so tangled up in 'em that I plumb lost myself. When Phil's daddy an' me was youngsters we used to ride from Camp Verde and Flagstaff clean to Date Creek without ever openin' a gate. But I can't see that men change much, though. They're good and bad, just like they've always been — an' I reckon always will be. There's been leaders and weaklin's and just betwixt and betweens in every herd of cattle or band of horses that ever I owned. You take Phil, now. He's exactly like his daddy was before him."

"His father must have been a fine man," said Patches, with quiet earnestness.

The Dean looked at him with an approving twinkle. "Fine?" For a few minutes, as they were rounding the turn of the road on the summit of the Divide where Phil and the stranger had met, the Dean looked away toward Granite Mountain. Then, as if thinking aloud, rather than purposely addressing his companion, he said, "John Acton — Honest John, as everybody called him — and I came to this country together when we were boys. Walked in, sir, with some pioneers from Kansas. We kept in touch with each other all the while we was growin' to be men; punched cattle for the same outfits most of the time; even did most of our courtin' together, for Phil's mother an' Stella were neighbors an' great friends over in Skull Valley. When we'd finally saved enough to get started we located homesteads close together back there in the Valley, an' as soon as we could get some sort of shacks built we married the girls and set up housekeepin'. Our stock ranged together, of course, but John sort of took care of the east side of the meadows an' I kept more to the west. When the children came along — John an' Mary had three before Phil, but only Phil lived — an' the stock had increased an' we'd built some decent houses, things seemed to be about as fine as possible. Then John went on a note for a man in Prescott. I tried my best to keep him out of it, but, shucks! he just laughed at me. You see, he was one of the best hearted men that ever lived — one of those men, you know, that just naturally believes in everybody.

"Well, it wound up after a-while by John losin' mighty nigh everything. We managed to save the homestead, but practically all the stock had to go. An' it wasn't more than a year after that till Mary died. We never did know just what was the matter with her — an' after that it seemed like John never was the same. He got killed in the rodeo that same fall — just wasn't himself somehow. I was with him when he died.

"Stella and me raised Phil — we don't know any difference between him and one of our own boys. The old homestead is his, of course, but Jim Reid's stock runs on the old range. Phil's got a few head that he works with mine — a pretty good bunch by now — for he's kept addin' to what his father left, an' I've paid him wages ever since he was big enough. Phil don't say much, even to Stella an' me, but I know he's figurin' on fixin' up the old home place some day."

After a long silence the Dean said again, as if voicing some conclusion of his unspoken thoughts: "Jim Reid is pretty well fixed, you see, an' Kitty bein' the only girl, it's natural, I reckon, that they should have ideas about her future, an' all that. I reckon it's natural, too, that the girl should find ranch life away out here so far from anywhere, a little slow after her three years at school in the East. She never says it, but somehow you can most always tell what Kitty's thinkin' without her speakin' a word."

"I have known people like that," said Patches, probably because there was so little that he could say.

"Yes, an' when you know Kitty, you'll say, like I always have, that if there's a man in Yavapai County that wouldn't ride the hoofs off the best horse in his outfit, night or day, to win a smile from her, he ought to be lynched."

That afternoon in Prescott they purchased an outfit for Patches, and the following day set out for the long return drive to the ranch.

They had reached the top of the hill at the western end of the meadow lane, when they saw a young woman, on a black horse, riding away from the gate that opens from the lane into the Pot-Hook-S meadow pasture, toward the ranch buildings on the farther side of the field.

As they drove into the yard at home, it was nearly supper time, and the men were coming from the corrals.

"Kitty's been over all the afternoon," Little Billy informed them promptly. "I told her all about you, Patches. She says she's just dyin' to see you."

Phil joined in the laugh, but Patches fancied that there was a shadow in the cowboy's usually sunny eyes as the young man looked at him to say, "That big horse of yours sure made me ride some today."

Chapter VI

THE DRIFT FENCE

*T*he education of Honorable Patches was begun without further delay. Because Phil's time was so fully occupied with his four-footed pupils, the Dean himself became the stranger's teacher, and all sorts of odd jobs about the ranch, from cleaning the pig pen to weeding the garden, were the text books. The man balked at nothing. Indeed, he seemed to find a curious, grim satisfaction in accomplishing the most menial and disagreeable tasks; and when he made mistakes, as he often did, he laughed at himself with such bitter, mocking humor that the Dean wondered.

"He's got me beat," the Dean confided to Stella. "There ain't nothin' that he won't tackle, an' I'm satisfied that the man never did a stroke of work before in his life. But he seems to be always tryin' experiments with himself, like he expected himself to play the fool one way or another, an' wanted to see if he would, an' then when he don't he's as surprised and tickled as a kid."

The Dean himself was not at all above assisting his new man in those experiments, and so it happened that day when Patches had been set to repairing the meadow pasture fence near the lower corrals.

The Dean, riding out that way to see how his pupil was progressing, noticed a particularly cross-tempered shorthorn bull that had wandered in from the near-by range to water at the house corral. But Phil and his helpers were in possession of the premises near the watering trough, and his shorthorn majesty was therefore even more than usual out of patience with the whole world. The corrals were between the bull and Patches, so that the animal had not noticed the man, and the Dean, chuckling to himself, and without attracting Patches' attention, quietly drove the ill-tempered beast into the enclosure and shut the gate.

Then, riding around the corral, the Dean called to the young man. When Patches stood beside his employer, the cattleman said, "Here's a blamed old bull that don't seem to be feelin' very well. I got him into the corral all right, but I'm so fat I can't reach him from the saddle. I wish you'd just halter him with this rope, so I can lead him up to the house and let Phil and the boys see what's wrong with him."

Patches took the rope and started toward the corral gate. "Shall I put it around his neck and make a hitch over his nose, like you do a horse?" he asked, glad for the opportunity to exhibit his newly acquired knowledge of ropes and horses and things.

"No, just tie it around his horns," the Dean answered. "He'll come, all right."

The bull, seeing a man on foot at the entrance to his prison, rumbled a deep-voiced threat, and pawed the earth with angry strength.

For an instant, Patches, with his hand on the latch of the gate, paused to glance from the dangerous-looking animal, that awaited his coming, to the Dean who sat on his horse just outside the fence. Then he slipped inside the corral and closed the gate behind him. The bull gazed at him a moment as if amazed at the audacity of this mere human, then lowered his head for the charge.

"Climb that gate, quick," yelled the Dean at the critical moment.

And Patches climbed — not a second too soon.

From his position of safety he smiled cheerfully at the Dean. "He came all right, didn't he?"

The Dean's full rounded front and thick shoulders shook with laughter, while Señor Bull dared the man on the gate to come down.

"You crazy fool," said the Dean admiringly, when he could speak. "Didn't you know any better than to go in there on foot?"

"But you said you wanted him," returned the chagrined Patches.

"What I wanted," chuckled the Dean, "was to see if you had nerve enough to tackle him."

"To tell the truth," returned Patches, with a happy laugh, "that's exactly what interested me."

But, while the work assigned to Patches during those first days of his stay on the Cross-Triangle was chiefly those odd jobs which called for little or no experience, his higher education was by no means neglected. A wise and gentle old cow-horse was assigned to him, and the Dean taught him the various parts of his equipment, their proper use, and how to care for them. And every day, sometimes in the morning, sometimes late in the afternoon, the master found some errand or business that would necessitate his pupil riding with him. When Phil or Mrs. Baldwin would inquire about the Dean's kindergarten, as they called it, the Dean would laugh with them, but always he would say stoutly, "Just you wait. He'll be as near ready for the rodeo this fall as them pupils in that kindergarten of Phil's. He takes to ridin' like the good Lord had made him specially for that particular job. He's just a natural-born horseman, 'or I don't know men. He's got the sense, he's got the nerve, an' he's got the disposition. He's goin' to make a top hand in a few months, if" — he always added with twinkling eyes — "he don't get himself killed tryin' some fool experiment on himself."

"I notice just the same that he always has plenty of help in his experimentin'," Mrs. Baldwin would return dryly, which saying indicted not only the Dean but Phil and every man on the Cross-Triangle, including Little Billy.

Then came that day when Patches was given a task that — the Dean assured him — is one of the duties of even the oldest and best qualified cowboys. Patches was assigned to the work of fence-riding. But when the Dean rode out with his pupil early that morning to where the drift fence begins at the corner of the big pasture, and explained that "riding a fence" meant, in ranch language, looking for breaks and repairing any such when found, he did not explain the peculiarities of that particular kind of fence.

"I told him to be sure and be back by night," he chuckled, as he explained Patches' absence at dinner to the other members of the household.

"That was downright mean of you, Will Baldwin," chided Stella, with her usual motherly interest in the comfort of her boys. "You know the poor fellow will lose himself, sure, out in that wild Tailholt Mountain country."

The boys laughed.

"We'll find him in the morning, all right, mother," reassured Phil.

"He can follow the fence back, can't he?" retorted the Dean. "Or, as far as that goes, old Snip will bring him home."

"If he knows enough to figger it out, or to let Snip have his head," said Curly.

"At any rate," the Dean maintained, "he'll learn somethin' about the country, an' he'll learn somethin' about fences, an' mebby he'll learn somethin' about horses. An' we'll see whether he can use his own head or not. There's nothin' like givin' a man a chance to find out things for himself sometimes. Besides, think what a chance he'll have for some of his experiments! I'll bet a yearling steer that when we do see him again, he'll be tickled to death at himself an' wonderin' how he had the nerve to do it."

"To do what?" asked Mrs. Baldwin.

"I don't know what," chuckled the Dean; "but he's bound to do some fool thing or other just to see if he can, and it'll be somethin' that nobody but him would ever think of doin', too."

But Honorable Patches did not get lost that day — that is, not too badly lost. There was a time, though — but that does not belong just here.

Patches was very well pleased with the task assigned to him that morning. For the first time he found himself trusted alone with a horse, on a mission that would keep him the full day in the saddle, and would take him beyond sight of the ranch house. Very bravely he set out, equipped with his cowboy regalia — except the riata, which the Dean, fearing experiments, had, at the last moment, thoughtfully borrowed — and armed with a fencing tool and staples. He was armed, too, with a brand-new "six-gun" in a spick and span holster, on a shiny belt of bright cartridges. The Dean had insisted on this, alleging that the embryo cowboy might want it to kill a sick cow or something.

Patches wondered if he would know a sick cow if he should meet one, or how he was to diagnose the case to ascertain if she were sick enough to kill.

The first thing he did, when the Dean was safely out of sight, was to dismount and examine his saddle girth. Always your real king of the cattle range is careful for the foundation of his throne. But there was no awkwardness, now, when he again swung to his seat. The young man was in reality a natural athlete. His work had already taken the soreness and stiffness out of his unaccustomed muscles, and he seemed, as the Dean had said, a born horseman. And as he rode, he looked about over the surrounding country with an expression on independence, freedom and fearlessness very different from the manner of the troubled man who had faced Phil Acton that night on the Divide. It was as though the spirit of the land was already working its magic within this man, too. He patted the holster at his side, felt the handle of the gun, lovingly fingered the bright cartridges in his shiny belt, leaned sidewise to look admiringly down at his fringed, leather chaps and spur ornamented boot heels, and wished for his riata — not forgetting, meanwhile, to scan the fence for places that might need his attention.

The guardian angel who cares for the "tenderfoot" was good to Patches that day, and favored him with many sagging wires and leaning or broken posts, so that he could not ride far. Being painstaking and conscientious in his work, he had made not more than four miles by the beginning of the afternoon. Then he found a break that would occupy him for two hours at least. With rueful eyes he surveyed the long stretch of dilapidated fence. It was time, he reflected, that the Dean sent someone to look after his property, and dismounting, he went to work, forgetting, in his interest in the fencing problem, to insure his horse's near-by attendance. Now, the best of cow-horses are not above taking advantage of their opportunities. Perhaps Snip felt that fence-riding with a tenderfoot was a little beneath the dignity of his cattle-punching years. Perhaps he reasoned that this man who was always doing such strange things was purposely dismissing him. Perhaps he was thinking of the long watering trough and the rich meadow grass at home. Or, perhaps again, the wise old Snip, feeling the responsibility of his part in training the Dean's pupil, merely thought to give his inexperienced master a lesson. However it happened, Patches looked up from his work some time later to find himself alone. In consternation, he stood looking about, striving to catch a glimpse of the vanished Snip. Save a lone buzzard that wheeled in curious circles above his head there was no living thing in sight.

As fast as his heavy, leather chaps and high-heeled, spur-ornamented boots would permit, he ran to the top of a knoll a hundred yards or so away. The wider range of country that came thus within the circle of his vision was as empty as it was silent. The buzzard wheeled nearer — the strange looking creature beneath it seemed so helpless that there might be in the situation something of vital interest to the tribe. Even buzzards must be about their business.

There are few things more humiliating to professional riders of the range than to be left afoot; and while Patches was far too much a novice to have acquired the peculiar and traditional tastes and habits of the clan of which he had that morning felt himself a member, he was, in this, the equal of the best of them. He thought of himself walking shamefaced into the presence of the Dean and reporting the loss of the horse. The animal might be recovered, he supposed, for he was still, Patches thought, inside the pasture which that fence enclosed. Still there was a chance that the runaway would escape through some break and never be found. In any case the vision of the grinning cowboys was not an attractive one. But at least, thought the amateur cowboy, he would finish the work entrusted to him. He might lose a horse for the Dean, but the Dean's fence should be repaired. So he set to work with a will, and, finishing that particular break, set out on foot to follow the fence around the field and so back to the lane that would lead him to the buildings and corrals of the home ranch.

For an hour he trudged along, making hard work of it in his chaps, boots, and spurs, stopping now and then to drive a staple or brace a post. The country was growing wilder and more broken, with cedar timber on the ridges and here and there a pine. Occasionally he could catch a glimpse of the black, forbidding walls of Tailholt Mountain. But Patches did not know that it was Tailholt. He only thought that he knew in which direction the home ranch lay. It seemed to him that it was a long, long way to the corner of the field — it must be a big pasture, indeed. The afternoon was well on when he paused on the summit of another ridge to rest. It, seemed to him that he had never in all his life been quite so warm. His legs ached. He was tired and thirsty and hungry. It was so still that the silence hurt, and that fence corner was nowhere in sight. He could not, now reach home before dark, even should he turn back; which, he decided grimly, he would not do. He would ride that fence if he camped three nights on the journey.

Suddenly he sprang to his feet, waving his hat, hallooing and yelling like a madman. Two horsemen were riding on the other side of the fence, along the slope of the next ridge, at the edge of the timber. In vain Patches strove to attract their attention. If they heard him, they gave no sign, and presently he saw them turn, ride in among the cedars, and disappear. In desperation he ran along the fence, down the hill, across the narrow little valley, and up the ridge over which the riders had gone. On the top of the ridge he stopped again, to spend the last of his breath in another series of wild shouts. But there was no answer. Nor could he be sure, even, which way the horsemen had gone.

Dropping down in the shade of a cedar, exhausted by his strenuous exertion, and wet with honest perspiration, he struggled for breath and fanned his hot face with his hat. Perhaps he even used some of the cowboy words that he had heard Curly and Bob employ when Little Billy was not around After the noise of his frantic efforts, the silence was more oppressive than ever. The Cross-Triangle ranch house was, somewhere, endless miles away.

Then a faint sound in the narrow valley below him caught his ear. Turning quickly, he looked back the way he had come. Was he dreaming, or was it all just a part of the magic of that wonderful land? A young woman was riding toward him — coming at an easy swinging lope — and, following, at the end of a riata, was the cheerfully wise and philosophic Snip.

Patches' first thought — when he had sufficiently recovered I from his amazement to think at all — was that the woman rode as he had never seen a woman ride before. Dressed in the divided skirt of corduroy, the loose, soft, grey shirt, gauntleted gloves, mannish felt hat, and boots, usual to Arizona horsewomen, she seemed as much at ease in the saddle as any cowboy in the land; and, indeed, she was.

As she came up the slope, the man in the shade of the cedar saw that she was young. Her lithe, beautifully developed body yielded to the movement of the spirited horse she rode with the unspoiled grace of health and youth. Still nearer, and he saw her clear cheeks glowing with the exercise and excitement, her soft, brown hair under the wide brim of the grey sombrero, and her dark eyes, shining with the fun of her adventure. Then she saw him, and smiled; and Patches remembered what the Dean had said: "If there's a man in Yavapai County who wouldn't ride the hoofs off the best horse in his outfit to win a smile from Kitty Reid, he ought to be lynched."

As the man stood, hat in hand, she checked her horse, and, in a voice that matched the smile so full of fun and the clean joy of living greeted him.

"You are Mr. Honorable Patches, are you not?"

Patches bowed. "Miss Reid, I believe?"

She frankly looked her surprise. "Why, how did you know me?"

"Your good friend, Mr. Baldwin, described you," he smiled.

She colored and laughed to hide her slight embarrassment. "The dear old Dean is prejudiced, I fear."

"Prejudiced he may be," Patches admitted, "but his judgment is unquestionable. And," he added gently, as her face grew grave and her chin lifted slightly, "his confidence in any man might be considered an endorsement, don't you think?"

"Indeed, yes," she agreed heartily, her slight coldness vanishing instantly. "The Dean and Stella told me all about you this afternoon, or I should not have ventured to introduce myself. I am very pleased to meet you, Mr. Patches," she finished with a mock formality that was delightful.

"And I am delighted to meet you, Miss Reid, for so many reasons that I can't begin to tell you of them," he responded laughing. "And now, may I ask what good magic brings you like a fairy in the story book to the rescue of a poor stranger in the hour of his despair? Where did you find my faithless Snip? How did you know where to find me? Where is the Cross-Triangle Ranch? How many miles is it to the nearest water? Is it possible for me to get home in time for supper?" Looking down at him she laughed as only Kitty Reid could laugh.

"You're making fun of me," he charged; "they all do. And I don't blame them in the least; I have been laughing at myself all day."

"I'll answer your last question first," she returned. "Yes, you can easily reach the Cross-Triangle in time for supper, if you start at once. I will explain the magic as we ride."

"You are going to show me the way?" he cried eagerly, starting toward his horse.

"I really think it would be best," she said demurely.

"Now I know you are a good fairy, or a guardian angel, or something like that," he returned, setting his foot in the stirrup to mount. Then suddenly he paused, with, "Wait a minute, please. I nearly forgot." And very carefully he examined the saddle girth to see that it was tight.

"If you had remembered to throw your bridle rein over Snip's head when you left him, you wouldn't have needed a guardian angel this time," she said.

He looked at her blankly over the patient Snip's back.

"And so that was what made him go away? I knew I had done some silly thing that I ought not. That's the only thing about myself that I am always perfectly sure of," he added as he mounted. "You see I can always depend upon myself to make a fool of myself. It was that bad place in the fence that did it." He pulled up his horse suddenly as they were starting. "And that reminds me; there is one thing you positively must tell me before I can go a foot, even toward supper. How much farther is it to the corner of this field?"

She looked at him in pretty amazement. "To the corner of this field?"

"Yes, I knew, of course, that if I followed the fence it was bound to lead me around the field and so back to where I started. That's why I kept on; I thought I could finish the job and get home, even if Snip did compel me to ride the fence on foot."

"But don't you know that this is a drift fence?" she asked, her eyes dancing with fun.

"That's what the Dean called it," he admitted. "But if it's drifting anywhere, it's going end on. Perhaps that's why I couldn't catch the corner."

"But there is no corner to a drift fence," she cried.

"No corner?"

She shook her head as if not trusting herself to speak.

"And it doesn't go around anything — there is no field?" Again she shook her head.

"Just runs away out in the country somewhere and stops?"

She nodded. "It must be eighteen or twenty miles from here to the end."

"Well, of all the silly fences!" he exclaimed, looking away to the mountain peaks toward which he had been so laboriously making his way. "Honestly, now, do you think that is any way for a respectable fence to act? And the Dean told me to be sure and get home before dark!"

Then they laughed together — laughed until their horses must have wondered.

As they rode on, she explained the purpose of the drift fence, and how it came to an end so many miles away and so far from water that the cattle do not usually find their way around it.

"And now the magic!" he said. "You have made a most unreasonable, unconventional and altogether foolish fence appear reasonable, proper and perfectly sane. Please explain your coming with Snip to my relief."

"Which was also unreasonable, unconventional and altogether foolish?" she questioned.

"Which was altogether wonderful, unexpected and delightful," he retorted.

"It is all perfectly simple," she explained. "Being rather —" She hesitated. "Well, rather sick of too much of nothing at all, you know, I went over to the Cross-Triangle right after dinner to visit a little with Stella — professionally."

"Professionally?" he asked.

She nodded brightly. "For the good of my soul. Stella's a famous soul doctor. The best ever except one, and she lives far away — away back east in Cleveland, Ohio."

"Yes, I know her, too," he said gravely.

And while they laughed at the absurdity of his assertion, they did not know until long afterward how literally true it was.

"Of course, I knew about you," she continued. "Phil told me how you tried to ride that unbroken horse, the last time he was at our house. Phil thinks you are quite a wonderful man."

"No doubt," said Patches mockingly. "I must have given a remarkable exhibition on that occasion." He was wondering just how much Phil had told her.

"And so, you see," she continued, "I couldn't very well help being interested in the welfare of the stranger who had come among us. Besides, our traditional western hospitality demanded it; don't you think?"

"Oh, certainly, certainly. You could really do nothing less than inquire about me," he agreed politely.

"And so, you see, Stella quite restored my soul health; or at least afforded me temporary relief."

He met the quizzing, teasing, laughing look in her eyes blankly. "You are making fun of me again," he said humbly. "I know I ought to laugh at myself, but —"

"Why, don't you understand?" she cried. "Dr. Stella administered a generous dose of talk about the only new thing that has happened in this neighborhood for months and months and months."

"Meaning me?" he asked.

"Well, are you not?" she retorted.

"I guess I am," he smiled. "Well, and then what?"

"Why, then I came away, feeling much better, of course."

"Yes?"

"I was feeling so much better I decided I would go home a roundabout way; perhaps to the top of Black Hill; perhaps up Horse Wash, where I might meet father, who would be on his way home from Fair Oaks where he went this morning."

"I see."

"Well, so I met Snip, who was on his way to the Cross-Triangle. I knew, of course, that old Snip would be your horse." She smiled, as though to rob her words of any implied criticism of his horsemanship.

"Exactly," he agreed understandingly.

"And I was afraid that something might have happened; though I couldn't see how that could be, either, with Snip. And so I caught him —"

He interrupted eagerly. "How?"

"Why, with my riata," she returned, in a matter-of-fact tone, wondering at his question.

"You caught my horse with your riata?" he repeated slowly.

"And pray how should I have caught him?" she asked.

"But — but, didn't he *run?*"

She laughed. "Of course he ran. They all do that once they get away from you. But Snip never could outrun my Midnight," she retorted.

He shook his head slowly, looking at her with frank admiration, as though, for the first time, he understood what a rare and wonderful creature she was.

"And you can ride and rope like that?" he said doubtfully.

She flushed hotly, and there was a spark of fire in the brown eyes. "I suppose you are thinking that I am coarse and mannish and all that," she said with spirit. "By your standards, Mr. Patches, I should have ridden back to the house, screaming, ladylike, for help."

"No, no," he protested. "That's not fair. I was thinking how wonderful you are. Why, I would give — what wouldn't I give to be able to do a thing like that!"

There was no mistaking his earnestness, and Kitty was all sunshine again, pardoning him with a smile.

"You see," she explained, "I have always lived here, except my three years at school. Father taught me to use a riata, as he taught me to ride and shoot, because — well — because it's all a part of this life, and very useful sometimes; just as it is useful to know about hotels and time-tables and taxicabs, in that other part of the world."

"I understand," he said gently. "It was stupid of me to notice it. I beg your pardon for interrupting the story of my rescue. You had just roped Snip while he was doing his best to outrun Midnight — simple and easy as calling a taxi — 'Number Two Thousand Euclid Avenue, please' — and there you are."

"Oh, do you know Cleveland?" she cried.

For an instant he was confused. Then he said easily, "Everybody has heard of the famous Euclid Avenue. But how did you guess where Snip had left me?"

"Why, Stella had told me that you were riding the drift fence," she answered, tactfully ignoring the evasion of her question. "I just followed the fence. So there was no magic about it at all, you see."

"I'm not so sure about the magic," he returned slowly.

"This is such a wonderful country — to me — that one can never be quite sure about anything. At least, I can't. But perhaps that's because I am such a new thing."

"And do you like it?" she asked, frankly curious about him.

"Like being a new thing?" he parried. "Yes and No."

"I mean do you like this wonderful country, as you call it?"

"I admire the people who belong to it tremendously," he returned. "I never met such men before — or such women," he finished with a smile.

"But, do you like it?" she persisted. "Do you like the life — your work — would you be satisfied to live here always?"

"Yes and No," he answered again, hesitatingly.

"Oh, well," she said, with, he thought, a little bitterness and rebellion, "it doesn't really matter to you whether you like it or not, because *you* are a man. If you are not satisfied with your environment, you can leave it — go away somewhere else — make yourself a part of some other life."

He shook his head, wondering a little at her earnestness. "That does not always follow. Can a man, just because he is a man, always have or do just what he likes?"

"If he's strong enough," she insisted. "But a woman must always do what other people like."

He was sure now that she was speaking rebelliously.

She continued, "Can't you, if you are not satisfied with this life here, go away?"

"Yes, but not necessarily to any life I might desire. Perhaps some sheriff wants me. Perhaps I am an escaped convict. Perhaps — oh, a thousand things."

She laughed aloud in spite of her serious mood. "What nonsense!"

"But, why nonsense? What do you and your friends know of me?"

"We know that you are not that kind of a man," she retorted warmly, "because" — she hesitated — "well, because you are *not* that sort of a man."

"Are you sure you don't mean because I am not man enough to make myself wanted very badly, even by the sheriff?" he asked, and Kitty could not mistake the bitterness in his voice.

"Why, Mr. Patches!" she cried. "How could you think I meant such a thing? Forgive me! I was only wondering foolishly what you, a man of education and culture, could find in this rough life that would appeal to you in any way. My curiosity is unpardonable, I suppose, but you must know that we are all wondering why you are here."

"I do not blame you," he returned, with that self-mocking smile, as though he were laughing at himself. "I told you I could always be depended upon to make a fool of myself. You see I am doing it now. I don't mind telling you this much — that I am here for the same reason that you went to visit Mrs. Baldwin this afternoon."

"For the good of your soul?" she asked gently.

"Exactly," he returned gravely. "For the good of my soul."

"Well, then, Mr. Honorable Patches, here's to your soul's good health!" she cried brightly, checking her horse and holding out her hand. "We part here. You can see the Cross-Triangle buildings yonder. I go this way."

He looked his pleasure, as he clasped her hand in hearty understanding of the friendship offered.

"Thank you, Miss Reid. I still maintain that the Dean's judgment is unquestionable."

She was not at all displeased with his reply.

"By the way," she said, as if to prove her friendship. "I suppose you know what to expect from Uncle Will and the boys when they learn of your little adventure?"

"I do," he answered, as if resigned to anything.

"And do you enjoy making fun for them?"

"I assure you, Miss Reid, I am very human."

"Well, then, why don't you turn the laugh on them?"

"But how?"

"They are expecting you to get into some sort of a scrape, don't you think?"

"They are always expecting that. And," he added, with that droll touch in his voice, "I must say I rarely disappoint them."

"I suspect," she continued, thoughtfully, "that the Dean purposely did not explain that drift fence to you."

"He has established precedents that would justify my thinking so, I'll admit."

"Well, then, why don't you ride cheerfully home and report the progress of your work as though nothing had happened?"

"You mean that you won't tell?" he cried.

She nodded gaily. "I told them this afternoon that it wasn't fair for you to have no one but Stella on your side."

"What a good Samaritan you are! You put me under an everlasting obligation to you."

"All right," she laughed. "I'm glad you feel that way about it. I shall hold that debt against you until some day when I am in dreadful need, and then I shall demand payment in full. Good-bye!"

And once again Kitty had spoken, in jest, words that held for them both, had they but known, great significance.

Patches watched until she was out of sight. Then he made his way happily to the house to receive, with a guilty conscience but with a light heart, congratulations and compliments upon his safe return.

That evening Phil disappeared somewhere, in the twilight. And a little later Jim Reid rode into the Cross-Triangle dooryard.

The owner of the Pot-Hook-S was a big man, tall and heavy, outspoken and somewhat gruff, with a manner that to strangers often seemed near to overbearing. When Patches was introduced, the big cattleman looked him over suspiciously, spoke a short word in response to Patches' commonplace, and abruptly turned his back to converse with the better-known members of the household.

For an hour, perhaps, they chatted about matters of general interest, as neighbors will; then the caller arose to go, and the Dean walked with him to his horse. When the two men were out of hearing of the people on the porch Reid asked in a low voice, "Noticed any stock that didn't look right lately, Will?"

"No. You see, we haven't been ridin' scarcely any since the Fourth. Phil and the boys have been busy with the horses every day, an' this new man don't count, you know."

"Who is he, anyway?" asked Reid bluntly.

"I don't know anymore than that he says his name is Patches."

"Funny name," grunted Jim.

"Yes, but there's a lot of funny names, Jim," the Dean answered quietly. "I don't know as Patches is any funnier than Skinner or Foote or Hogg, or a hundred other names, when you come to think about it. We ain't just never happened to hear it before, that's all."

"Where did you pick him up?"

"He just came along an' wanted work. He's green as they make 'em, but willin', an' he's got good sense, too."

"I'd go slow 'bout takin' strangers in," said the big man bluntly.

"Shucks!" retorted the Dean. "Some of the best men I ever had was strangers when I hired 'em. Bein' a stranger ain't nothin' against a man. You and me would be strangers if we was to go many miles from Williamson Valley. Patches is a good man, I tell you. I'll stand for him, all right. Why, he's been out all day, alone, ridin' the drift fence, just as good any old-timer."

"The drift fence!"

"Yes, it's in pretty bad shape in places."

"Yes, an' I ran onto a calf over in Horse Wash, this afternoon, not four hundred yards from the fence on the Tailholt side, fresh-branded with the Tailholt iron, an' I'll bet a thousand dollars it belongs to a Cross-Triangle cow."

"What makes you think it was mine?" asked the Dean calmly.

"Because it looked mighty like some of your Hereford stock, an' because I came on through the Horse Wash gate, an' about a half mile on this side, I found one of your cows that had just lost her calf."

"They know we're busy an' ain't ridin' much, I reckon," mused the Dean.

"If I was you, I'd put some hand that I knew to ridin' that drift fence," returned Jim significantly, as he mounted his horse to go.

"You're plumb wrong, Jim," returned the Dean earnestly. "Why, the man don't know a Cross-Triangle from a Five-Bar, or a Pot-Hook-S."

"It's your business, Will; I just thought I'd tell you," growled Reid. "Good-night!"

"Good-night, Jim! I'm much obliged to you for ridin' over."

Chapter VII

THINGS THAT ENDURE

*W*hen Kitty Reid told Patches that it was her soul sickness, from too much of nothing at all, that had sent her to visit Mrs. Baldwin that afternoon, she had spoken more in earnest than in jest. More than this, she had gone to the Cross-Triangle hoping to meet the stranger, of whom she had heard so much. Phil had told Kitty that she would like Patches. As Phil had put it, the man spoke her language; he could talk to her of people and books and those things of which the Williamson Valley folk knew so little.

But as she rode slowly homeward after leaving Patches, she found herself of two minds regarding the incident. She had enjoyed meeting the man; he had interested and amused her; had taken her out of herself, for she was not slow to recognize that the man really did belong to that world which was so far from the world of her childhood. And she was glad for the little adventure that, for one afternoon, at least, had broken the dull, wearying monotony of her daily life. But the stranger, by the very fact of his belonging to that other world, had stimulated her desire for those things which in her home life and environment she so greatly missed. He had somehow seemed to magnify the almost unbearable commonplace narrowness of her daily routine. He had made her even more restless, disturbed and dissatisfied. It had been to her as when one in some foreign country meets a citizen from one's old home town. And for this Kitty was genuinely sorry. She did not wish to feel as she did about her home and the things that made the world of those she loved. She had tried honestly to still the unrest and to deny the longing. She had wished many times, since her return from the East, that she had never left her home for those three years in school. And yet, those years had meant much to her; they had been wonderful years; but they seemed, somehow — now that they were past and she was home again — to have brought her only that unrest and longing.

From the beginning of her years until that first great crisis in her life — her going away to school — this world into which she was born had been to Kitty an all-sufficient world. The days of her childhood had been as carefree and joyous, almost, as the days of the young things of her father's roaming herds. As her girlhood years advanced, under her mother's wise companionship and careful teaching, she had grown into her share of the household duties and into a knowledge of woman's part in the life to which she belonged, as naturally as her girlish form had put on the graces of young womanhood. The things that filled the days of her father and mother, and the days of her neighbors and friends, had filled her days. The things that were all in all to those she loved had been all in all to her. And always, through those years, from her earliest childhood to her young womanhood, there was Phil, her playmate, schoolmate, protector, hero, slave. That Phil should be her boy sweetheart and young man lover had seemed as natural to Kitty as her relation to her parents. There had never been anyone else but Phil. There never could be — she was sure, in those days — anyone else.

In Kitty's heart that afternoon, as she rode, so indifferent to the life that called from every bush and tree and grassy hill and distant mountain, there was sweet regret, deep and sincere, for those years that were now, to her, so irrevocably gone. Kitty did not know how impossible it was for her to ever wholly escape the things that belonged to her childhood and youth. Those things of her girlhood, out of which her heart and soul had been fashioned, were as interwoven in the fabric of her being as the vitality, strength and purity of the clean, wholesome, outdoor life of those same years were wrought into the glowing health and vigor and beauty of her physical womanhood.

And then had come those other years — the maturing, ripening years — when, from the simple, primitive and enduring elements of life, she had gone to live amid complex, cultivated and largely fanciful standards and values. In that land of Kitty's birth a man is measured by the measure of his manhood; a woman is ranked by the quality of her womanhood. Strength and courage, sincerity, honesty, usefulness — these were the prime essentials of the man life that Kitty had, in those years of her girlhood, known; and these, too, in their feminine expressions, were the essentials of the woman life. But from these the young woman had gone to be educated in a world where other things are of first importance. She had gone to be taught that these are not the essential elements of manhood and womanhood. Or, at least, if she was not to be deliberately so taught, these things would be so ignored and neglected and overlooked in her training, that the effect on her character would be the same. In that new world she was to learn that men and women are not to be measured by the standards of manhood and womanhood — that they were to be rated, not for strength, but for culture; not for courage, but for intellectual cleverness; not for sincerity, but for manners; not for honesty, but for success; not for usefulness, but for social position, which is most often determined by the degree of uselessness. It was as though the handler of gems were to attach no value whatever to the weight of the diamond itself, but to fix the worth of the stone wholly by the cutting and polish that the crystal might receive.

At first, Kitty had been excited, bewildered and fascinated by the glittering, sparkling, ever-changing, many-faceted life. Then she had grown weary and homesick. And then, as the months had passed, and she had been drawn more and more by association and environment into the world of down-to-dateism she, too, began to regard the sparkle of the diamond as the determining factor in the value of the gem. And when the young woman had achieved this, they called her education finished, and sent her back to the land over which Granite Mountain, grey and grim and fortresslike, with its ranks of sentinel bills? keeps enduring and unchanging watch.

During those first glad days of Kitty's homecoming she had been eagerly interested in everything. The trivial bits of news about the small doings of her old friends had been delightful. The home life, with its simple routine and its sweet companionship, had been restful and satisfying. The very scenes of her girlhood had seemed to welcome her with a spirit of genuineness and steadfastness that had made her feel as one entering a safe home harbor after a long and adventurous voyage to faraway and little-known lands. And Phil, in the virile strength of his manhood, in the simple bigness of his character, and in his enduring and unchanging love, had made her feel his likeness to the primitive land of his birth.

But when the glad excitement of those first days of her return were past, when the meetings with old friends were over and the tales of their doings exhausted, then Kitty began to realize what her education, as they called it, really meant. The lessons of those three years were not to be erased from her life as one would erase a mistake in a problem or a misspelled word. The tastes, habits of thought and standards of life, the acquirement of which constituted her culture, would not be denied. It was inevitable that there should be a clash between the claims of her home life and the claims of that life to which she now felt that she also belonged.

However odious comparisons may be, they are many times inevitable. Loyally, Kitty tried to magnify the worth of those things that in her girlhood had been the supreme things in her life, but, try as she might, they were now, in comparison with those things which her culture placed first, of trivial importance. The virile strength and glowing health of Phil's unspoiled manhood — beautiful as the vigorous life of one of the wild horses from which he had his nickname — were overshadowed, now, by the young man's inability to clothe his splendid body in that fashion which her culture demanded. His simple and primitive views of life — as natural as the instinct which governs all creatures in his God-cultivated world — were now unrefined, ignoble, inelegant. His fine nature and unembarrassed intelligence, which found in the wealth of realities amid which he lived abundant food for his intellectual life, and which enabled him to see clearly, observe closely and think with such clean-cut directness, beside the intellectuality of those schooled in the thoughts of others, appeared as ignorance and illiteracy. The very fineness and gentleness of his nature were now the distinguishing marks of an uncouth and awkward rustic.

With all her woman heart Kitty had fought against these comparisons — and continued to make them. Everything in her nature that belonged to Granite Mountain — that was, in short, the product of that land — answered to Phil's call, as instinctively as the life of that land calls and answers Its mating calls. Everything that she had acquired in those three years of a more advanced civilization denied and repulsed him. And now her meeting with Patches had stirred the warring forces to renewed activity, and in the distracting turmoil of her thoughts she found herself hating the land she loved, loathing the life that appealed to her with such insistent power, despising those whom she so dearly esteemed and honored, and denying the affection of which she was proud with a true woman's tender pride.

Kitty was aroused from her absorption by the shrill boyish yells of her two younger brothers, who, catching sight of their sister from the top of one of the low hills that edge the meadow bottom lands, were charging recklessly down upon her.

As the clatter and rumble of those eight flying hoofs drew nearer and nearer, Midnight, too, "came alive," as the cowboys say, and tossed his head and pranced with eager impatience.

"Where in the world have you been all the afternoon?" demanded Jimmy, with twelve-year-old authority, as his pony slid to a halt within a foot or two of his sister's horse.

And, "We wanted you to go with us, to see our coyote traps," reproved Conny — two years younger than his brother — as his pinto executed a like maneuver on the other side of the excited Midnight.

"And where is Jack?" asked the young woman mischievously, as she smilingly welcomed the vigorous lads.

"Couldn't he help?"

Jack was the other member of the Reid trio of boys — a lusty four-year-old who felt himself equal to any venture that interested his brothers.

Jimmy grinned. "Aw, mama coaxed him into the kitchen with something to eat while me and Conny sneaked down to the corral and saddled up and beat it."

Big sister's dark eyebrows arched in shocked inquiry, "*Me* and Conny?"

"That is, Conny and I," amended Jimmy, with good-natured tolerance of his sister's whims.

"You see, Kitty," put in Conny, "this hero coyote traps pin' ain't just fun. It's business. Dad's promised us three dollars for every scalp, an' we're aimin' to make a stake. We didn't git a blamed thing, today, though."

Sister's painful and despairing expression was blissfully ignored as Jimmy stealthily flicked the long romal at the end of his bridle reins against Midnight's flank.

"Gee!" observed the tickled youngster, as Kitty gave all her attention to restraining the fretting and indignant horse, "ol' Midnight is sure some festive, ain't he?"

"I'll race you both to the big gate," challenged Kitty.

"For how much?" demanded Jimmy quickly.

"You got to give us fifty yards start," declared Conny, leaning forward in his saddle and shortening his reins.

"If I win, you boys go straight to bed tonight, when it's time, without fussing," said Kitty, "and I'll give you to that oak bush yonder."

"Good enough! You're on!" they shouted in chorus, and loped away.

As they passed the handicap mark, another shrill, defiant yell came floating back to where Kitty sat reining in her impatient Midnight. At the signal, the two ponies leaped from a lope into a full run, while Kitty loosed the restraining rein and the black horse stretched away in pursuit. Spurs ring, shouting, entreating, the two lads urged their sturdy mounts toward the goal, and the pintos answered gamely with all that they had. Over knolls and washes, across arroyos and gullies they flew, sure-footed and eager, neck and neck, while behind them, drawing nearer and nearer, came the black, with body low, head outstretched and limbs that moved apparently with the timed regularity and driving power of a locomotive's piston rod. As she passed them, Kitty shouted a merry "Come on!"

which they answered with redoubled exertion and another yell of hearty boyish admiration for the victorious Midnight and his beautiful rider.

"Doggone that black streak!" exclaimed Jimmy, his eyes dancing with fun as they pulled up at the corral gate.

"He opens and shuts like a blamed ol' jack rabbit," commented Conny. "Seemed like we was just a-sittin' still watchin' you go by."

Kitty laughed, teasingly, and unconsciously slipped into the vernacular as she returned, "Did you kids think you were a-horseback?"

"You just wait, Miss," retorted the grinning Jimmy, as he opened the big gate. "I'll get a horse some day that'll run circles around that ol' black scound'el."

And then, as they dismounted at the door of the saddle room in the big barn, he added generously, "You scoot on up to the house, Kitty; I'll take care of Midnight. It must be gettin' near supper time, an' I'm hungry enough to eat a raw dog."

At which alarming statement Kitty promptly scooted, stopping only long enough at the windmill pump for a cool, refreshing drink.

Mrs. Reid, with sturdy little Jack helping, was already busy in the kitchen. She was a motherly woman, rather below Kitty's height, and inclined somewhat to a comfortable stoutness. In her face was the gentle strength and patience of those whose years have been spent in home-making, without the hardness that is sometimes seen in the faces of those whose love is not great enough to soften their tail. One knew by the light in her eyes whenever she spoke of Kitty, or, indeed, whenever the girl's name was mentioned, how large a place her only daughter held in her mother heart.

While the two worked together at their homely task, the girl related in trivial detail the news of the neighborhood, and repeated faithfully the talk she had had with the mistress of the Cross-Triangle, answering all her mother's questions, replying with careful interest to the older woman's comments, relating all that was known or guessed, or observed regarding the stranger. But of her meeting with Patches, Kitty said little; only that she had met him as she was coming home. All during the evening meal, too, Patches was the principal topic of the conversation, though Mr. Reid, who had arrived home just in time for supper, said little.

When supper was over, and the evening work finished, Kitty sat on the porch in the twilight, looking away across the wide valley meadows, toward the light that shone where the walnut trees about the Cross-Triangle ranch house made a darker mass in the gathering gloom. Her father had gone to call upon the Dean. The men were at the bunk-house, from which their voices came low and indistinct. Within the house the mother was coaxing little Jack to bed. Jimmy and Conny, at the farther end of the porch, were planning an extensive campaign against coyotes, and investing the unearned profits of their proposed industry.

Kitty's thoughts were many miles away. In that bright and stirring life — so far from the gloomy stillness of her home land, where she sat so alone — what gay pleasures held her friends? Amid what brilliant scenes were they spending the evening, while she sat in her dark and silent world alone? As her memory pictured the lights, the stirring movement, the music, the merry-voiced talk, the laughter, the gaiety, the excitement, the companionship of those whose lives were so full of interest, her heart rebelled at the dull emptiness of her days. As she watched the evening dusk deepen into the darkness of the night, and the outlines of the familiar landscape fade and vanish in the thickening gloom, she felt the dreary monotony of the days and years that were to come, blotting out of her life all tone and color and forms of brightness and beauty.

Then she saw, slowly emerging from the shadows of the meadow below, a darker shadow — mysterious, formless — that seemed, as it approached, to shape itself out of the very darkness through which it came, until, still dim and indistinct, a horseman was opening the meadow gate. Before the cowboy answered Jimmy's boyish "Hello!" Kitty knew that it was Phil.

The young woman's first impulse was to retreat to the safe seclusion of her own room. But, even as she arose to her feet, she knew how that would hurt the man who had always been so good to her; and so she went generously down the walk to meet him where he would dismount and leave his horse.

"Did you see father?" she asked, thinking as she spoke how little there was for them to talk about.

"Why, no. What's the matter?" he returned quickly, pausing as if ready to ride again at her word.

She laughed a little at his manner. "There is nothing the matter. He just went over to see the Dean, that's all."

"I must have missed him crossing the meadow," returned Phil. "He always goes around by the road."

Then, when he stood beside her, he added gently, "But there is something the matter, Kitty. What is it? Lonesome for the bright lights?"

That was always Phil's way, she thought. He seemed always to know instinctively her every mood and wish.

"Perhaps I was a little lonely," she admitted. "I am glad that you came."

Then they were at the porch, and her ambitious brothers were telling Phil in detail their all-absorbing designs against the peace of the coyote tribe, and asking his advice. Mrs. Reid came to sit with them a-while, and again the talk followed around the narrow circle of their lives, until Kitty felt that she could bear no more. Then Mrs. Reid, more merciful than she knew, sent the boys to bed and retired to her own room.

"And so you are tired of us all, and want to go back," mused Phil, breaking one of the long, silent periods that in these days seemed so often to fall upon them when they found themselves alone.

"That's not quite fair, Phil," she returned gently. "You know it's not that."

"Well, then, tired of this" — his gesture indicated the sweep of the wide land — "tired of what we are and what we do?"

The girl stirred uneasily, but did not speak.

"I don't blame you," he continued, as if thinking aloud. "It must seem mighty empty to those who don't really know it."

"And don't I know it?" challenged Kitty. "You seem to forget that I was born here — that I have lived here almost as many years as you."

"But just the same you don't know," returned Phil gently. "You see, dear, you knew it as a girl, the same as I did when I was a boy. But now — well, I know it as a man, and you as a woman know something that you think is very different."

Again that long silence lay a barrier between them. Then Kitty made the effort, hesitatingly. "Do you love the life so very, very much, Phil?"

He answered quickly. "Yes, but I could love any life that suited you."

"No — no," she returned hurriedly, "that's not — I mean — Phil, why are you so satisfied here? There is so little for a man like you."

"So little!" His voice told her that her words had stung. "I told you that you did not know. Why, everything that a man has a right to want is here. All that life can give anywhere is here — I mean all of life that is worth having. But I suppose," he finished lamely, "that it's hard for you to see it that way — now. It's like trying to make a city man understand why a fellow is never lonesome just because there's no crowd around. I guess I love this life and am satisfied with it just as the wild horses over there at the foot of old Granite love it and are satisfied."

"But don't you feel, sometimes, that if you had greater opportunities — don't you sometimes wish that you could live where —" She paused at a loss for words. Phil somehow always made the things she craved seem so trivial.

"I know what you mean," he answered. "You mean, don't the wild horses wish that they could live in a fine stable, and have a lot of men to feed and take care of them, and rig them out with fancy, gold-mounted harness, and let them prance down the streets for the crowds to see? No; horses have more sense than that. It takes a human to make that kind of a fool of himself. There's only one thing in the world that would make me want to try it, and I guess you know what that is."

His last words robbed his answer of its sting, and she said gently, "You are bitter tonight, Phil. It is not like you."

He did not answer.

"Did something go wrong today?" she persisted.

He turned suddenly to face her, and spoke with a passion unusual to him. "I saw you at the ranch this afternoon — as you were riding away. You did not even look toward the corral where you knew I was at work; and it seemed like all the heart went clear out of me. Oh, Kitty, girl, can't we bring back the old days as they were before you went away?"

"Hush, Phil," she said, almost as she would have spoken to one of her boy brothers.

But he went on recklessly. "No, I'm going to speak tonight. Ever since you came home you have refused to listen to me — you have put me off — made me keep still. I want you to tell me, Kitty, if I were like Honorable Patches, would it make any difference?"

"I do not know Mr. Patches," she answered.

"You met him today; and you know what I mean. Would it make any difference if I were like him?"

"Why, Phil, dear, how can I answer such a question? I do not know."

"Then it's not because I belong here in this country instead of back East in some city that has made you change?"

"I have changed, I suppose, because I have become a woman, Phil, as you have become a man."

"Yes, I have become a man," he returned, "but I have not changed, except that the boy's love has become a man's love. Would it make any difference, Kitty, if you cared more for the life here — I mean if you were contented here — if these things that mean so much to us all, satisfied you?"

Again she answered, "I do not know, Phil. How can I know?"

"Will you try, Kitty — I mean try to like your old home as you used to like it?"

"Oh, Phil, I have tried. I do try," she cried. "But I don't think it's the life that I like or do not like that makes the difference. I am sure, Phil, that if I could" — she hesitated, then went on bravely — "if I could give you the love you want, nothing else would matter. You said you could like any life that suited me. Don't you think that I could be satisfied with any life that suited the man I loved?"

"Yes," he said, "you could; and that's the answer."

"What is the answer?" she asked.

"Love, just love, Kitty — anyplace with love is a good place, and without love no life can satisfy. I am glad you said that. It was what I wanted you to say. I know now what I have to do. I am like Patches. I have found my job." There was no bitterness in his voice now.

The girl was deeply moved, but — "I don't think I quite understand, Phil," she said.

"Why, don't you see?" he returned. "My job is to win your love — to make you love me — for myself — for just what I am — as a man — and not to try to be something or to live some way that I think you would like. It's the man that you must love, and not what he does or where he lives. Isn't that it?"

"Yes," she answered slowly. "I am sure that is so. It must be so, Phil."

He rose to his feet abruptly. "All right," he said, almost roughly. "I'll go now. But don't make any mistake, Kitty. You're mine, girl, mine, by laws that are higher than the things they taught you at school. And you are going to find it out. I am going to win you — just as the wild things out there win their mates. You are going to come to me, girl, because you are mine — because you are my mate."

And then, as she, too, arose, and they stood for a silent moment facing each other, the woman felt his strength, and in her woman heart was glad — glad and proud, though she could not give all that he asked.

As she watched him ride away into the night, and the soft mystery of the darkness out of which he had come seemed to take his shadowy form again to itself, she wondered — wondered with regret in the thought — would he, perhaps, go thus out of her life? Would he?

When Phil turned his horse into the meadow pasture at home the big bay, from somewhere in the darkness, trumpeted his challenge. A low laugh came from near by, and in the light of the stars Phil saw a man standing by the pasture fence. As he went toward the shadowy figure the voice of Patches followed the laugh.

"I'll bet that was Stranger."

"I know it was," answered Phil. "What's the matter that you're not in bed?"

"Oh, I was just listening to the horses out there, and thinking," returned Patches.

"Thinking about your job?" asked Phil quietly.

"Perhaps," admitted the other.

"Well, you have no reason to worry; you'll ride him all right," said the cowboy.

"I wish I could be as sure," the other returned doubt fully.

And they both knew that they were using the big bay horse as a symbol.

"And I wish I was as sure of making good at my job, as I am that you will win out with yours," returned Phil.

Patches' voice was very kind as he said reflectively, "So, you have a job, too. I am glad for that."

"Glad?"

"Yes," the tall man placed a hand on the other's shoulder as they turned to walk toward the house, "because, Phil, I have come to the conclusion that this old world is a mighty empty place for the man who has nothing to do."

"But there seems to be a lot of fellows who manage to keep fairly busy doing nothing, just the same, don't you think?" replied Phil with a low laugh.

"I said *man*'," retorted Patches, with emphasis.

"That's right," agreed Phil. "A man just naturally requires a man's job."

"And," mused Patches, "when it's all said and done, I suppose there's only one genuine, simon-pure, full-sized man's job in the world."

"And I reckon that's right, too," returned the cowboy.

Chapter VIII

CONCERNING BRANDS

A few days after Jim Reid's evening visit to the Dean two cowboys from the Diamond-and-a-Half outfit, on their way to Cherry Creek, stopped at the ranch for dinner.

The well-known, open-handed Baldwin hospitality led many a passing rider thus aside from the main valley road and through the long meadow lane to the Cross-Triangle table. Always there was good food for man and horse, with a bed for those who came late in the day; and always there was a hearty welcome and talk under the walnut trees with the Dean. And in all that broad land there was scarce a cowboy who, when riding the range, would not look out for the Dean's cattle with almost the same interest and care that he gave to the animals bearing the brand of his own employer.

So it was that these riders from the Tonto Flats country told the Dean that in looking over the Cross-Triangle cattle watering at Toohey they had seen several cases of screwworms.

"We doped a couple of the worst, and branded a calf for you," said "Shorty" Myers.

And his companion, Bert Wilson, added, as though apologizing, "We couldn't stop any longer because we got to make it over to Wheeler's before mornin'."

"Much obliged, boys," returned the Dean. Then, with his ever-ready jest, "Sure you put the right brand on that calf?"

"We-all ain't ridin' for no Tailholt Mountain outfit this season," retorted Bert dryly, as they all laughed at the Dean's question.

And at the cowboy's words Patches, wondering, saw the laughing faces change and looks of grim significance flash from man to man.

"Anybody seen anything over your way lately?" asked the Dean quietly.

In the moment of silence that followed the visitors looked questioningly from the face of Patches to the Dean and then to Phil. Phil smiled his endorsement of the stranger, and "Shorty" said, "We found a couple of fresh-branded calves what didn't seem to have no mothers last week, and Bud Stillwell says some things look kind o' funny over in the D.1 neighborhood."

Another significant silence followed. To Patches, it seemed as the brooding hush that often precedes a storm. He had not missed those questioning looks of the visitors, and had seen Phil's smiling endorsement, but he could not, of course, understand. He could only wonder and wait, for he felt intuitively that he must not speak. It was as though these strong men who had received him so generously into their lives put him, now, outside their circle, while they considered business of grave moment to themselves.

"Well, boys," said the Dean, as if to dismiss the subject, "I've been in this cow business a good many years, now, an' I've seen all kinds of men come an' go, but I ain't never seen the man yet that could get ahead very far without payin' for what he got. Some time, one way or another, whether he's so minded or not, a man's just naturally got to pay."

"That law is not peculiar to the cattle business, either, is it, Mr. Baldwin?" The words came from Patches, and as they saw his face, it was their turn to wonder.

The Dean looked straight into the dark eyes that were so filled with painful memories, and wistful desire. "Sir?"

"I mean," said Patches, embarrassed, as though he had spoken involuntarily, "that what you say applies to those who live idly — doing no useful work whatever — as well as to those who are dishonest in business of any kind, or who deliberately steal outright. Don't you think so?"

The Dean — his eyes still fixed on the face of the new man — answered slowly, "I reckon that's so, Patches. When you come to think about it, it *must* be so. One way or another every man that takes what he ain't earned has to pay for it."

"Who is he?" asked the visitors of Curly and Bob, as they went for their horses, when the meal was over.

The Cross-Triangle men shook their heads.

"Just blew in one day, and the Dean hired him," said Bob.

"But he's the handiest man with his fists that's ever been in this neck of the woods. If you don't believe it, just you start something," added Curly with enthusiasm.

"Found it out, did you?" laughed Bert.

"In something less than a minute," admitted Curly.

"Funny name!" mused "Shorty."

Bob grinned. "That's what Curly thought — at first."

"And then he took another think, huh?"

"Yep," agreed Curly, "he sure carries the proper credentials to make any name that he wants to wear good enough for me."

The visitors mounted their horses, and sat looking appraisingly at the tall figure of Honorable Patches, as that gentleman passed them at a little distance, on his way to the barn.

"Mebby you're right," admitted "Shorty," "but he sure talks like a schoolmarm, don't he?"

"He sure ain't no puncher," commented Bert.

"No, but I'm gamblin' that he's goin' to be," retorted Curly, ignoring the reference to Patches' culture.

"Me, too," agreed Bob.

"Well, we'll all try him out this fall rodeo"; and "better not let him drift far from the home ranch for a while," laughed the visitors. "So long!" and they were away.

Before breakfast the next morning Phil said to Patches, "Catch up Snip, and give him a feed of grain. You'll ride with me today."

At Patches' look of surprise he explained laughingly, "I'm going to give my school a little vacation, and Uncle Will thinks it's time you were out of the kindergarten."

Later, as they were crossing the big pasture toward the country that lies to the south, the foreman volunteered the further information that for the next few weeks they would ride the range.

"May I ask what for?" said Patches, encouraged by the cowboy's manner.

It was one of the man's peculiarities that he rarely entered into the talk of his new friends when their work was the topic of conversation. And he never asked questions except when alone with Phil or the Dean, and then only when led on by them. It was not that he sought to hide his ignorance, for he made no pretenses whatever, but his reticence seemed, rather, the result of a curious feeling of shame that he had so little in common with these men whose lives were so filled with useful labor. And this, if he had known, was one of the things that made them like him. Men who live in such close daily touch with the primitive realities of life, and who thereby acquire a simple directness, with a certain native modesty, have no place in their hearts for — to use their own picturesque vernacular — a "four-flusher."

Phil tactfully did not even smile at the question, but answered in a matter-of-fact tone. "To look out for screw-*worms, brand a calf here and there, keep the water holes open, and look out for the stock generally."

"And you mean," questioned Patches doubtfully, "that *I* am to ride with you?"

"Sure. You see, Uncle Will thinks you are too good a man to waste on the odd jobs around the place, and so I'm going to get you in shape for the rodeo this fall."

The effect of his words was peculiar. A deep red colored Patches' face, and his eyes shone with a glad light, as he faced his companion. "And you — what do you think about it, Phil?" he demanded.

The cowboy laughed at the man's eagerness. "Me? Oh, I think just as I have thought all the time — ever since you asked for a job that day in the corral."

Patches drew a long breath, and, sitting very straight in the saddle, looked away toward Granite Mountain; while Phil, watching him curiously, felt something like kindly pity in his heart for this man who seemed to hunger so for a man's work, and a place among men.

Just outside the Deep Wash gate of the big pasture, a few cattle were grazing in the open flat. As the men rode toward them, Phil took down his riata while Patches watched him questioningly.

"We may as well begin right here," said the cowboy. "Do you see anything peculiar about anything in that bunch?"

Patches studied the cattle in vain.

"What about that calf yonder?" suggested Phil, leisurely opening the loop of his rope. "I mean that six-months youngster with the white face."

Still Patches hesitated.

Phil helped him again. "Look at his ears."

"They're not marked," exclaimed Patches.

"And what should they be marked?" asked the teacher.

"Under-bit right and a split left, if he belongs to the Cross-Triangle," returned the pupil proudly, and in the same breath he exclaimed, "He is not branded either."

Phil smiled approval. "That's right, and we'll just fix him now, before somebody else beats us to him." He moved his horse slowly toward the cattle as he spoke.

"But," exclaimed Patches, "how do you know that he belongs to the Cross-Triangle?"

"He doesn't," returned Phil, laughing. "He belongs to me."

"But I don't see how you can tell."

"I know because I know the stock," Phil explained, "and because I happen to remember that particular calf, in the rodeo last spring. He got away from us, with his mother, in the cedars and brush over near the head of Mint Wash. That's one of the things that you have to learn in this business, you see. But, to be sure we're right, you watch him a minute, and you'll see him go to a Five-Bar cow. The Five-Bar is my iron, you know — I have a few head running with Uncle Will's."

Even as he spoke, the calf, frightened at their closer approach, ran to a cow that was branded as Phil had said, and the cow, with unmistakable maternal interest in her offspring, proved the ownership of the calf.

"You see?" said Phil. "We'll get that fellow now, because before the next rodeo he'll be big enough to leave his mother, and then; if he isn't branded, he'll be a maverick, and will belong to anybody that puts an iron on him."

"But couldn't someone brand him now, with their brand, and drive him away from his mother?" asked Patches.

"Such things have been known to happen, and that not a thousand miles from here, either," returned Phil dryly. "But, really, you know, Mr. Patches, it isn't done among the best people."

Patches laughed aloud at his companion's attempt at a simpering affectation. Then he watched with admiration while the cowboy sent his horse after the calf and, too quickly for an inexperienced eye to see just how it was done, the deft riata stretched the animal by the heels.

With a short "hogging" rope, which he carried looped through a hole cut in the edge of his chaps near the belt, Phil tied the feet of his victim, before the animal had recovered from the shock of the fall; and then, with Patches helping, proceeded to build a small fire of dry grass and leaves and sticks from a near-by bush. From his saddle, Phil took a small iron rod, flattened at one end, and only long enough to permit its being held in the gloved hand when the flattened end was hot — a running iron, he called it, and explained to his interested pupil, as he thrust it into the fire, how some of the boys used an iron ring for range branding.

"And is there no way to change or erase a brand?" asked Patches, while the iron was heating.

"Sure there is," replied Phil. And sitting on his heels, cowboy fashion, he marked on the ground with a stick.

"Look! This is the Cross-Triangle brand: —; and this: —, the Four-Bar-M, happens to be Nick Cambert's iron, over at Tailholt Mountain. Now, can't you see how, supposing I were Nick, and this calf were branded with the Cross-Triangle, I could work the iron over into my brand?"

Patches nodded. "But is there no way to detect such a fraud?"

"It's a mighty hard thing to prove that an iron has bees worked over," Phil answered slowly. "About the only sure way is to catch the thief in the act."

"But there are the earmarks," said Patches, a few moments later, when Phil had released the branded and marked calf — "the earmarks and the brand wouldn't agree."

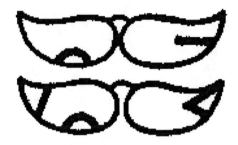

"They would if I were Nick," said the cowboy. Then he added quickly, as if regretting his remark, "Our earmark is an under-bit right and a split left, you said. Well, the Four-Bar-M earmark is a crop and an under-bit right and a swallow-fork left." With the point of his iron now he again marked in the dirt. "Here's your Cross-Triangle: — ; and here's your Pour-Bar-M: —."

"And if a calf branded with a Tailholt iron were to be found following a Cross-Triangle cow, then what?" came Patches' very natural question.

"Then," returned the foreman of the Cross-Triangle grimly, "there would be a mighty good chance for trouble."

"But it seems to me," said Patches, as they rode on, "that it would be easily possible for a man to brand another man's calf by mistake."

"A man always makes a mistake when he puts his iron on another man's property," returned the cowboy shortly.

"But might it not be done innocently, just the same!" persisted Patches.

"Yes, it might," admitted Phil.

"Well, then, what would you do if you found a calf, that you knew belonged to the Dean, branded with some other man's brand? I mean, how would you proceed?"

"Oh, I see what you are driving at," said Phil in quite a different tone. "If you ever run on to a case, the first thing for you to do is to be dead sure that the misbranded calf belongs to one of our cows. Then, if you are right, and it's not too far, drive the cow and calf into the nearest corral and report it. If you can't get them to a corral without too much trouble, just put the Cross-Triangle on the calf's ribs. When he shows up in the next rodeo, with the right brand on his ribs, and some other brand where the right brand ought to be — you'll take pains to remember his natural markings, of course — you will explain the circumstances, and the owner of the iron that was put on him by mistake will be asked to vent his brand. A brand is vented by putting the same brand on the animal's shoulder. Look! There's one now." He pointed to an animal a short distance away. "See, that steer is branded Diamond-and-a-Half on hip and shoulder, and Cross-Triangle on his ribs. Well, when he was a yearling he belonged to the Diamond-and-a-Half outfit. We picked him up in the rodeo, away over toward Mud Tanks. He was running with our stock, and Stillwell didn't want to go to the trouble of taking him home — about thirty miles it is — so he sold him to Uncle Will, and vented his brand, as you see."

"I see," said Patches, "but that's different from finding a calf misbranded."

"Sure. There was no question of ownership there," agreed Phil.

"But in the case of the calf," the cowboy's pupil persisted, "if it had left its mother when the man owning the iron was asked to vent it, there would be no way of proving the real ownership."

"Nothing but the word of the man who found the calf with its mother, and, perhaps, the knowledge of the men who knew the stock."

"What I am getting at," smiled Patches, "is this: it would come down at last to a question of men, wouldn't it?"

"That's where most things come to in, the end in this country, Patches. But you're right. With owners like Uncle Will, and Jim Reid, and Stillwell, and dozens of others; and with cowboys like Curly and Bob and Bert and 'Shorty,' there would be no trouble at all about the matter."

"But with others," suggested Patches.

"Well," said Phil slowly, "there are men in this country, who, if they refused to vent a brand under such circumstances, would be seeing trouble, and mighty quick, too."

"There's another thing that we've got to watch out for, just now," Phil continued, a few minutes later, "and that is, 'sleepers'. We'll suppose," he explained, "that I want to build up my, bunch of Five-Bars, and that I am not too particular about how I do it. Well, I run on to an unbranded Pot-Hook-S calf that looks good to me, but I don't dare put my iron on him because he's too young to leave his mother. If I let him go until he is older, some of Jim Reid's riders will brand him, and, you see, I never could work over the Pot-Hook-S iron into my Five-Bar. So I earmark the calf with the owner's marks, and don't brand him at all. Then he's a sleeper. If the Pot-Hook-S boys see him, they'll notice that he's earmarked all right, and very likely they'll take it for granted that he's branded, or, perhaps let him go anyway. Before the next rodeo I run on to my sleeper again, and he's big enough now to take away from the cow, so all I have to do is to change the earmarks and brand him with my iron. Of course, I wouldn't get all my sleepers, but — the percentage would be in my favor. If too many sleepers show up in the rodeo, though, folks would get mighty suspicious that someone was too handy with his knife. We got a lot of sleepers in the last rodeo," he concluded quietly.

And Patches, remembering what Little Billy had said about Nick Cambert and Yavapai Joe, and with the talk of the visiting cowboys still fresh in his mind, realized that he was making progress in his education.

Riding leisurely, and turning frequently aside for a nearer view of the cattle they sighted here and there, they reached Toohey a little before noon. Here, in a rocky hollow of the hills, a small stream wells from under the granite walls, only to lose itself a few hundred yards away in the sands and gravel of the wash. But, short as its run in the daylight is, the water never fails. And many cattle come from the open range that lies on every side, to drink, and, in summertime, to spend the heat of the day, standing in the cool, wet sands or lying in the shade of the giant sycamores that line the bank opposite the bluff. There are corrals near-by and a rude cook-shack under the wide-spreading branches of an old walnut tree; and the ground of the flat open space, a little back from the water, is beaten bare and hard by the thousands upon thousands of cattle that have at many a past rodeo-time been gathered there.

The two men found, as the Diamond-and-a-Half riders had said, several animals suffering from those pests of the Arizona ranges, the screwworms. As Phil explained to Patches while they watered their horses, the screwworm is the larva of a blowfly bred in sores on living animals. The unhealed wounds of the branding iron made the calves by far the most numerous among the sufferers, and were the afflicted animals not treated the loss during the season would amount to considerable.

"Look here, Patches," said the cowboy, as his practiced eyes noted the number needing attention. "I'll tell you what we'll do. We'll just run this hospital bunch into the corral, and you can limber up that riata of yours."

And so Patches learned not only the unpleasant work of cleaning the worm-infested sores with chloroform, but received his first lesson in the use of the cowboy's indispensable tool, the riata.

"What next?" asked Patches, as the last calf escaped through the gate which he had just opened, and ran to find the waiting and anxious mother.

Phil looked at his companion, and laughed. Honorable Patches showed the effect of his strenuous and bungling efforts to learn the rudiments of the apparently simple trick of roping a calf. His face was streaked with sweat and dust, his hair disheveled, and his clothing soiled and stained. But his eyes were bright, and his bearing eager and ready.

"What's the matter?" he demanded, grinning happily at his teacher. "What fool thing have I done now?"

"You're doing fine," Phil returned. "I was only thinking that you don't look much like the man I met up on the Divide that evening."

"I don't feel much like him, either, as far as that goes," returned Patches.

Phil glanced up at the sun. "What do you say to dinner? It must be about that time."

"Dinner?"

"Sure. I brought some jerky — there on my saddle — and some coffee. There ought to be an old pot in the shack yonder. Some of the boys don't bother, but I never like to miss a feed unless it's necessary." He did not explain that the dinner was really a thoughtful concession to his companion.

"Ugh!" ejaculated Patches, with a shrug of disgust, the work they had been doing still fresh in his mind. "I couldn't eat a bite."

"You think that now," retorted Phil, "but you just go down to the creek, drink all you can hold, wash up, and see how quick you'll change your mind when you smell the coffee."

And thus Patches received yet another lesson — a lesson in the art of forgetting promptly the most disagreeable features of his work — an art very necessary to those who aspire to master real work of any sort whatever.

When they had finished their simple meal, and lay stretched full length beneath the overhanging limbs of the age-old tree that had witnessed so many stirring scenes, and listened to so many campfire tales of ranch and range, they talked of things other than their work. In low tones, as men who feel a mystic and not-to-be-explained bond of fellowship — with half-closed eyes looking out into the untamed world that lay before them — they spoke of life, of its mystery and meaning. And Phil, usually so silent when any conversation touched himself, and so timid always in expressing his own self thoughts, was strangely moved to permit this man to look upon the carefully hidden and deeper things of his life. But upon his cherished dream — upon his great ambition — he kept the door fast closed. The time for that revelation of himself was not yet.

"By the way, Phil," said Patches, when at last his companion signified that it was time for them to go. "Where were you educated? I don't think that I have heard you say."

"I have no education," returned the young man, with a laugh that, to Patches, sounded a bitter note. "I'm just a common cow-puncher, that's all."

"I beg your pardon," returned the other, "but I thought from the books you mentioned —"

"Oh, the books! Why, you see, some four years ago a real, honest-to-goodness book man came out to this country for his health, and brought his disease along with him."

"His disease?" questioned Patches.

Phil smiled. "His books, I mean. They killed him, and I fell heir to his trouble. He was a good fellow, all right — we all liked him — might have been a man if he hadn't been so much of a scholar. I was curious, at first, just to see what it was that had got such a grip on him; and then I got interested myself. About that time, too, there was a reason why I thought it might be a good thing for me; so I sent for more, and have made a fairly good job of it in the past three years. I don't think that there's any danger, though, of the habit getting the grip on me that it had on him," he reflected with a whimsical grin. "It was our book friend who first called Uncle Will the Dean."

"The title certainly fits him well," remarked Patches. "I don't wonder that it stuck. I suppose you received yours for your riding?"

"Mine?"

"'Wild Horse Phil,' I mean," smiled the other.

Phil laughed. "Haven't you heard that yarn yet? I reckon I may as well tell you. No, wait!" he exclaimed eagerly. "We have lots of time. We'll ride south a little way and perhaps I can show you."

As they rode away up the creek, Patches wondered much at his companion's words and at his manner, but the cowboy shook his head at every question, answering, simply, "Wait."

Soon they had left the creek bed — passing through a rock gateway at the beginning of the little stream — and were riding up a long, gently sloping hollow between two low but rugged ridges. The crest of the rocky wall on their left was somewhat higher than the ridge on their right, but, as the floor of the long, narrow hollow ascended, the sides of the little valley became correspondingly lower. Patches noticed that his companion was now keenly alert and watchful. He sat his horse easily, but there was a certain air of readiness in his poise, as though he anticipated sudden action, while his eyes searched the mountain sides with eager expectancy.

They had nearly reached the upper end of the long slope when Phil abruptly reined his horse to the left and rode straight up that rugged, rock-strewn mountain wall. To Patches it seemed impossible that a horse could climb such a place; but he said nothing, and wisely gave Snip his head. They were nearly at the top — so near, in fact, that Phil could see over the narrow crest — when the cowboy suddenly checked his horse and slipped from the saddle. With a gesture he bade his companion follow his example, and in a moment Patches stood beside him. Leaving their horses, they crept the few remaining feet to the summit. Crouching low, then lying prone, they worked their way to the top of a huge rounded rock, from which they could look over and down upon the country that lies beyond.

Patches uttered a low exclamation, but Phil's instant grip on his arm checked further speech.

From where they lay, they looked down upon a great mountain basin of gently rolling, native grass land. From the foot of that rocky ridge, the beautiful pasture stretches away, several miles, to the bold, grey cliffs and mighty, towering battlements of Granite Mountain. On the south, a range of dark hills, and to the north, a series of sharp peaks, form the natural boundaries.

"Do you see them?" whispered Phil.

Patches looked at him inquiringly. The stranger's interest in that wonderful scene had led him to overlook that which held his companion's attention.

"There," whispered Phil impatiently, "on the side of that hill there — they're not more than four hundred yards away, and they're working toward us."

"Do you mean those horses?" whispered Patches, amazed at his companion's manner.

Phil nodded.

"Do they belong to the Cross-Triangle?" asked Patches, still mystified.

"The Cross-Triangle!" Phil chuckled. Then, with a note of genuine reverence in his voice, he added softly, "They belong to God, Mr. Honorable Patches."

Then Patches understood. "Wild horses!" he ejaculated softly.

There are few men, I think, who can look without admiration upon a beautifully formed, noble spirited horse. The glorious pride and strength and courage of these most kingly of God's creatures — even when they are in harness and subject to their often inferior masters — compel respect and a degree of appreciation. But seen as they roam free in those pastures that, since the creation, have never been marred by plow or fence — pastures that are theirs by divine right, and the sunny slopes and shady groves and rocky nooks of which constitute their kingdom — where, in their lordly strength, they are subject only to the dictates of their own being, and, unmutilated by human cruelty, rule by the power and authority of Nature's laws — they stir the blood of the coldest heart to a quicker flow, and thrill the mind of the dullest with admiring awe.

"There's twenty-eight in that bunch," whispered Phil. "Do you see that big black stallion on guard — the one that throws up his head every minute or two for a look around?"

Patches nodded. There was no mistaking the watchful leader of the band.

"He's the chap that gave me my title, as you call it," chuckled Phil. "Come on, now, and we'll see them in action; then I'll tell you about it."

He slipped from the rock and led the way back to the saddle horses.

Riding along the ridge, just under the crest, they soon reached the point where the chain of low peaks merges into the hills that form the southern boundary of the basin, and so came suddenly into full view of the wild horses that were feeding on the slopes a little below.

As the two horsemen appeared, the leader of the band threw up his head with a warning call to his fellows.

Phil reined in his horse and motioned for Patches to do the same.

For several minutes, the black stallion held his place, as motionless as the very rocks of the mountain side, gazing straight at the mounted men as though challenging their right to cross the boundary of his kingdom, while his retainers stood as still, waiting his leadership. With his long, black mane and tail rippling and waving in the breeze that swept down from Blair Pass and across the Basin, with his raven-black coat glistening in the sunlight with the sheen of richest satin where the swelling muscles curved and rounded from shadow to high light, and with his poise of perfect strength and freedom, he looked, as indeed he was, a prince of his kind — a lord of the untamed life that homes in those God-cultivated fields.

Patches glanced at his companion, as if to speak, but struck by the expression on the cowboy's face, remained silent. Phil was leaning a little forward in his saddle, his body as perfect in its poise of alert and graceful strength as the body of the wild horse at which he was gazing with such fixed interest. The clear, deeply tanned skin of his cheeks glowed warmly with the red of his clean, rich blood, his eyes shone with suppressed excitement, his lips, slightly parted, curved in a smile of appreciation, love and reverence for the unspoiled beauty of the wild creature that he himself, in so many ways, unconsciously resembled.

And Patches — bred and schooled in a world so far from this world of primitive things — looking from Phil to the wild horse, and back again from the stallion to the man, felt the spirit and the power that made them kin — felt it with a, to him, strange new feeling of reverence, as though in the perfect, unspoiled life-strength of man and horse he came in closer touch with the divine than he had ever known before.

Then, without taking his eyes from the object of his almost worship, Phil said, "Now, watch him, Patches, watch him!"

As he spoke, he moved slowly toward the band, while Patches rode close by his side.

At their movement, the wild stallion called another warning to his followers, and went a few graceful paces toward the slowly approaching men. And then, as they continued their slow advance, he wheeled with the smooth grace of a swallow, and, with a movement so light and free that he seemed rather to skim over the surface of the ground than to tread upon it, circled here and there about his band, assembling them in closer order, flying, with ears flat and teeth bared and mane and tail tossing, in lordly fury at the laggards, driving them before him, but keeping always between his charges and the danger until they were at what he evidently judged to be, for their inferior strength, a distance of safety. Then again he halted his company and, moving alone a short way toward the horsemen, stood motionless, watching their slow approach.

Again Phil checked his horse. "God!" he exclaimed under his breath. "What a sight! Oh, you beauty! You beauty!"

But Patches was moved less by the royal beauty of the wild stallion than by the passionate reverence that vibrated in his companion's voice.

Again the two horsemen moved forward; and again the stallion drove his band to a safe distance, and stood waiting between them and their enemies.

Then the cowboy laughed aloud — a hearty laugh of clean enjoyment. "All right, old fellow, I'll just give you a whirl for luck," he said aloud to the wild horse, apparently forgetting his human companion.

And Patches saw him shorten his reins, and rise a little in his stirrups, while his horse, as though understanding, gathered himself for a spring. In a flash Patches was alone, watching as Phil, riding with every ounce of strength that his mount could command, dashed straight toward the band.

For a moment, the black stallion stood watching the now rapidly approaching rider. Then, wheeling, he started his band, driving them imperiously, now, to their utmost speed, and then, as though he understood this new maneuver of the cowboy, he swept past his running companions, with the clean, easy flight of an arrow, and taking his place at the head of his charges led them away toward Granite Mountain.

Phil stopped, and Patches could see him watching, as the wild horses, with streaming manes and tails, following their leader, who seemed to run with less than half his strength, swept away across the rolling hillsides, growing smaller and smaller in the distance, until, as dark, swiftly moving dots, they vanished over the sky line.

"Wasn't that great?" cried Phil, when he had loped back to his companion. "Did you see him go by the bunch like they were standing still?"

"There didn't seem to be much show for you to catch him," said Patches.

"Catch him!" exclaimed Phil. "Did you think I was trying to catch him? I just wanted to see him go. The horse doesn't live that could put a man within roping distance of anyone in that bunch on a straightaway run, and the black can run circles around the whole outfit. I had him once, though."

"You caught that black!" exclaimed Patches — incredulously.

Phil grinned. "I sure had him for a little while."

"But what is he doing out here running loose, then?" demanded the other. "Got away, did he?"

"Got away, nothing. Fact is, he belongs to me right now, in a way, and I wouldn't swap him for any string of cow-horses that I ever saw."

Then, as they rode toward the home ranch, Phil told the story that is known throughout all that country.

"It was when the black was a yearling," he said. "I'd had my eye on him all the year, and so had some of the other boys who had sighted the band, for you could see, even when he was a colt, what he was going to be. The wild horses were getting rather too numerous that season, and we planned a chase to thin them out a little, as we do every two or three years. Of course, everybody was after the black; and one day, along toward the end of the chase, when the different bands had been broken up and scattered pretty much, I ran onto him. I was trailing an old grey up that draw — the way we went today, you know, and all at once I met him as he was coming over the top of the hill, right where you and I rode onto him. It was all so sudden that for a minute he was rattled as bad as I was; and, believe me, I was shaking like a leaf. I managed to come to, first, though, and hung my rope on him before he could get started. I don't know to this day where the old grey that I was after went. Well, sir; he fought like a devil, and for a spell we had it around and around until I wasn't dead sure whether I had him or he had me. But he was only a yearling then, you see, and I finally got him down."

Phil paused, a peculiar expression on his face. Patches waited silently.

"Do you know," said the cowboy, at last, hesitatingly, "I can't explain it — and I don't talk about it much, for it was the strangest thing that ever happened to me — but when I looked into that black stallion's eyes, and he looked me straight in the face, I never felt so sorry for anything in my life. I was sort of ashamed like — like — well, like I'd been caught holding up a church, you know, or something like that. We were all alone up there, just him and me, and while I was getting my wind, and we were sizing each other up, and I was feeling that way, I got to thinking what it all meant to him — to be broken and educated — and — well — civilized, you know; and I thought what a horse he would be if he was left alone to live as God made him, and so — well —" He paused again with an embarrassed laugh.

"You let him go?" cried Patches.

"It's God's truth, Patches. I couldn't do anything else — I just couldn't. One of the boys came up just in time to catch me turning him loose, and, of course, the whole outfit just naturally raised hell about it. You see, in a chase like that, we always bunch all we get and sell them off to the highest bidder, and every man in the outfit shares alike. The boys figured that the black was worth more than any five others that were caught, and so you couldn't blame them for feeling sore. But I fixed it with them by turning all my share into the pot, so they couldn't kick. That, you see, makes the black belong to me, in a way, and it's pretty generally understood that I propose to take care of him. There was a fellow, riding in the rodeo last fall, that took a shot at him one day, and — well — he left the country right after it happened and hasn't been seen around here since."

The cowboy grinned as his companion's laugh rang out.

"Do you know," Phil continued in a low tone, a few minutes later, "I believe that horse knows me yet. Whenever I am over in this part of the country I always have a look at him, if he happens to be around, and we visit a little, as we did today. I've got a funny notion that he likes it as much as I do, and, I can't tell how it is, but it sort of makes me feel good all over just to see him. I reckon you think I'm some fool," he finished with another short laugh of embarrassment, "but that's the way I feel — and that's why they call me 'Wild Horse Phil'."

For a little they rode in silence; then Patches spoke, gravely, "I don't know how to tell you what I think, Phil, but I understand, and from the bottom of my heart I envy you."

And the cowboy, looking at his companion, saw in the man's eyes something that reminded him of that which he had seen in the wild horse's eyes, that day when he had set him free. Had Patches, too, at some time in those days that were gone, been caught by the riata of circumstance or environment, and in some degree robbed of his God-inheritance? Phil smiled at the fancy, but, smiling, felt its truth; and with genuine sympathy felt this also to be true, that the man might yet, by the strength that was deepest within him, regain that which he had lost.

And so that day, as the man from the ranges and the man from the cities rode together, the feeling of kinship that each had instinctively recognized at their first meeting on the Divide was strengthened. They knew that a mutual understanding which could not have been put into words of any tongue or land was drawing them closer together.

A few days later the incident occurred that fixed their friendship — as they thought — for all time to come.

Chapter IX
THE TAILHOLT MOUNTAIN OUTFIT

*P*hil and Patches were riding that day in the country about Old Camp. Early in the afternoon, they heard the persistent bawling of a calf, and upon riding toward the sound, found the animal deep in the cedar timber, which in that section thickly covers the ridges. The calf was freshly branded with the Tailholt iron. It was done, Phil said, the day before, probably in the late afternoon. The youngster was calling for his mother.

"It's strange, she is not around somewhere," said Patches.

"It would be more strange if she was," retorted the cowboy shortly, and he looked from the calf to the distant Tailholt Mountain, as though he were considering some problem which he did not, for some reason, care to share with his companion.

"There's not much use to look for her," he added, with grim disappointment. "That's always the way. If we had ridden this range yesterday, instead of away over there in the Mint Wash country — I am always about a day behind."

There was something in the manner and in the quiet speech of the usually sunny-tempered foreman that made his companion hesitate to ask questions, or to offer comment with the freedom that he had learned to feel that first day of their riding together. During the hours that followed Phil said very little, and when he did speak his words were brief and often curt, while, to Patches, he seemed to study the country over which they rode with unusual care. When they had eaten their rather gloomy lunch, he was in the saddle again almost before Patches had finished, with seemingly no inclination for their usual talk.

The afternoon, was nearly gone, and they were making their way homeward when they saw a Cross-Triangle bull that had evidently been hurt in a fight. The animal was one of the Dean's much-prized Herefords, and the wound needed attention.

"We've got to dope that," said Phil, "or the screwworms will be working in it sure." He was taking down his riata and watching the bull, who was rumbling a sullen, deep-voiced challenge, as he spoke.

"Can I help?" asked Patches anxiously, as he viewed the powerful beast, for this was the first full-grown animal needing attention that he had seen in his few days' experience.

"No," returned Phil. "Just keep in the clear, that's all. This chap is no calf, and he's sore over his scrap. He's on the prod right now."

It all happened in a few seconds.

The cowboy's horse, understanding from long experience that this threatening mark for his master's riata was in no gentle frame of mind, fretted uneasily as though dreading his part in the task before them. Patches saw the whirling rope leave Phil's hand, and saw it tighten, as the cowboy threw the weight of his horse against it; and then he caught a confused vision — a fallen, struggling horse with a man pinned to the ground beneath him, and a wickedly lowered head, with sharp horns and angry eyes, charging straight at them.

Patches did not think — there was no time to think. With a yell of horror, he struck deep with both spurs, and his startled, pain-maddened horse leaped forward. Again he spurred cruelly with all his strength, and the next bound of his frenzied mount carried him upon those deadly horns. Patches remembered hearing a sickening rip, and a scream of fear and pain, as he felt the horse under him rise in the air. He never knew how he managed to free himself, as he fell backward with his struggling mount, but he distinctly saw Phil regain his saddle while his horse was in the very act of struggling to its feet, and he watched with anxious interest as the cowboy forced his excited mount in front of the bull to attract the beast's wicked attention. The bull, accepting the tantalizing challenge, charged again, and Patches, with a thrill of admiration for the man's coolness and skill, saw that Phil was coiling his riata, even while his frightened horse, with terrific leaps, avoided those menacing horns. The bull stopped, shook his head in anger over his failure, and looked back toward the man on foot. But again that horse and rider danced temptingly before him, so close that it seemed he could not fail, and again he charged, only to find that his mad rush carried him still further from the helpless Patches. And by now, Phil had recovered his riata, and the loop was whirling in easy circles about his head. The cow-horse, as though feeling the security that was in that familiar motion of his master's arm, steadied himself, and, in the few active moments that followed, obedient to every signal of his rider, did his part with almost human intelligence.

When the bull was safely tied, Phil went to the frightfully injured horse, and with a merciful bullet ended the animal's suffering. Then he looked thoughtfully at Patches, who stood gazing ruefully at the dead animal, as though he felt himself to blame for the loss of his employer's property. A slight smile lightened the cowboy's face, as he noticed his companion's troubled thought.

"I suppose I've done it now," said Patches, as though expecting well-merited censure.

Phil's smile broadened. "You sure have," he returned, as he wiped the sweat from his face. "I'm much obliged to you."

Patches looked at him in confused embarrassment.

"Don't you know that you saved my life?" asked Phil dryly.

"But — but, I killed a good horse for the Dean," stammered Patches.

To which the Dean's foreman returned with a grin, "I reckon Uncle Will can stand the loss — considering."

This relieved the tension, and they laughed together.

"But tell me something, Patches," said Phil, curiously. "Why didn't you shoot the bull when he charged me?"

"I didn't think of it," admitted Patches. "I didn't really think of anything."

The cowboy nodded with understanding approval. "I've noticed that the man to tie to, in sudden trouble, is the man who doesn't have to think; the man, I mean, who just does the right thing instinctively, and waits to think about it afterwards when there's time."

Patches was pleased. "I did the right thing, then?"

"It was the only thing you *could* do to save my life," returned Phil seriously. "If you had tried to use your gun — even if you could have managed to hit him — you wouldn't have stopped him in time. If you had been where you could have put a bullet between his eyes, it might have worked, but" — he smiled again — "I'm mighty glad you didn't think to try any experiments. Tell me something else," he added. "Did you realize the chance you were taking for yourself?"

Patches shook his head. "I can't say that I realized anything except that you were in a bad fix, and that it was up to me to do something quick. How did it happen, anyway?" He seemed anxious to turn the conversation.

"Diamond stepped in that hole there," explained Phil. "When he turned over I sure thought it was all day for me. Believe me, I won't forget this, Patches."

For another moment there was an embarrassed silence; then Patches said, "What puzzles me is, why you didn't take a shot at him, after you were up, instead of risking your neck again trying to rope him."

"Why, there was no use killing a good bull, as long as there was any other way. It's my business to keep him alive; that's what I started in to do, wasn't it?" And thus the cowboy, in a simple word or two, stated the creed of his profession, a creed that permits no consideration of personal danger or discomfort when the welfare of the employer's property is at stake.

When they had removed saddle and bridle from the dead horse and had cleaned the ugly wound in the bull's side, Phil said, "Now, Mr. Honorable Patches, you'd better move on down the wash a piece, and get out of sight behind one of those cedars. This fellow is going to get busy again when I let him up. I'll come along when I've got rid of him."

A little later, as Phil rode out of the cedars toward Patches, a deep, bellowing challenge came from up the wash.

"He's just telling us what he'll do to us the next chance he gets," chuckled Phil. "Hop up behind me now and we'll go home."

The gloom, that all day had seemed to overshadow Phil, was effectually banished by the excitement of the incident, and he was again his sunny, cheerful self. As they rode, they chatted and laughed merrily. Then, suddenly, as it had happened that morning, the cowboy was again grim and silent.

Patches was wondering what had so quickly changed his companion's mood, when he caught sight of two horsemen, riding along the top of the ridge that forms the western side of the wash, their course paralleling that of the Cross-Triangle men, who were following the bed of the wash.

When Patches directed Phil's attention to the riders, the cowboy said shortly, "I've been watching them for the last ten minutes." Then, as if regretting the manner of his reply, he added more kindly, "If they keep on the way they're going, we'll likely meet them about a mile down the wash where the ridge breaks."

"Do you know them?" asked Patches curiously.

"It's Nick Cambert and that poor, lost dog of a Yavapai Joe," Phil answered.

"The Tailholt Mountain outfit," murmured Patches, watching the riders on the ridge with quickened interest. "Do you know, Phil, I believe I have seen those fellows before."

"You have!" exclaimed Phil. "Where? When?"

"I don't know how to tell you where," Patches replied, "but it was the day I rode the drift fence. They were on a ridge, across a little valley from me."

"That must have been this same Horse Wash that we're following now," replied Phil; "it widens out a bit below here. What makes you think it was Nick and Joe?"

"Why, those fellows up there look like the two that I saw, one big one and one rather lightweight. They were the same distance from me, you know, and — yes — I am sure those are the same horses."

"Pretty good, Patches, but you ought to have reported it when you got home."

"Why, I didn't think it of any importance."

"There are two rules that you must follow, always," said the cowboy, "if you are going to learn to be a top hand in this business. The first is: to see everything that there is to see, and to see everything about everything that you see. And the second is: to remember it all. I don't mind telling you, now, that Jim Reid found a calf, fresh-branded with the Tailholt iron, that same afternoon, in that same neighborhood; and that, on our side of the drift fence, he ran onto a Cross-Triangle cow that had lost her calf. There come our friends now."

The two horsemen were riding down the side of the hill at an angle that would bring about the meeting which Phil had foreseen. And Patches immediately broke the first of the two rules, for, while watching the riders, he did not notice that his companion loosened his gun in its holster.

Nick Cambert was a large man, big-bodied and heavy, with sandy hair, and those peculiar light blue eyes which do not beget confidence. But, as the Tailholt Mountain men halted to greet Phil, Patches gave to Nick little more than a passing glance, so interested was he in the big man's companion.

It is doubtful if blood, training, environment, circumstances, the fates, or whatever it is that gives to men individuality, ever marked a man with less manhood than was given to poor Yavapai Joe. Standing erect, he would have been, perhaps, a little above medium height, but thin and stooped, with a half-starved look, as he slouched listlessly in the saddle, it was almost impossible to think of him as a matured man.

The receding chin, and coarse, loosely opened mouth, the pale, lifeless eyes set too closely together under a low forehead, with a ragged thatch of dead, mouse-colored hair, and a furtive, sneaking, lost-dog expression, proclaimed him the outcast that he was.

The big man eyed Patches as he greeted the Cross-Triangle's foreman. "Howdy, Phil!"

"Hello, Nick!" returned Phil coldly. "Howdy, Joe!"

The younger man, who was gazing stupidly at Patches, returned the salutation with an unintelligible mumble, and proceeded to roll a cigarette.

"You folks at the Cross-Triangle short of horses?" asked Nick, with an evident attempt at jocularity, alluding to the situation of the two men, who were riding one horse.

"We got mixed up with a bull back yonder," Phil explained briefly.

"They can sure put a horse out o' the game mighty quick sometimes," commented the other. "I've lost a few that way myself. It's about as far from here to my place as it is to Baldwin's, or I'd help you out. You're welcome, you know."

"Much obliged," returned Phil, "but we'll make it home all right. I reckon we'd better be moving, though. So long!"

"Adios!"

Throughout this brief exchange of courtesies, Yavapai Joe had not moved, except to puff at his cigarette; nor had he ceased to regard Patches with a stupid curiosity. As Phil and Patches moved away, he still sat gazing after the stranger, until he was aroused by a sharp word from Nick, as the latter turned his horse toward Tailholt Mountain. Without changing his slouching position in the saddle, and with a final slinking, sidewise look toward Patches, the poor fellow obediently trailed after his master.

Patches could not resist the impulse to turn for another look at the wretched shadow of manhood that so interested him.

"Well, what do you think of that pair?" asked Phil, breaking in upon his companion's preoccupation.

Patches shrugged his shoulders much as he had done that day of his first experience with the screwworms; then he said quietly, "Do you mind telling me about them, Phil?"

"Why, there's not much to tell," returned the cowboy. "That is, there's not much that anybody knows for certain. Nick was born in Yavapai County. His father, old George Cambert, was one of the kind that seems honest enough, and industrious, too, but somehow always just misses it. They moved away to some place in Southern California when Nick was about grown. He came back six years ago, and located over there at the foot of Tailholt Mountain, and started his Four-Bar-M iron; and, one way or another, he's managed to get together quite a bunch of stock. You see, his expenses don't amount to anything, scarcely. He and Joe bach in an old shack that somebody built years ago, and they do all the riding themselves. Joe's not much force, but he's handier than you'd think, as long as there's somebody around to tell him what to do, and sort of back him up. Nick, though, can do two men's work any day in the year."

"But it's strange that a man like Nick would have anything to do with such a creature as that poor specimen," mused Patches. "Are they related in any way?"

"Nobody knows," answered Phil. "Joe first showed up at Prescott about four years ago with a man by the name of Dryden, who claimed that Joe was his son. They camped just outside of town, in some dirty old tents, and lived by picking up whatever was lying around loose. Dryden wouldn't work, and, naturally, no one would have Joe. Finally Dryden was sent up for robbing a store, and Joe nearly went with him. They let him off, I believe, because it was proved pretty well that he was only Dryden's tool, and didn't have nerve enough to do any real harm by himself. He drifted around for several months, living like a stray cur, until Nick took him in tow. Nick treats him shamefully, abuses him like a beast, and works him like a slave. The poor devil stays on with him because he doesn't know what else to do, I suppose."

"Is he always like we saw him today?" asked Patches, who seemed strangely interested in this bit of human drift. "Doesn't he ever talk?"

"Oh, yes, he'll talk all right, when Nick isn't around, or when there are not too many present. Get off somewhere alone with him, after he gets acquainted a little, and he's not half such bad company as he looks. I reckon that's the main reason why Nick keeps him. You see, no decent cow-puncher would dare work at Tailholt Mountain, and a man gets mighty lonesome living so much alone. But Joe never talks about where he came from, or who he is; shuts up like a clam if you so much as mention anything that looks like you were trying to find out about him. He's not such a fool as he looks, either, so far as that goes, but he's always got that sneaking, coyote sort of look, and whatever he does he does in that same way."

"In other words," commented Patches thoughtfully, "poor Joe must have someone to depend on; taken alone he counts no more than a cipher."

"That's it," said Phil. "With somebody to feed him, and think for him, and take care of him, and be responsible for him, in some sort of a way, he makes almost one."

"After all, Phil," said Patches, with bitter sarcasm, "poor Yavapai Joe is not so much different from hundreds of men that I know. By their standards he should be envied."

Phil was amazed at his companion's words, for they seemed to hint at something in the man's past, and Patches, so far as his reticence upon any subject that approached his own history, was always as silent as Yavapai Joe himself.

"What do you mean by that?" Phil demanded. "What sort of men do you mean?"

"I mean the sort that never do anything of their own free wills; the sort that have someone else to think for them, and feed them, and take care of them and take all the responsibility for what they do or do not do. I mean those who are dependents, and those who aspire to be dependent. I can't see that it makes any essential difference whether they have inherited wealth and what we call culture, or whether they are poverty-stricken semi-imbeciles like Joe; the principle is the same."

As they dismounted at the home corral gate, Phil looked at his companion curiously. "You seem mighty interested in Joe," he said, with a smile.

"I am," retorted Patches. "He reminds me of — of someone I know," he finished, with his old, self-mocking smile. "I have a fellow feeling for him, the same as you have for that wild horse, you know. I'd like to take him away from Nick, and see if it would be possible to make a real man of him," he mused, more to himself than to his companion.

"I don't believe I'd try any experiments along that line, Patches," cautioned Phil. "You've got to have something to build on when you start to make a man. The raw material is not in Joe, and, besides," he added significantly, "folks might not understand."

Patches laughed bitterly. "I have my hands full now."

The next morning the foreman said that he would give that day to the horses he was training, and sent Patches, alone, after the saddle and bridle which they had left near the scene of the accident.

"You can't miss finding the place again," he said to Patches; "just follow up the wash. You'll be back by noon — if you don't try any experiments," he added laughing.

Patches had ridden as far as the spot where he and Phil had met the Tailholt Mountain men, and was thirsty. He thought of the distance he had yet to go, and then of the return back to the ranch, in the heat of the day. He remembered that Phil had told him, as they were riding out the morning before, of a spring a little way up the small side canyon that opens into the main wash through that break in the ridge. For a moment he hesitated; then he turned aside, determined to find the water.

Riding perhaps two hundred yards into that narrow gap In the ridge, he found the way suddenly becoming steep and roughly strewn with boulders, and, thinking to make better time, left his horse tied to a bush in the shadow of the rocky wall, while he climbed up the dry watercourse on foot. He found, as Phil had said, that it was not far. Another hundred yards up the boulder-strewn break in the ridge, and he came out into a beautiful glade, where he found the spring, clear and cold, under a moss-grown rock, in the deep shade of an old gnarled and twisted cedar. Gratefully he threw himself down and drank long and deep; then sat for a few moments' rest, before making his way back to his horse. The moist, black earth of the cuplike hollow was roughly trampled by the cattle that knew the spot, and there were well-marked trails leading down through the heavy growth of brush and trees that clothed the hillsides. So dense was this forest growth, and so narrow the glade, that the sunlight only reached the cool retreat through a network of leaves and branches, in ever-shifting spots and bars of brightness. Nor could one see very far through the living screens.

Patches was on the point of going, when he heard voices and the sound of horses' feet somewhere above. For a moment he sat silently listening. Then he realized that the riders were approaching, down one of the cattle trails. A moment more, and he thought he recognized one of the voices. There was a low, murmuring, whining tone, and then a rough, heavy voice, raised seemingly in anger. Patches felt sure, now, that he knew the speakers; and, obeying one of those impulses that so often prompted his actions, he slipped quietly into the dense growth on the side of the glade opposite the approaching riders. He was scarcely hidden — a hundred feet or so from the spring — when Nick Cambert and Yavapai Joe rode into the glade.

If Patches had paused to think, he likely would have disdained to play the part of a hidden spy; but he had acted without thinking, and no sooner was he concealed than he realized that it was too late. So he smiled mockingly at himself, and awaited developments. He had heard and seen enough, since he had been in the Dean's employ, to understand the suspicion in which the owner of the Four-Bar-M iron was held; and from even his few days' work on the range in company with Phil, he had come to understand how difficult it was for the cattlemen to prove anything against the man who they had every reason to believe was stealing their stock. It was the possibility of getting some positive evidence, and of thus protecting his employer's property, that had really prompted him to take advantage of the chance situation.

As the two men appeared, it was clear to the hidden observer that the weakling had in some way incurred his master's displeasure. The big man's face was red with anger, and his eyes were hard and cruel, while Joe had more than aver the look of a lost dog that expects nothing less than a curse and a kick.

Nick drank at the spring, then turned back to his companion, who had not dismounted, but sat on his horse cringing and frightened, trying, with fluttering fingers, to roll a cigarette. A moment the big man surveyed his trembling follower; then, taking a heavy quirt from his saddle, he said with a contemptuous sneer, "Well, why don't you get your drink?"

"I ain't thirsty, Nick," faltered the other.

"You ain't thirsty?" mocked the man with a jeering laugh. "You're lying, an' you know it. Get down!"

"Hones' to God, Nick, I don't want no drink," whimpered Joe, as his master toyed with the quirt suggestively.

"Get down, I tell you!" commanded the big man.

Joe obeyed, his thin form shaking with fear, and stood shrinking against his horse's side, his fearful eyes fixed on the man.

"Now, come here."

"Don't, Nick; for God's sake! don't hit me. I didn't mean no harm. Let me off this time, won't you, Nick?"

"Come here. You got it comin', damn you, an' you know it. Come here, I say!"

As if it were beyond his power to refuse, the wretched creature took a halting step or two toward the man whose brutal will dominated him; then he paused and half turned, as if to attempt escape. But that menacing voice stopped him.

"Come here!"

Whimpering and begging, with disconnected, unintelligible words, the poor fellow again started toward the man with the quirt.

At the critical moment a quiet, well-schooled voice interrupted the scene.

"I beg your pardon, Mr. Cambert!"

Nick whirled with an oath of surprise and astonishment, to face Patches, who was coming leisurely toward him from the bushes above the spring.

"What are you doin' here?" demanded Nick, while his victim slunk back to his horse, his eyes fixed upon the intruder with dumb amazement.

"I came for a drink," returned Patches coolly. "Excellent water, isn't it? And the day is really quite warm — makes one appreciate such a delightfully cool retreat, don't you think?"

"Heard us comin' an' thought you'd play the spy, did you?" growled the Tailholt Mountain man.

Patches smiled. "Really, you know, I am afraid I didn't think much about it," he said gently. "I'm troubled that way, you see," he explained, with elaborate politeness. "Often do things upon impulse, don't you know — beastly embarrassing sometimes."

Nick glared at this polite, soft-spoken gentleman, with half-amused anger. "I heard there was a dude tenderfoot hangin' 'round the Cross-Triangle," he said, at last. "You're sure a hell of a fine specimen. You've had your drink; now s'pose you get a-goin'."

"I beg pardon?" drawled Patches, looking at him with innocent inquiry.

"Vamoose! Get out! Go on about your business."

"Really, Mr. Cambert, I understood that this was open range —" Patches looked about, as though carefully assuring himself that he was not mistaken in the spot.

The big man's eyes narrowed wickedly. "It's closed to you, all right." Then, as Patches did not move, "Well, are you goin', or have I got to start you?" He took a threatening step toward the intruder.

"No," returned Patches easily, "I am certainly not going — not just at present — and," he added thoughtfully, "if I were you, I wouldn't try to start *anything.*"

Something in the extraordinary self-possession of this soft-spoken stranger made the big man hesitate. "Oh, you wouldn't, heh?" he returned. "You mean, I s'pose, that you propose to interfere with my business."

"If, by your business, you mean beating a man who is so unable to protect himself, I certainly propose to interfere."

For a moment Nick glared at Patches as though doubting his own ears. Then rage at the tenderfoot's insolence mastered him. With a vile epithet, he caught the loaded quirt in his hand by its small end, and strode toward the intruder.

But even as the big man swung his wicked weapon aloft, a hard fist, with the weight of a well-trained and well-developed shoulder back of it, found the point of his chin with scientific accuracy. The force of the blow, augmented as it was by Nick's weight as he was rushing to meet it, was terrific. The man's head snapped back, and he spun half around as he fell, so that the uplifted arm with its threatening weapon was twisted under the heavy bulk that lay quivering and harmless.

Patches coolly bent over the unconscious man and extracted his gun from the holster. Then, stepping back a few paces, he quietly waited.

Yavapai Joe, who had viewed the proceedings thus far with gaping mouth and frightened wonder, scrambled into his saddle and reined his horse about, as if to ride for his life.

"Wait, Joe!" called Patches sharply.

The weakling paused in pitiful indecision.

"Nick will be all right in a few minutes," continued the stranger, reassuringly. "Stay where you are."

Even as he spoke, the man on the ground opened his eyes. For a moment he gazed about, collecting his shocked and scattered senses. Then, with a mad roar, he got to his feet and reached for his gun, but when his hand touched the empty holster a look of dismay swept over his heavy face, and he looked doubtfully toward Patches, with a degree of respect and a somewhat humbled air.

"Yes, I have your gun," said Patches soothingly. "You see, I thought it would be best to remove the temptation. You don't really want to shoot me, anyway, you know. You only think you do. When you have had time to consider it all, calmly, you'll thank me; because, don't you see, I would make you a lot more trouble dead than I could possibly, alive. I don't think that Mr. Baldwin would like to have me all shot to pieces, particularly if the shooting were done by someone from Tailholt Mountain. And I am quite sure that 'Wild Horse Phil' would be very much put out about it."

"Well, what do you want?" growled Nick. "You've got the drop on me. What are you after, anyway?"

"What peculiar expressions you western people use!" murmured Patches sweetly. "You say that I have got the drop on you; when, to be exact, you should have said that you got the drop *from* me — do you see? Good, isn't it?"

Nick's effort at self-control was heroic.

Patches watched him with an insolent, taunting smile that goaded the man to reckless speech.

"If you didn't have that gun, I'd —" the big man began, then stopped, for, as he spoke, Patches placed the weapon carefully on a rock and went toward him barehanded.

"You would do what?"

At the crisp, eager question that came in such sharp contrast to Patches' former speech, Nick hesitated and drew back a step.

Patches promptly moved a step nearer; and his words came, now, in answer to the unfinished threat with cutting force. "What would you do, you big, hulking swine? You can bully a weakling not half your size; you can beat a helpless incompetent like a dog; you can bluster, and threaten a tenderfoot when you think he fears you; you can attack a

man with a loaded quirt when you think him unable to defend himself;
— show me what you can do *now.* ”

The Tailholt Mountain man drew back another step.

Patches continued his remarks. “You are a healthy specimen, you are.
You have the frame of a bull with the spirit of a coyote and the courage
of a sucking dove. Now — in your own vernacular — get a-goin’. Vamoose!
Get out! I want to talk to your superior over there.”

Sullenly Nick Cambert mounted his horse and turned away toward
one of the trails leading out from the little arena.

“Come along, Joe!” he called to his follower.

“No, you don’t,” Patches cut in with decisive force. “Joe, stay where
you are!”

Nick paused. “What do you mean by that?” he growled.

“I mean,” returned Patches, “that Joe is free to go with you, or not,
as he chooses. Joe,” he continued, addressing the cause of the contro-
versy, “you need not go with this man. If you wish, you can come with
me. I’ll take care of you; and I’ll give you a chance to make a man of
yourself.”

Nick laughed coarsely. “So, that’s your game, is it? Well, it won’t work.
I know now why Bill Baldwin’s got you hangin’ ’round, pretendin’
you’re a tenderfoot, you damned spy. Come on, Joe.” He turned to ride
on; and Joe, with a slinking, sidewise look at Patches, started to follow.

Again Patches called, “Wait, Joe!” and his voice was almost pleading.
“Can’t you understand, Joe? Come with me. Don’t be a dog for any
man. Let me give you a chance. Be a man, Joe — for God’s sake, be a
man! Come with me.”

“Well,” growled Nick to his follower, as Patches finished, “are you
comin’ or have I got to go and get you?”

With a sickening, hangdog look Joe mumbled something and rode
after his master.

As they disappeared up the trail, Nick called back, “I’ll get you yet,
you sneakin’ spy.”

“Not after you’ve had time to think it over,” answered Patches
cheerfully. “It would interfere too much with your *real* business. I’ll leave
your gun at the gate of that old corral up the wash. Good-bye, Joe!”

For a few moments longer the strange man stood in the glade,
listening to the vanishing sounds of their going, while that mirthless,
self-mocking smile curved his lips.

“Poor devil!” he muttered sadly, as he turned at last to make his way
back to his horse. “Poor Joe! I know just how he feels. It’s hard — it’s
beastly hard to break away.”

"I'm afraid I have made trouble for you, sir," Patches said ruefully to the Dean, as he briefly related the incident to his employer and to Phil that afternoon. "I'm sorry; I really didn't stop to think."

"Trouble!" retorted the Dean, his eyes twinkling approval, while Phil laughed joyously. "Why, man, we've been prayin' for trouble with that blamed Tailholt Mountain outfit. You're a plumb wonder, young man. But what in thunder was you aimin' to do with that ornery Yavapai Joe, if he'd a' took you up on your fool proposition?"

"Really, to tell the truth," murmured Patches, "I don't exactly know. I fancied the experiment would be interesting; and I was so sorry for the poor chap that I —" he stopped, shamefaced, to join in the laugh.

But, later, the Dean and Phil talked together privately, with the result that during the days that followed, as Patches and his teacher rode the range together, the pupil found revolver practice added to his studies.

The art of drawing and shooting a "six-gun" with quickness and certainty was often a useful part of the cowboy's training, Phil explained cheerfully. "In the case, for instance, of a mix-up with a bad steer, when your horse falls, or something like that, you know."

Chapter X
THE RODEO

As the remaining weeks of the summer passed, Patches spent the days riding the range with Phil, and, under the careful eye of that experienced teacher, made rapid progress in the work he had chosen to master. The man's intense desire to succeed, his quick intelligence, with his instinct for acting without hesitation, and his reckless disregard for personal injury, together with his splendid physical strength, led him to a mastery of the details of a cowboy's work with remarkable readiness.

Occasionally the two Cross-Triangle riders saw the men from Tailholt Mountain, sometimes merely sighting them in the distance, and, again, meeting them face to face at some watering place or on the range. When it happened that Nick Cambert was thus forced to keep up a show of friendly relations with the Cross-Triangle, the few commonplaces of the country were exchanged, but always the Tailholt Mountain man addressed his words to Phil, and, save for surly looks, ignored the foreman's companion. He had evidently — as Patches had said that he would — come to realize that he could not afford to arouse the cattlemen to action against him, as he would certainly have done, had he attempted to carry out his threat to "get" the man who had so humiliated him.

But Patches' strange interest in Yavapai Joe in no way lessened. Always he had a kindly word for the poor unfortunate, and sought persistently to win the weakling's friendship. And Phil seeing this wondered, but held his peace.

Frequently Kitty Reid, sometimes alone, often with the other members of the Reid household, came across the big meadow to spend an evening at the neighboring ranch. Sometimes Phil and Patches, stopping at the Pot-Hook-S home ranch, at the close of the day, for a drink at the windmill pump, would linger a while for a chat with Kitty, who would come from the house to greet them. And now and then Kitty, out for a ride on Midnight, would chance to meet the two Cross-Triangle men on the range, and so would accompany them for an hour or more.

And thus the acquaintance between Patches and the girl grew into friendship; for Kitty loved to talk with this man of the things that play so large a part in that life which so appealed to her; and, with Phil's ever-ready and hearty endorsement of Patches, she felt safe in permitting the friendship to develop. And Patches, quietly observing, with now and then a conversational experiment — at which game he was an adepts — came to understand, almost as well as if he had been told, Phil's love for Kitty and her attitude toward the cowboy — her one-time schoolmate and sweetheart. Many times when the three were together, and the talk, guided by Kitty, led far from Phil's world, the cowboy would sit a silent listener, until Patches would skillfully turn the current back to the land of Granite Mountain and the life in which Phil had so vital a part.

In the home-life at the Cross-Triangle, too, Patches gradually came to hold his own peculiar place. His cheerful helpfulness, and gentle, never-failing courtesy, no less than the secret pain and sadness that sometimes, at some chance remark, drove the light from his face and brought that wistful look into his eyes, won Mrs. Baldwin's heart. Many an evening under his walnut trees, with Stella and Phil and Curly and Bob and Little Billy near, the Dean was led by the rare skill and ready wit of Patches to open the book of his kindly philosophy, as he talked of the years that were past. And sometimes Patches himself, yielding to temptation offered by the Dean, would speak in such vein that the older man came to understand that this boy, as he so often called him, had somewhere, somehow, already experienced that Gethsemane which soon or late — the Dean maintains — leaves its shadow upon us all. The cowboys, for his quick and genuine appreciation of their skill and knowledge, as well as for his unassuming courage, hearty good nature and ready laugh, took him into their fellowship without question or reserve, while Little Billy, loyal ever to his ideal, "Wild Horse Phil," found a large place in his boyish heart for the tenderfoot who was so ready always to recognize superior wisdom and authority.

So the stranger found his place among them, and in finding it, found also, perhaps, that which he most sorely needed.

[Illustration:]

When rodeo time came Patches was given a "string" of horses and, through the hard, grilling work that followed, took his place among the riders. There was no leisurely roaming over the range now, with only an occasional short dash after some animal that needed the "iron" or the "dope can;" but systematically and thoroughly the thirty or forty cowboys covered the country — mountain and mesa and flat, and wash and timbered ridge and rocky pass — for many miles in every direction.

In this section of the great western cattle country, at the time of my story, the round-ups were cooperative. Each of the several ranchers whose cattle, marked by the owner's legally recorded brand, ranged over a common district that was defined only by natural boundaries, was represented in the rodeo by one or two or more of his cowboys, the number of his riders being relative to the number of cattle marked with his iron. This company of riders, each with from three to five saddle horses in his string, would assemble at one of the ranches participating in the rodeo. From this center they would work until a circle of country within riding distance was covered, the cattle gathered and "worked" — or, in other words, sorted — and the animals belonging to the various owners disposed of as the representatives were instructed by their employers. Then the rodeo would move to another ranch, and would so continue until the entire district of many miles was covered. The owner or the foreman of each ranch was in charge of the rodeo as long as the riders worked in his territory. When the company moved to the next point, this loader took his place in the ranks, and cheerfully received his orders from some comrade, who, the day before, had been as willingly obedient to him. There was little place in the rodeo for weak, incompetent or untrustworthy men. Each owner, from his long experience and knowledge of men, sent as his representatives the most skillful and conscientious riders that he could secure. To make a top hand at a rodeo a man needed to be, in the truest sense, a man.

Before daylight, the horse wrangler had driven in the saddle band, and the men, with nose bags fashioned from grain sacks, were out in the corral to give the hard-working animals their feed of barley. The grey quiet of the early dawn was rudely broken by the sounds of the crowding, jostling, kicking, squealing band, mingled with the merry voices of the men, with now and then a shout of anger or warning as the cowboys moved here and there among their restless four-footed companions; and always, like a deep undertone, came the sound of trampling, iron-shod hoofs.

Before the sky had changed to crimson and gold the call sounded from the ranch house, "Come and get it!" and laughing and joking in friendly rivalry, the boys rushed to breakfast. It was no dainty meal of toast and light cereals that these hardy ones demanded. But huge cuts of fresh-killed beef, with slabs of bread, and piles of potatoes, and stacks of hot cakes, and buckets of coffee, and whatever else the hard-working Chinaman could lay his hands on to satisfy their needs. As soon as each man reached the utmost limit of his capacity, he left the table without formality, and returned to the corral, where, with riata or persuasion, as the case demanded, he selected from his individual string of horses his first mount for the day.

By the time the sun was beginning to gild the summit of old Granite Mountain's castlelike walls, and touch with glorious color the peaks of the neighboring sentinel hills, the last rider had saddled, and the company was mounted and ready for their foreman's word. Then to the music of jingling spurs, tinkling bridle chains, squeaking saddle leather, and the softer swish and rustle and flap of chaps, romals and riatas, they rode forth, laughing and joking, still, with now and then a roaring chorus of shouting comment or wild yells, as some half-broken horse gave an exhibition of his prowess in a mad effort to unseat his grinning rider.

Soon the leader would call the name of a cowboy, known to be particularly familiar with the country which was to be the scene of that day's work, and telling him to take two or three or more men, as the case might be, would direct him to ride over a certain section, indicating the assigned territory by its natural marks of valley or flat or wash or ridge, and designating the point where the cattle would first be brought together. The cowboy named would rein his horse aside from the main company, calling the men of his choice as he did so, and a moment later with his companions would be lost to sight. A little farther, and again the foreman would name a rider, and, telling him to pick his men, would assign to him another section of the district to be covered, and this cowboy, with his chosen mates, would ride away. These smaller groups would, in their turn, separate, and thus the entire company of riders would open out like a huge fan to sweep the countryside.

It was no mere pleasure canter along smoothly graded bridle paths or well-kept country highways that these men rode. From roughest rock-strewn mountain side and tree-clad slope, from boulder-piled watercourse and tangled brush, they must drive in the scattered cattle. At reckless speed, as their quarry ran and turned and dodged, they must hesitate at nothing. Climbing to the tops of the hills, scrambling catlike to the ragged crests of the ridges, sliding down the bluffs, jumping deep arroyos, leaping brush and boulders, twisting, dodging through the timber, they must go as fast as the strength and endurance of their mounts would permit. And so, gradually, as the sun climbed higher above the peaks and crags of Old Granite, the great living fan of men and horses closed, the courses of the widely scattered riders leading them, with the cattle they had found, to the given point.

And now, the cattle, urged by the active horsemen, came streaming from the different sections to form the herd, and the quiet of the great range was broken by the bawling of confused and frightened calves, the lowing of anxious mothers, the shrill, long-drawn call of the steers, and the deep bellowing of the bulls, as the animals, so rudely driven from their peaceful feeding grounds, moved restlessly within the circle of guarding cowboys, while cows found their calves, and the monarchs of the range met in fierce combat.

A number of the men — those whose mounts most needed the rest — were now left to hold the herd, or, perhaps, to move it quietly on to some other point, while the others were again sent out to cover another section of the territory included in that day's riding. As the hours passed, and the great fan of horsemen opened and closed, sweeping the cattle scattered over the range into the steadily growing herd, the rodeo moved gradually toward some chosen open flat or valley that afforded a space large enough for the operations that followed the work of gathering. At this "rodeo ground" a man would be waiting with fresh mounts for the riders, and, sometimes, with lunch. Quickly, those whose names were called by the foreman would change their saddles from dripping, exhausted horses to fresh animals from their individual strings, snatch a hasty lunch — often to be eaten in the saddle — and then, in their turn, would hold the cattle while their companions followed their example.

Then came the fast, hot work of "parting" the cattle. The representatives from one of the ranches interested would ride in among the cattle held by the circle of cowboys, and, following their instructions, would select such animals bearing their employer's brand as were wanted, cutting them out and passing them through the line of guarding riders, to be held in a separate group. When the representatives of one owner had finished, they were followed by the men who rode for some other outfit; and so on, until the task of "parting" was finished.

As the afternoon sun moved steadily toward the skyline of the western hills, the tireless activity of men and horses continued. The cattle, as the mounted men moved among them, drifted about, crowding and jostling, in uneasy discontent, with sometimes an indignant protest, and many attempts at escape by the more restless and venturesome. When an animal was singled out, the parting horses, chosen and prized for their quickness, dashed here and there through the herd with fierce leaps and furious rushes, stopping short in a terrific sprint to whirl, flashlike, and charge in another direction, as the quarry dodged and doubled. And now and then an animal would succeed for the moment in passing the guard line, only to be brought back after a short, sharp chase by the nearest cowboy. From the rodeo ground, where for long years the grass had been trampled out, the dust, lifted by the trampling thousands of hoofs in a dense, choking cloud, and heavy with the pungent odor of warm cattle and the smell of sweating horses, rising high into the clear air, could be seen from miles away, while the mingled voices of the bellowing, bawling herd, with now and then the shrill, piercing yells of the cowboys, could be heard almost as far.

When this part of the work was over, some of the riders set out to drive the cattle selected to the distant home ranch corrals, while others of the company remained to brand the calves and to start the animals that were to have their freedom until the next rodeo time back to the open range. And so, at last — often not until the stars were out — the riders would dismount at the home corrals of the ranch that, at the time, was the center of their operations, or, perhaps, at some rodeo camping ground.

At supper the day's work was reviewed with many a laugh and jest of pointed comment, and then, those whose horses needed attention because of saddle sores or, it might be, because of injuries from some fall on the rocks, busied themselves at the corral, while others met for a friendly game of cards, or talked and yarned over restful pipe or cigarette. And then, bed and blankets, and, all too soon, the reveille sounded by the beating hoofs of the saddle band as the wrangler drove them in, announced the beginning of another day.

Not infrequently there were accidents — from falling horses — from angry bulls — from ill-tempered steers, or excited cows — or, perhaps, from a carelessly handled rope in some critical moment. Horses were killed; men with broken limbs, or with bodies bruised and crushed, were forced to drop out; and many a strong horseman who rode forth in the morning to the day's work, laughing and jesting with his mates, had been borne by his grave and silent comrades to some quiet resting place, to await, in long and dreamless sleep, the morning of that last great rodeo which, we are told, shall gather us all.

Day after day, as Patches rode with these hardy men, Phil watched him finding himself and winning his place among the cowboys. They did not fail, as they said, to "try him out." Nor did Phil, in these trials, attempt in any way to assist his pupil. But the men learned very quickly, as Curly had learned at the time of Patches' introduction, that, while the new man was always ready to laugh with them when a joke was turned against himself, there was a line beyond which it was not well to go. In the work he was, of course, assigned only to such parts as did not require the skill and knowledge of long training and experience. But he did all that was given him to do with such readiness and skill, thanks to Phil's teaching, that the men wondered. And this, together with his evident ability in the art of defending himself, and the story of his strange coming to the Cross-Triangle, caused not a little talk, with many and varied opinions as to who he was, and what it was that had brought him among them. Strangely enough, very few believed that Patches' purpose in working as a cowboy for the Dean was simply to earn an honest livelihood. They felt instinctively — as, in fact, did Phil and the Dean — that there was something more beneath it all than such a commonplace.

Nick Cambert, who, with Yavapai Joe, rode in the rodeo, carefully avoided the stranger. But Patches, by his persistent friendly interest in the Tailholt Mountain man's follower, added greatly to the warmth of the discussions and conjectures regarding himself. The rodeo had reached the Pot-Hook-S Ranch, with Jim Reid in charge, when the incident occurred which still further stimulated the various opinions and suggestions as to the new man's real character and mission.

They were working the cattle that day on the rodeo ground just outside the home ranch corral. Phil and Curly were cutting out some Cross-Triangle steers, when the riders, who were holding the cattle, saw them separate a nine-months-old calf from the herd, and start it, not toward the cattle they had already cut out, but toward the corral.

Instantly everybody knew what had happened.

The cowboy nearest the gate did not need Phil's word to open it for his neighbor next in line to drive the calf inside.

Not a word was said until the calves to be branded were also driven into the corral. Then Phil, after a moment's talk with Jim Reid, rode up to Nick Cambert, who was sitting on his horse a little apart from the group of intensely interested cowboys. The Cross-Triangle foreman's tone was curt. "I reckon I'll have to trouble you to vent your brand on that Cross-Triangle calf, Nick."

The Tailholt Mountain man made no shallow pretense that he did not understand. "Not by a damn sight," he returned roughly. "I ain't raisin' calves for Bill Baldwin, an' I happen to know what I'm talkin' about this trip. That's a Four-Bar-M calf, an' I branded him myself over in Horse Wash before he left the cow. Some of your punchers are too damned handy with their runnin' irons, Mr. Wild Horse Phil."

For a moment Phil looked at the man, while Jim Reid moved his horse nearer, and the cowboys waited, breathlessly. Then, without taking his eyes from the Tailholt Mountain man's face, Phil called sharply:

"Patches, come here!"

There was a sudden movement among the riders, and a subdued murmur, as Patches rode forward.

"Is that calf you told me about in the corral, Patches?" asked Phil, when the man was beside him.

"Yes, sir; that's him over there by that brindle cow." Patches indicated the animal in question.

"And you put our iron on him?" asked Phil, still watching Nick.

"I did," returned Patches, coolly.

"Tell us about it," directed the Dean's foreman.

And Patches obeyed, briefly. "It was that day you sent me to fix the fence on the southwest corner of the big pasture. I saw a bunch of cattle a little way outside the fence, and went to look them over. This calf was following a Cross-Triangle cow."

"Are you sure?"

"Yes, sir. I watched them for half an hour."

"What was in the bunch?"

"Four steers, a Pot-Hook-S bull, five cows and this calf. There were three Five-Bar cows, one Diamond-and-a-Half and one Cross-Triangle. The calf went to the Cross-Triangle cow every time. And, besides, he is marked just like his mother. I saw her again this afternoon while we were working the cattle."

Phil nodded. "I know her."

Jim Reid was watching Patches keenly, with a quiet look now and then at Nick.

The cowboys were murmuring among themselves.

"Pretty good work for a tenderfoot!"

"Tenderfoot, hell!"

"They've got Nick this trip."

"Got nothin'! Can't you see it's a frame-up?"

Phil spoke to Nick. "Well, are satisfied? Will you vent your brand?"

The big man's face was distorted with passion. "Vent nothin'," he roared. "On the word of a damned sneakin' tenderfoot! I —"

He stopped, as Patches, before Phil could check the movement, pushed close to his side.

In the sudden stillness the new man's cool, deliberate voice sounded clearly. "I am positive that you made a mistake when you put your iron on that calf, Mr. Cambert. And," he added slowly, as though with the kindest possible intention, "I am sure that you can safely take my word for it without further question."

For a moment Nick glared at Patches, speechless. Then, to the amazement of every cowboy in the corral, the big man mumbled a surly something, and took down his riata to rope the calf and disclaim his ownership of the animal.

Jim Reid shook his head in puzzled doubt.

The cowboys were clearly divided.

"He's too good a hand for a tenderfoot," argued one; "carried that off like an old-timer."

"'Tain't like Nick to lay down so easy for anybody," added another.

"Nick's on to something about Mr. Patches that we ain't next to," insisted a third.

"Or else we're all bein' strung for a bunch of suckers," offered still another.

"You boys just hold your horses, an' ride easy," said Curly. "My money's still on Honorable Patches."

And Bob added his loyal support with his cheerful "Me, too!"

"It all looked straight enough," Jim Reid admitted to the Dean that evening, "but I can't get away from the notion that there was some sort of an understanding between your man an' that damned Tailholt Mountain thief. It looked like it was all too quiet an' easy somehow; like it had been planned beforehand."

The Dean laughingly told his neighbor that he was right; that there was an understanding between Patches and Nick, and then explained by relating how Patches had met the Tailholt Mountain men that day at the spring.

When the Dean had finished the big cowman asked several very suggestive questions. How did the Dean know that Patches' story was anything more than a cleverly arranged tale, invented for the express purpose of allaying any suspicion as to his true relationship with Nick? If Patches' character was so far above suspicion, why did he always dodge any talk that might touch his past? Was it necessary or usual for men to keep so close-mouthed about themselves? What did the Dean, or anyone else, for that matter, really know about this man who had appeared so strangely from nowhere, and had given a name even that was so plainly a ridiculous invention? The Dean must remember that the suspicion as to the source of Nick's too rapidly increasing herds had, so far, been directed wholly against Nick himself, and that the owner of the Four-Bar-M iron was not altogether a fool. It was quite time, Reid argued, for Nick to cease his personal activities, and to trust the actual work of branding to some confederate whose movements would not be so closely questioned. In short, Reid had been expecting some stranger to seek a job with some of the ranches that were in a position to contribute to the Tailholt Mountain outfit, and, for his part, he would await developments before becoming too enthusiastic over Honorable Patches.

All of which the good Dean found very hard to answer.

"But look here, Jim," he protested, "don't you go makin' it unpleasant for the boy. Whatever you think, you don't know anymore than the rest of us. If we're guessin' on one side, you're guessin' on the other. I admit that what you say sounds reasonable; but, hang it, I like Patches. As for his name — well — we didn't use to go so much on names, in this country, you know. The boy may have some good reason for not talkin' about himself. Just give him a square chance; don't put no burrs under his saddle blanket — that's all I'm askin'."

Jim laughed. The speech was so characteristic of the Dean, and Jim Reid loved his old friend and neighbor, as all men did, for being, as was commonly said, "so easy."

"Don't worry, Will," he answered. "I'm not goin' to start anything. If I should happen to be right about Mr. Honorable Patches, he's exactly where we want him. I propose to keep my eye on him, that's all. And I think you an' Phil had better do the same."

Chapter XI
AFTER THE RODEO

*A*s the fall rodeo swept on its way over the wide ranges, the last reluctant bits of summer passed, and hints of the coming winter began to appear The yellow glory of the goldenrod, and the gorgeous banks of color on sunflower flats faded to earthy russet and brown; the white cups of the Jimson weed were broken and lost; the dainty pepper-grass, the thin-leafed grama-grass, and the heavier bladed bear-grass of the great pasture lands were dry and tawny; and the broom-weed that had tufted the rolling hills with brighter green, at the touch of the first frost, turned a dull and somber grey; while the varied beauties of the valley meadows became even as the dead and withered leaves of the Dean's walnut trees that, in falling, left the widespread limbs and branches so bare.

Then the rodeo and the shipping were over; the weeks of the late fall range riding were past — and it was winter.

From skyline to skyline the world was white, save for the dark pines upon the mountain sides, the brighter cedars and junipers upon the hills and ridges, and the living green of the oak brush, that, when all else was covered with snow, gave the cattle their winter feed.

More than ever, now, with the passing of the summer and fall, Kitty longed for the stirring life that, in some measure, had won her from the scenes of her home and from her homeland friends. The young woman's friendship with Patches — made easy by the fact that the Baldwins had taken him so wholly into their hearts — served to keep alive her memories of that world to which she was sure he belonged, and such memories did not tend to make Kitty more contented and happy in Williamson Valley.

Toward Phil, Kitty was unchanged. Many times her heart called for him so insistently that she wished she had never learned to know any life other than that life to which they had both been born. If only she had not spent those years away from home — she often told herself —

it would all have been so different. She could have been happy with Phil — very happy — if only she had remained in his world. But now — now she was afraid — afraid for him as well as for herself. Her friendship with Patches had, in so many ways, emphasized the things that stood between her and the man whom, had it not been for her education, she would have accepted so gladly as her mate.

Many times when the three were together, and Kitty had led the talk far from the life with which the cowboy was familiar, the young woman was forced, against the wish of her heart, to make comparisons. Kitty did not understand that Phil — unaccustomed to speaking of things outside his work and the life interests of his associates, and timid always in expressing his own thoughts — found it very hard to reveal the real wealth of his mind to her when she assumed so readily that he knew nothing beyond his horses and cattle. But Patches, to whom Phil had learned to speak with little reserve, understood. And, knowing that the wall which the girl felt separated her from the cowboy was built almost wholly of her own assumptions, Patches never lost an opportunity to help the young woman to a fuller acquaintance with the man whom she thought she had known since childhood.

During the long winter months, many an evening at the Cross-Triangle, at the Reid home, or, perhaps, at some neighborhood party or dance, afforded Kitty opportunities for a fuller understanding of Phil, but resulted only in establishing a closer friendship with Patches.

Then came the spring.

The snow melted; the rains fell; the washes and creek channels were filled with roaring floods; hill and ridge and mountain slope and mesa awoke to the new life that was swelling in every branch and leaf and blade; the beauties of the valley meadow appeared again in fresh and fragrant loveliness; while from fence-post and bush and grassy bank and new-leaved tree the larks and mocking birds and doves voiced their glad return.

And, with the spring, came a guest to the Cross-Triangle Ranch — another stranger.

Patches had been riding the drift fence, and, as he made his way toward the home ranch, in the late afternoon, he looked a very different man from the Patches who, several months before, had been rescued by Kitty from a humiliating experience with that same fence.

The fact that he was now riding Stranger, the big bay with the blazed face, more than anything else, perhaps, marked the change that had come to the man whom the horse had so viciously tested, on that day when they began together their education and work on the Cross-Triangle Ranch.

No one meeting the cowboy, who handled his powerful and wild spirited mount with such easy confidence and skill, would have identified him with the white-faced, well-tailored gentleman whom Phil had met on the Divide. The months of active outdoor life had given his tall body a lithe and supple strength that was revealed in his every movement, while wind and sun had stained his skin that deep tan which marks those who must face the elements every waking hour. Prom tinkling bridle chain and jingling spur, to the coiled riata, his equipment showed the unmistakable marks of use. His fringed chaps, shaped, by many a day in the saddle, to his long legs, expressed experience, while his broad hat, soiled by sweat and dust, had acquired individuality, and his very jumper — once blue but now faded and patched — disclaimed the tenderfoot.

Riding for a little way along the top of the ridge that forms the western edge of the valley, Patches looked down upon the red roofs of the buildings of the home ranch, and smiled as he thought of the welcome that awaited him there at the close of his day's work. The Dean and Stella, with Little Billy, and Phil, and the others of the home circle, had grown very dear to this strong man of whom they still knew nothing; and great as was the change in his outward appearance and manner, the man himself knew that there were other changes as great. Honorable Patches had not only acquired a name and a profession, but in acquiring them he had gained something of much greater worth to himself. And so he was grateful to those who, taking him on trust, had helped him more than they knew.

He had left the ridge, and was halfway across the flat toward the corrals, when Little Billy, spurring old Sheep in desperate energy, rode wildly out to meet him.

As the lad approached, he greeted his big friend with shrill, boyish shouts, and Patches answered with a cowboy yell which did credit to his training, while Stranger, with a wild, preliminary bound into the air, proceeded, with many weird contortions, to give an exhibition which fairly expressed his sentiments.

Little Billy grinned with delight. "Yip! Yip! Yee-e-e!" he shrilled, for Stranger's benefit. And then, as the big horse continued his manifestations, the lad added the cowboy's encouraging admonition to the rider. "Stay with him, Patches! Stay with him!"

Patches laughingly stayed with him. "What you aimin' to do, pardner" — he asked good-naturedly, when Stranger at last consented to keep two feet on the ground at the same time — "tryin' to get me piled?"

"Shucks!" retorted the youngster admiringly. "I don't reckon any-thing could pile you, *now*. I come out to tell you that we got company," he added, as, side by side, they rode on toward the corrals.

Patches was properly surprised. "Company!" he exclaimed.

Little Billy grinned proudly. "Yep. He's a man — from way back East somewhere. Uncle Will brought him out from town. They got here just after dinner. I don't guess he's ever seen a ranch before. Gee! but won't we have fun with him!"

Patches face was grave as he listened. "How do you know he is from the East, Billy?" he asked, concealing his anxious interest with a smile at his little comrade.

"Heard Uncle Will tell Phil and Kitty."

"Oh, Kitty is at the house, too, is she?"

Billy giggled. "She an' Phil's been off somewheres ridin' together most all day; they just got back a while ago. They was talkin' with the company when I left. Phil saw you when you was back there on the ridge, an' I come on out to tell you."

Phil and Kitty were walking toward their horses, which were standing near the corral fence, as Patches and Little Billy came through the gate.

The boy dropped from his saddle, and ran on into the house to tell his Aunt Stella that Patches had come, leaving Sheep to be looked after by whoever volunteered for the service. It was one of Little Billy's humiliations that he was not yet tall enough to saddle or bridle his own horse, and the men tactfully saw to it that his mount was always ready in the morning, and properly released at night, without any embarrass-ing comments on the subject.

Patches checked his horse, and without dismounting greeted his friends. "You're not going?" he said to Kitty, with a note of protest in his voice. "I haven't seen you for a week. It's not fair for Phil to take advantage of his position and send me off somewhere alone while he spends his time riding over the country with you."

They laughed up at him as he sat there on the big bay, hat in hand, looking down into their upturned faces with the intimate, friendly interest of an older brother.

Patches noticed that Kitty's eyes were bright with excitement, and that Phil's were twinkling with suppressed merriment.

"I must go, Patches," said the young woman. "I ought to have gone two hours ago; but I was so interested that the time slipped away before I realized."

"We have company," explained Phil, looking at Patches and deliber-ately closing one eye — the one that Kitty could not see. "A distinguished guest, if you please. I'll loan you a clean shirt for supper; that is, if mother lets you eat at the same table with him."

"Phil, how can you!" protested Kitty.

The two men laughed, but Phil fancied that there was a hint of anxiety in Patches' face, as the man on the horse said, "Little Billy broke the news to me. Who is he?"

"A friend of Judge Morris in Prescott," answered Phil. "The Judge asked Uncle Will to take him on the ranch for a while. He and the Judge were —"

Kitty interrupted with enthusiasm. "It is Professor Parkhill, Patches, the famous professor of aesthetics, you know: Everard Charles Parkhill. And he's going to spend the summer in Williamson Valley! Isn't it wonderful!"

Phil saw a look of relief in his friend's face as Patches answered Kitty with sympathetic interest. "It certainly will be a great pleasure, Miss Reid, especially for you, to have one so distinguished for his scholarship in the neighborhood. Is Professor Parkhill visiting Arizona for his health?"

Something in Patches' voice caused Phil to turn hastily aside.

But Kitty, who was thinking how perfectly Patches understood her, noticed nothing in his grave tones save his usual courteous deference.

"Partly because of his health," she answered, "but he is going to prepare a series of lectures, I understand. He says that in the crude and uncultivated mentalities of our —"

"Here he is now," interrupted Phil, as the distinguished guest of the Cross-Triangle appeared, coming slowly toward them.

Professor Everard Charles Parkhill looked the part to which, from his birth, he had been assigned by his overcultured parents. His slender body, with its narrow shoulders and sunken chest, frail as it was, seemed almost too heavy for his feeble legs. His thin face, bloodless and sallow, with a sparse, daintily trimmed beard and weak watery eyes, was characterized by a solemn and portentous gravity, as though, realizing fully the profound importance of his mission in life, he could permit no trivial thought to enter his bald, domelike head. One knew instinctively that in all the forty-five or fifty years of his little life no happiness or joy that had not been scientifically sterilized and certified had ever been permitted to stain his super-aesthetic soul.

As he came forward, he gazed at the long-limbed man on the big bay horse with a curious eagerness, as though he were considering a strange and interesting creature that could scarcely be held to belong to the human race.

"Professor Parkhill," said Phil coolly, "you were saying that you had never seen a genuine cowboy in his native haunt. Permit me to introduce a typical specimen, Mr. Honorable Patches. Patches, this is Professor Parkhill."

"Phil," murmured Kitty, "how can you?"

The Professor was gazing at Patches as though fascinated. And Patches, his weather-beaten face as grave as the face of a wooden Indian, stared back at the Professor with a blank, open-mouthed and wild-eyed expression of rustic wonder that convulsed Phil and made Kitty turn away to hide a smile.

"Howdy! Proud to meet up with you, mister," drawled the typical specimen of the genus cowboy. And then, as though suddenly remembering his manners, he leaped to the ground and strode awkwardly forward, one hand outstretched in greeting, the other holding fast to Stranger's bridle rein, while the horse danced and plunged about with reckless indifference to the polite intentions of his master.

The Professor backed fearfully away from the dangerous looking horse and the equally formidable-appearing cowboy. Whereat Patches addressed Stranger with a roar of savage wrath.

"Whoa! You consarned, square-headed, stiff-legged, squint-eyed, lop-eared, four-flusher, you. Whoa, I tell you! Cain't you see I'm a-wantin' to shake hands with this here man what the boss has interduced me to?"

Phil nearly choked. Kitty was looking unutterable things. They did not know that Patches was suffering from a reaction caused by the discovery that he had never before met Professor Parkhill.

"You see, mister," he explained gravely, advancing again with Stranger following nervously, "this here fool horse ain't used to strangers, no how, 'specially them as don't look, as you might say, just natural like." He finished with a sheepish grin, as he grasped the visitor's soft little hand and pumped it up and down with virile energy. Then, staring with bucolic wonder at the distinguished representative of the highest culture, he asked, "Be you an honest-to-God professor? I've heard about such, but I ain't never seen one before."

The little man replied hurriedly, but with timid pride, "Certainly, sir; yes, certainly."

"You be!" exclaimed the cowboy, as though overcome by his nearness to such dignity. "Excuse me askin', but if you don't mind, now — what be you professor of?"

The other answered with more courage, as though his soul found strength in the very word: "Aesthetics."

The cowboy's jaw dropped, his mouth opened in gaping awe, and he looked from the professor to Phil and Kitty, as if silently appealing to them to verify this startling thing which he had heard. "You don't say!" he murmured at last in innocent admiration. "Well, now, to think of a little feller like you a-bein' all that! But jest what be them there esteticks what you're professor of — if you don't mind my askin'?"

The distinguished scholar answered promptly, in his best platform voice, "The science or doctrine of the nature of beauty and of judgments of tastes."

At this, Stranger, with a snort of fear, stood straight up on his hind legs, and Professor Parkhill scuttled to a position of safety behind Phil.

"Excuse me, folks," said Patches. "I'm just naturally obliged to 'tend to this here thing what thinks he's a hoss. Come along, you ornery, pigeon-toed, knock-kneed, sway-backed, wooly-haired excuse, you. You ain't got no more manners 'n a measly coyote."

The famous professor of aesthetics stood with Phil and Kitty watching Patches as that gentleman relieved the dancing bay of the saddle, and led him away through the corrals to the gate leading into the meadow pasture.

"I beg pardon," murmured the visitor in his thin, little voice, "but what did I understand you to say is the fellow's name?"

"Patches; Honorable Patches," answered Phil.

"How strange! how extraordinarily strange! I should be very interested to know something of his ancestry, and, if possible, to trace the origin of such a peculiar name."

Phil replied with exaggerated concern. "For heaven's sake, sir, don't say anything about the man's name in his hearing."

"He — he is dangerous, you mean?"

"He is, if he thinks anyone is making light of his name. You should ask some of the boys who have tried it."

"But I — I assure you, Mr. Acton, I had no thought of ridicule — far from it. Oh, very far from it."

Kitty was obliged to turn away. She arrived at the corral in time to meet Patches, who was returning.

"You ought to be ashamed," she scolded. But in spite of herself her eyes were laughing.

"Yes, ma'am," said Patches meekly, hat in hand.

"How could you do such a thing?" she demanded.

"How could I help doing it?"

"How could you help it?"

"Yes. You saw how he looked at me. Really, Miss Reid, I couldn't bear to disappoint him so cruelly. Honestly, now, wasn't I exactly what he expected me to be? I think you should compliment me. Didn't I do it very well?"

"But, he'll think you're nothing but a cowboy," she protested.

"Fine!" retorted Patches, quickly. "I thank you, Miss Reid; that is really the most satisfactory compliment I have ever received."

"You're mocking me now," said Kitty, puzzled by his manner.

"Indeed, I am not. I am very serious," he returned. "But here he comes again. With your gracious permission, I'll make my exit. Please don't explain to the professor. It would humiliate me, and think how it would shock and disappoint him!"

Lifting his saddle from the ground and starting toward the shed, he said in a louder tone, "Sure, I won't ferget, Miss Kitty; an' you kin tell your paw that there bald-faced steer o' his'n, what give us the slip last rodeo time, is over in our big pasture. I sure seen him thar today."

During the days immediately following that first meeting, Kitty passed many hours with Professor Parkhill. Phil and his cowboys were busy preparing for the spring rodeo. Mrs. Baldwin was wholly occupied with ministering to the animal comforts of her earthly household. And the Dean, always courteous and kind to his guest, managed, nevertheless, to think of some pressing business that demanded his immediate and personal attention whenever the visitor sought to engage him in conversation. The professor, quite naturally holding the cattleman to be but a rude, illiterate and wholly materialistic creature, but little superior in intellectual and spiritual powers to his own beasts, sought merely to investigate the Dean's mental works, with as little regard for the Dean's feelings as a biologist would show toward a hug. The Dean confided to Phil and Patches, one day when he had escaped to the blacksmith shop where the men were shoeing their horses, that the professor was harmlessly insane. "Just think," he exploded, "of the poor, little fool livin' in Chicago for three years, an' never once goin' out to the stockyards even!"

It remained, therefore, for Kitty — the only worshiper of the professor's gods in Williamson Valley — to supply that companionship which seems so necessary even to those whose souls are so far removed from material wants. In short, as Little Billy put it, with a boy's irreverence, "Kitty rode herd on the professor." And, strangely enough to them all, Kitty seemed to like the job.

Either because her friendship with Patches — which had some to mean a great deal to Kitty — outweighed her respect and admiration for the distinguished object of his fun, or because she waited for some opportunity to make the revelation a punishment to the offender, the young woman did not betray the real character of the cowboy to the stranger. And the professor, thanks to Phil's warning, not only refrained from investigating the name of Patches, but carefully avoided Patches himself.

In the meantime, the "typical specimen" was forced to take a small part in the table talk lest he betray himself. So marked was this that Mrs. Baldwin one day, not understanding, openly chided him for being so "glum." Whereupon the Dean — to whom Phil had thoughtfully explained — teased the deceiver unmercifully, with many laughingly alleged reasons for his "grouch," while Curly and Bob, attributing their comrade's manner to the embarrassing presence of the stranger, grinned sympathetically; and the professor himself — unconsciously agreeing with the cowboys — with kindly condescension tried to make the victim of his august superiority as much at ease as possible; which naturally, for the Dean and Phil, added not a little to the situation.

Then the spring rodeo took the men far from the home ranch, and for several weeks the distinguished guest of the Cross-Triangle was left almost wholly to the guardianship of the young woman who lived on the other side of the big meadows.

It was the last day of the rodeo, when Phil rode to the home ranch, late in the afternoon, to consult with the Dean about the shipping. Patches and the cowboys who were to help in the long drive to the railroad were at Toohey with the cattle. While the cowboys were finishing their early breakfast the next morning, the foreman returned, and Patches knew, almost before Phil spoke, that something had happened. They shouted their greetings as he approached, but he had no smile for their cheery reception, nor did he answer, even, until he had ridden close to the group about the campfire. Then, with a short "mornin', boys," he dismounted and stood with the bridle reins in his hand.

At his manner a hush fell over the little company, and they watched him curiously.

"No breakfast, Sam," he said, shortly, to the Chinaman. "Just a cup of coffee." Then to the cowboys, "You fellows saddle up and get that bunch of cattle to moving. We'll load at Skull Valley."

Sam brought his coffee and he drank it as he stood, while the men hurriedly departed for their horses. Patches, the last to go, paused a moment, as though to speak, but Phil prevented him with a gruff order. "Get a move on you, Patches. Those cars will be there long before we are."

And Patches, seeing the man's face dark and drawn with pain, moved away without a word.

"Great snakes," softly ejaculated Curly a few moments later, as Patches stooped to take his saddle from where it lay on the ground beside Curly's. "What do you reckon's eatin' the boss? Him an' the Dean couldn't 'a' mixed it last night, could they? Do you reckon the Dean crawled him about somethin'?"

Patches shook his head with a "Search me, pardner," as he turned to his horse.

"Somethin's happened sure," muttered the other, busy with his saddle blanket. "Sufferin' cats! but I felt like he'd poured a bucket of ice water down my neck!" He drew the cinch tight with a vigorous jerk that brought a grunt of protest from his mount. "That's right," he continued, addressing the horse, "hump yourself, an' swell up and grunt, damn you; you ought to be thankin' God that you ain't nothin' but a hoss, nohow, with no feelin' 'cept what's in your belly." He dropped the heavy stirrup with a vicious slap, and swung to his seat. "If Phil's a-goin' to keep up the way he's startin', we'll sure have a pleasant little ol' ride to Skull Valley. Oh, Lord! but I wisht I was a professor of them there exeticks, or somethin' nice and gentle like, jest for today, anyhow."

Patches laughed. "Think you could qualify, Curly?"

The cowboy grinned as they rode off together. "So far as I've noticed the main part of the work, I could. The shade of them walnut trees at the home ranch, or the Pot-Hook-S front porch, an' a nice easy rockin' chair with fat cushions, or mebby the buckboard onct in a while, with Kitty to do the drivin' — Say, this has sure been some little ol' rodeo, ain't it? I ain't got a hoss in my string that can more'n stand up, an' honest to God, Patches, I'm jest corns all over. How's your saddle feel, this mornin'?"

"It's got corns, too," admitted Patches. "But there's Phil; we'd better be riding."

All that day Phil kept to himself, speaking to his companions only when speech could not be avoided, and then with the fewest possible words. That night, he left the company as soon as he had finished his supper, and went off somewhere alone, and Patches heard him finding his bed, long after the other members of the outfit were sound asleep. And the following day, through the trying work of loading the cattle, the young foreman was so little like himself that, had it not been that his men were nearly all old-time, boyhood friends who had known him all his life, there would surely have been a mutiny.

It was late in the afternoon, when the last reluctant steer was prodded and pushed up the timbered runway from the pens, and crowded into the car. Curly and Bob were going with the cattle train. The others would remain at Skull Valley until morning, when they would start for their widely separated homes. Phil announced that he was going to the home ranch that night.

"You can make it home sometime tomorrow, Patches," he finished, when he had said good-bye to the little group of men with whom he had lived and worked in closest intimacy through the long weeks of the rodeo. He reined his horse about, even as he spoke, to set out on his long ride.

The Cross-Triangle foreman was beyond hearing of the cowboys when Patches overtook him. "Do you mind if I go back to the Cross-Triangle with you tonight, Phil?" the cowboy asked quietly.

Phil checked his horse and looked at his friend a moment without answering. Then, in a kindlier tone than he had used the past two days, he said, "You better stay here with the boys, and get your night's rest, Patches. You have had a long hard spell of it in this rodeo, and yesterday and today have not been exactly easy. Shipping is always hell, even when everybody is in a good humor," he smiled grimly.

"If you do not object, I would really like to go," said Patches simply.

"But your horse is as tired as you ought to be," protested Phil.

"I'm riding Stranger, you know," the other answered.

To which Phil replied tersely, "Let's be riding, then."

The cowboys, who had been watching the two men, looked at each other in amazement as Phil and Patches rode away together.

"Well, what do you make of that?" exclaimed one.

"Looks like Honorable Patches was next," commented another.

"Us old-timers ain't in it when it comes to associatin' with the boss," offered a third.

"You shut up on that line," came sharply from Curly. "Phil ain't turnin' us down for nobody. I reckon if Patches is fool enough to want to ride to the Cross-Triangle tonight Phil ain't got no reason for stoppin' him. If any of you punchers wants to make the ride, the way's open, ain't it?"

"Now, don't you go on the prod, too," soothed the other. "We wasn't meanin' nothin' agin Phil."

"Well, what's the matter with Patches?" demanded the Cross-Triangle man, whose heart was sorely troubled by the mystery of his foreman's mood.

"Ain't nobody *said* as there was anything the matter. Fact is, don't nobody *know* that there is."

And for some reason Curly had no answer.

"Don't it jest naturally beat thunder the way he's cottoned up to that yellow dog of a Yavapai Joe?" mused another, encouraged by Curly's silence. "Three or four of the boys told how they'd seen 'em together off an' on, but I didn't think nothin' of it until I seen 'em myself when we was workin' over at Tailholt. It was one evenin' after supper. I went down to the corral to fix up that Pedro horse's back, when I heard voices kind o' low like. I stopped a minute, an' then sort o' eased along in the dark, an' run right onto 'em where they was a-settin' in the door o' the

saddle room, cozy as you please. Yavapai sneaked away while I was gettin'
the lantern an' lightin' it, but Patches, he jest stayed an' held the light
for me while I fixed ol' Pedro, jest as if nothin' had happened."

"Well," said Curly sarcastically, "what *had* happened?"

"I don't know-nothin' — mebby."

"If Patches was what some o' you boys seem to think, do you reckon
he'd be a-ridin' for the Cross-Triangle?" demanded Curly.

"He might, an' he mightn't," retorted two or three at once.

"Nobody can't say nothin' in a case like that until the showdown,"
added one. "I don't reckon the Dean knows anymore than the rest of
us."

"Unless Patches is what some of the other boys are guessin'," said
another.

"Which means," finished Curly, in a tone of disgust, "that we've got
to millin' 'round the same old ring again. Come on, Bob; let's see what
they've got for supper. That engine'll happen along directly, an' we'll be
startin' hungry."

Phil Acton was not ignorant of the different opinions that were held
by the cattlemen regarding Honorable Patches. Nor, as the responsible
foreman of the Cross-Triangle, could he remain indifferent to them.
During those first months of Patches' life on the ranch, when the
cowboy's heart had so often been moved to pity for the stranger who
had come to them apparently from some painful crisis in his life, he
had laughed at the suspicions of his old friends and associates. But as
the months had passed, and Patches had so rapidly developed into a
strong, self-reliant man, with a spirit of bold recklessness that was
marked even among those hardy riders of the range, Phil forgot, in a
measure, those characteristics that the stranger had shown at the beginning of their acquaintance. At the same time, the persistent suspicions
of the cattlemen, together with Patches' curious, and, in a way, secret
interest in Yavapai Joe, could not but have a decided influence upon
the young man who was responsible for the Dean's property.

It was inevitable, under the circumstances, that Phil's attitude toward
Patches should change, even as the character of Patches himself had
changed. While the foreman's manner of friendship and kindly regard
remained, so far, unaltered, and while Phil still, in his heart, believed in
his friend, and — as he would have said — "would continue to back his
judgment until the showdown," nevertheless that spirit of intimacy
which had so marked those first days of their work together had
gradually been lost to them. The cowboy no longer talked to his
companion, as he had talked that day when they lay in the shade of the
walnut tree at Toohey, and during the following days of their range

riding. He no longer admitted his friend into his inner life, as he had done that day when he told Patches the story of the wild stallion. And Patches, feeling the change, and unable to understand the reason for it, waited patiently for the time when the cloud that had fallen between them should lift.

So they rode together that night, homeward bound, at the end of the long, hard weeks of the rodeo, in the deepening gloom of the day's passing, in the hushed stillness of the wild land, under the wide sky where the starry sentinel hosts were gathering for their ever-faithful watch. And as they rode, their stirrups often touching, each was alone with his own thoughts. Phil, still in the depth of his somber mood, brooded over his bitter trouble. Patches, sympathetically wondering, silently questioning, wished that he could help.

There are times when a man's very soul forces him to seek companionship. Alone in the night with this man for whom, even at that first moment of their meeting on the Divide, he had felt a strange sense of kinship, Phil found himself drifting far from the questions that had risen to mar the closeness of their intimacy. The work of the rodeo was over; his cowboy associates, with their suggestive talk, were far away. Under the influence of the long, dark miles of that night, and the silent presence of his companion, the young man, for the time being, was no longer the responsible foreman of the Cross-Triangle Ranch. In all that vast and silent world there was, for Phil Acton, only himself, his trouble, and his friend.

And so it came about that, little by little, the young man told Patches the story of his dream, and of how it was now shattered and broken.

Sometimes bitterly, as though he felt injustice; sometimes harshly, as though in contempt for some weakness of his own; with sentences broken by the pain he strove to subdue, with halting words and long silences, Phil told of his plans for rebuilding the home of his boyhood, and of restoring the business that, through the generosity of his father, had been lost; of how, since his childhood almost, he had worked and saved to that end; and of his love for Kitty, which had been the very light of his dream, and without which for him there was no purpose in dreaming. And the man who rode so close beside him listened with a fuller understanding and a deeper sympathy than Phil knew.

"And now," said Phil hopelessly, "it's all over. I've sure come to the end of my string. Reid has put the outfit on the market. He's going to sell out and quit. Uncle Will told me night before last when I went home to see about the shipping."

"Reid is going to sell!" exclaimed Patches; and there was a curious note of exultation in his voice which Phil did not hear. Neither did Phil see that his companion was smiling to himself under cover of the darkness.

"It's that damned Professor Parkhill that's brought it about," continued the cowboy bitterly. "Ever since Kitty came home from the East she has been discontented and dissatisfied with ranch life. I was all right when she went away, but when she came back she discovered that I was nothing but a cow-puncher. She has been fair, though. She has tried to get back where she was before she left and I thought I would win her again in time. I was so sure of it that it never troubled me. You have seen how it was. And you have seen how she was always wanting the life that she had learned to want while she was away — the life that you came from, Patches. I have been mighty glad for your friendship with her, too, because I thought she would learn from you that a man could have all that is worth having in *that* life, and still be happy and contented *here*. And she would have learned, I am sure. She couldn't help seeing it. But now that damned fool who knows no more of real manhood than I do of his profession has spoiled it all."

"But Phil, I don't understand. What has Parkhill to do with Reid's selling out?"

"Why, don't you see?" Phil returned savagely. "He's the supreme representative of the highest highbrowed culture, isn't he? He's a lord high admiral, duke, or potentate of some sort, in the world of loftiest thought, isn't he? He lives, moves and has his being in the lofty realms of the purely spiritual, doesn't he? He's cultured, and cultivated, and spiritualized, until he vibrates nothing but pure soul — whatever that means — and he's refined himself, and mental-disciplined himself, and soul-dominated himself, until there's not an ounce of red blood left in his carcass. Get him between you and the sun, after what he calls a dinner, and you can see every material mouthful that he, has disgraced himself by swallowing. He's not human, I tell you; he's only a kind of a he-ghost, and ought to be fed on sterilized moonbeams and pasteurized starlight."

"Amen!" said Patches solemnly, when Phil paused for lack of breath. "But, Phil, your eloquent characterization does not explain what the he-ghost has to do with the sale of the Pot-Hook-S outfit."

Phil's voice again dropped into its hopeless key as he answered. "You remember how, from the very first, Kitty — well — sort of worshiped him, don't you?"

"You mean how she worshiped his aesthetic cult, don't you?" corrected Patches quietly.

"I suppose that's it," responded Phil gloomily. "Well, Uncle Will says that they have been together mighty near every day for the past three months, and that about half of the time they have been over at Kitty's home. He has discovered, he says, that Kitty possesses a rare and wonderful capacity for absorbing the higher truths of the more purely intellectual and spiritual planes of life, and that she has a marvelously developed appreciation of those ideals of life which are so far removed from the base and material interests and passions which belong to the mere animal existence of the common herd."

"Oh, hell!" groaned Patches.

"Well, that's what he told Uncle Will," returned Phil stoutly. "And he has harped on that string so long, and yammered so much to Jim and to Kitty's mother about the girl's wonderful intellectuality, and what a record-breaking career she would have if only she had the opportunity, and what a shame, and a loss to the world it is for her to remain buried in these soul-dwarfing surroundings, that they have got to believing it themselves. You see, Kitty herself has in a way been getting them used to the idea that Williamson Valley isn't much of a place, and that the cow business doesn't rank very high among the best people. So Jim is going to sell out, and move away somewhere, where Kitty can have her career, and the boys can grow up to be something better than low-down cow-punchers like you and me. Jim is able to retire anyway."

"Thanks, Phil," said Patches quietly.

"What for?"

"Why, for including me in your class. I consider it a compliment, and" — he added, with a touch of his old self-mocking humor — "I think I know what I am saying — better, perhaps, than the he-ghost knows what he talks about."

"It may be that you do," returned Phil wearily, "but you can see where it all puts me. The professor has sure got me down and hog-tied so tight that I can't even think."

"Perhaps, and again, perhaps not," returned Patches. "Reid hasn't found a buyer for the outfit yet, has he?"

"Not yet, but they'll come along fast enough. The Pot-Hook-S Ranch is too well known for the sale to hang fire long."

The next day Phil seemed to slip back again, in his attitude toward Patches, to the temper of those last weeks of the rodeo. It was as though the young man — with his return to the home ranch and to the Dean and their talks and plans for the work — again put himself, his personal convictions and his peculiar regard for Patches, aside, and became the unprejudiced foreman, careful for his employer's interests.

Patches very quickly, but without offense, found that the door, which his friend had opened in the long dark hours of that lonely night ride, had closed again; and, thinking that he understood, he made no attempt to force his way. But, for some reason, Patches appeared to be in an unusually happy frame of mind, and went singing and whistling about the corrals and buildings as though exceedingly well pleased with himself and with the world.

The following day was Sunday. In the afternoon, Patches was roaming about the premises, keeping at a safe distance from the walnut trees in front of the house, where the professor had cornered the Dean, thus punishing both Patches and his employer by preventing one of their long Sunday talks which they both so much enjoyed. Phil had gone off somewhere to be alone, and Mrs. Baldwin was reading aloud to Little Billy. Honorable Patches was left very much to himself.

From the top of the little hill near the corrals, he looked across the meadow at exactly the right moment to see someone riding away from the neighboring ranch. He watched until he was certain that whoever it was was not coming to the Cross-Triangle — at least, not by way of the meadow lane. Then, smiling to himself, he went to the big barn and saddled a horse — there are always two or three that are not turned out in the pasture — and in a few minutes was riding leisurely away on the Simmons road, along the western edge of the valley. An hour later he met Kitty Reid, who was on her way from Simmons to the Cross-Triangle.

The young woman was sincerely glad to meet him.

"But you were going to Simmons, were you not?" she asked, as he reined his horse about to ride with her.

"To be truthful, I was going to Simmons if I met anyone else, or if I had not met you," he answered. Then, at her puzzled look, he explained, "I saw someone leave your house, and guessed that it was you. I guessed, too, that you would be coming this way."

"And you actually rode out to meet me?"

"Actually," he smiled.

They chatted about the rodeo, and the news of the countryside — for it had been several weeks since they had met — and so reached the point of the last ridge before you come to the ranch. Then Patches asked, "May we ride over there on the ridge, and sit for a while in the shade of that old cedar, for a little talk? It's early yet, and it's been ages since we had a powwow."

Reaching the point which Patches had chosen, they left their horses and made themselves comfortable on the brow of the hill, overlooking the wide valley meadow and the ranches.

"And now," said Kitty, looking at him curiously, "what's the talk, Mr. Honorable Patches?"

"Just you," said Patches, gravely.

"Me?"

"Your own charming self," he returned.

"But, please, good sir, what have I done?" she asked. "Or, perhaps, it's what have I not done?"

"Or perhaps," he retorted, "it's what you are going to do."

"Oh!"

"Miss Reid, I am going to ask you a favor — a great favor."

"Yes?"

"You have known me now almost a year."

"Yes."

"And, yet, to be exact, you do not know me at all."

She did not answer, but looked at him steadily.

"And that, in a way," he continued, "makes it easy for me to ask the favor; that is, if you feel that you can trust me ever so little — trust me, I mean, to the extent of believing me sincere."

"I know that you are sincere, Patches," she answered, gravely.

"Thank you," he returned. Then he said gently, "I want you to let me talk to you about what is most emphatically none of my business. I want you to let me ask you impertinent questions. I want you to talk to me about" — he hesitated; then finished with meaning — "about your career."

She felt his earnestness, and was big enough to understand, and be grateful for the spirit that prompted his words.

"Why, Patches," she cried, "after all that your friendship has meant to me, these past months, I could not think any question that you would ask impertinent Surely you know that, don't you?"

"I hoped that you would feel that way. And I know that I would give five years of my life if I knew how to convince you of the truth which I have learned from my own bitter experience, and save you from — from yourself."

She could not mistake his earnestness and in spite of herself the man's intense feeling moved her deeply.

"Save me from myself?" she questioned. "What in the world do you mean, Patches?"

"Is it true," he asked, "that your father is offering the ranch for sale, and that you are going out of the Williamson Valley life?"

"Yes, but it is not such a sudden move as it seems. We have often talked about it at home — father and mother and I."

"But the move is to be made chiefly on your account, is it not?"

She flushed a little at this, but answered stoutly. "Yes. I suppose that is true. You see, being the only one in our family to have the advantages of — well — the advantages that I have had, it was natural that I should

— Surely you have seen, Patches, how discontented and dissatisfied I have been with the life here! Why, until you came there was no one to whom I could talk, even — no one, I mean, who could understand."

"But what is it that you want, or expect to find, that you may not have right here?"

Then she told him all that he had expected to hear. Told him earnestly, passionately, of the life she craved, and of the sordid, commonplace narrowness and emptiness — as she saw it — of the life from which she sought to escape. And as she talked the man's good heart was heavy with sadness and pity for her.

"Oh, girl, girl," he cried, when she had finished. "Can't you — won't you — understand? All that you seek is right here — everywhere about you — waiting for you to make it your own, and with it you may have here those greater things without which no life can be abundant and joyous. The culture and the intellectual life that is dependent upon mere environment is a crippled culture and a sickly life. The mind that cannot find its food for thought wherever it may be planed will never hobble very far on crutches of superficial cults and societies. You are leaving the substance, child, for the shadow. You are seeking the fads and fancies of shallow idlers, and turning your back upon eternal facts. You are following after silly fools who are chasing bubbles over the edge of God's good world. Believe me, girl, I know — God! but I do know what that life, stripped of its tinseled and spangled show, means. Take the good grain, child, and let the husks go."

As the man spoke, Kitty watched him as though she were intently interested; but, in truth, her thoughts were more on the speaker than on what he said.

"You are in earnest, aren't you, Patches?" she murmured softly.

"I am," he returned sharply, for he saw that she was not even considering what he had said. "I know how mistaken you are; I know what it will mean to you when you find how much you have lost and how little you have gained."

"And how am I mistaken? Do I not know what I want? Am I not better able than anyone else to say what satisfies me and what does not?"

"No," he retorted, almost harshly, "you are not. You *think* it is the culture, as you call it, that you want; but if that were really it, you would not go. You would find it here. The greatest minds that the world has ever known you may have right here in your home, on your library table. And you may listen to their thoughts without being disturbed by the magpie chatterings of vain and shallow pretenders. You are attracted by the pretentious forms and manners of that life; you think that because a certain class of people, who have nothing else to do, talk a certain jargon, and profess to follow certain teachers — who, nine times out of ten, are charlatans or fools — that they are the intellectual and spiritual leaders of the race. You are mistaking the very things that prevent intellectual and spiritual development for the things you think you want."

She did not answer his thought, but replied to his words. "And supposing I am mistaken, as you say. Still, I do not see why it should matter so to you."

He made a gesture of hopelessness and sat for a moment in silence. Then he said slowly, "I fear you will not understand, but did you ever hear the story of how 'Wild Horse Phil' earned his title?"

She laughed. "Why, of course. Everybody knows about that. Dear, foolish old Phil — I shall miss him dreadfully." "Yes," he said significantly, "you will miss him. The life you are going to does not produce Phil Actons."

"It produced an Honorable Patches," she retorted slyly.

"Indeed it did *not,*" he answered quickly. "It produced —" He checked himself, as though fearing that he would say too much.

"But what have Phil and his wild horse to do with the question?" she asked.

"Nothing, I fear. Only I feel about your going away as Phil felt when he gave the wild horse its freedom."

"I don't think I understand," she said, genuinely puzzled.

"I said you would not," he retorted bluntly, "and that's why you are leaving all this." His gesture indicated the vast sweep of country with old Granite Mountain in the distance.

Then, with a nod and a look he indicated Professor Parkhill, who was walking toward them along the side of the ridge skirting the scattered cedar timber. "Here comes a product of the sort of culture to which you aspire. Behold the ideal manhood of your higher life! When the intellectual and spiritual life you so desire succeeds in producing racial fruit of that superior quality, it will have justified its existence — and will perish from the earth."

Even as Patches spoke, he saw something just beyond the approaching man that made him start as if to rise to his feet.

It was the unmistakable face of Yavapai Joe, who, from behind an oak bush, was watching the professor.

Patches, glancing at Kitty, saw that she had not noticed.

Before the young woman could reply to her companion's derisive remarks, the object which had prompted his comments arrived within speaking distance.

"I trust I am not intruding," began the professor, in his small, thin voice. Then as Patches, his eyes still on that oak bush, stood up, the little man added, with hasty condescension, "Keep your seat, my man; keep your seat. I assure you it is not my purpose to deprive you of Miss Reid's company."

Patches grinned. By that "my man" he knew that Kitty had not enlightened her teacher as to the "typical cowboy's" real character.

"That's all right, perfessor," he said awkwardly. "I just seen a maverick over yonder a-piece. I reckon I'd better mosey along an' have a closer look at him. Me an' Kitty here warn't talkin' nothin' important, nohow. Just a gassin' like. I reckon she'd ruther go on home with you, anyhow, an' it's all right with me."

"Maverick!" questioned the professor. "And what, may I ask, is a maverick?"

"Hit's a critter what don't belong to nobody," answered Patches, moving toward his horse.

At the same moment Kitty, who had risen, and was looking in the direction from which the professor had come, exclaimed, "Why, there's Yavapai Joe, Patches. What is he doing here?"

She pointed, and the professor, looking, caught a glimpse of Joe's back as the fellow was slinking over the ridge.

"I reckon mebby he wants to see me 'bout somethin' or other," Patches returned, as he mounted his horse. "Anyway, I'm a-goin' over that-a-way an' see. So long!"

Patches rode up to Joe just as the Tailholt Mountain man regained his horse on the other side of the ridge.

"Hello, Joe!" said the Cross-Triangle rider, easily.

The wretched outcast was so shaken and confused that he could scarcely find the stirrup with his foot, and his face was pale and twitching with excitement. He looked at Patches, wildly, but spoke in a sullen tone. "What's he doin' here? What does he want? How did he get to this country, anyhow?"

Patches was amazed, but spoke calmly. "Whom do you mean, Joe?"

"I mean that man back there, Parkhill — Professor Parkhill. What's he a-lookin' for hangin' 'round here? You can tell him it ain't no use — I —" He stopped suddenly, and with a characteristic look of cunning, turned away.

Patches rode beside him for some distance, but nothing that he could say would persuade the wretched creature to explain.

"Yes, I know you're my friend, all right, Patches," he answered. "You sure been mighty friendly ter me, an' I ain't fergettin' it. But I ain't a-tellin' nothin' to nobody, an' it ain't a-goin' to do you no good to go askin' him 'bout me, neither."

"I'm not going to ask Professor Parkhill anything, Joe," said Patches shortly.

"You ain't?"

"Certainly not; if you don't want me to know. I'm not trying to find out about anything that's none of my business."

Joe looked at him with a cunning leer. "Oh, you ain't, ain't you? Nick 'lows that you're sure —" Again he caught himself. "But I ain't a-tellin' nothin' to nobody."

"Well, have *I* ever asked you to tell me anything?" demanded Patches.

"No, you ain't — that's right — you sure been square with me, Patches, an' I ain't fergettin' it. Be you sure 'nuf my friend, Patches? Honest-to-God, now, be you?"

His question was pitiful, and Patches assured the poor fellow that he had no wish to be anything but his friend, if only Yavapai Joe would accept his help.

"Then," said Joe pleadingly, "if you mean all that you been sayin' about wantin' to help me, you'll do somethin' fer me right now."

"What can I do, Joe?"

"You kin promise me that you won't say nothin' to nobody 'bout me an' him back there."

Patches, to demonstrate his friendliness, answered without thought, "Certainly, I'll promise that, Joe."

"You won't tell nobody?"

"No, I won't say a word."

The poor fellow's face revealed his gratitude. "I'm obliged to you, Patches, I sure am, an' I ain't fergettin' nothin', either. You're my friend, all right, an' I'm your'n. I got to be a-hittin' it up now. Nick'll jest nachally gimme hell for bein' gone so long."

"Good-bye, Joe!"

"So long, Patches! An' don't you get to thinkin' that I'm fergettin' how me an' you is friends."

When Patches reviewed the incident, as he rode back to the ranch, he questioned if he had done right in promising Joe. But, after all, he reassured himself, he was under no obligation to interfere with what was clearly none of his business. He could not see that the matter in any possible way touched his employer's interests. And, he reflected, he had already tried the useless experiment of meddling with other people's affairs, and he did not care to repeat the experience.

That evening Patches asked Phil's permission to go to Prescott the next day. It would be the first time that he had been to town since his coming to the ranch and the foreman readily granted his request.

A few minutes later as Phil passed through the kitchen, Mrs. Baldwin remarked, "I wonder what Patches is feeling so gay about. Ever since he got home from the rodeo he's been singin' an' whistlin' an' grinnin' to himself all the time. He went out to the corral just now as merry as a lark."

Phil laughed. "Anybody would be glad to get through with that rodeo, mother; besides, he is going to town tomorrow."

"He is? Well, you mark my words, son, there's somethin' up to make him feel as good as he does."

And then, when Phil had gone on out into the yard, Professor Parkhill found him.

"Mr. Acton," began the guest timidly, "there is a little matter about which I feel I should speak to you."

"Very well, sir," returned the cowboy.

"I feel that it would be better for me to speak to you rather than to Mr. Baldwin, because, well, you are younger, and will, I am sure, understand more readily."

"All right; what is it, Professor?" asked Phil encouragingly, wondering at the man's manner.

"Do you mind — ah — walking a little way down the road?"

As they strolled out toward the gate to the meadow road, the professor continued:

"I think I should tell you about your man Patches."

Phil looked at his companion sharply. "Well, what about him?"

"I trust you will not misunderstand my interest, Mr. Acton, when I say that it also includes Miss Reid."

Phil stopped short. Instantly Mrs. Baldwin's remark about Patches' happiness, his own confession that he had given up all hope of winning Kitty, and the thought of the friendship which he had seen developing during the past months, with the realization that Patches belonged to that world to which Kitty aspired — all swept through his mind. He was looking at the man beside him so intently that the professor said again uneasily:

"I trust, Mr. Acton, that you will understand."

Phil laughed shortly. "I think I do. But just the same you'd better explain. What about Patches and Miss Reid, sir?"

The professor told how he had found them together that afternoon.

"Oh, is that all?" laughed Phil.

"But surely, Mr. Acton, you do not think that a man of that fellow's evident brutal instincts is a fit associate for a young woman of Miss Reid's character and refinement."

"Perhaps not," admitted Phil, still laughing, "but I guess Kitty can take care of herself."

"I do not agree with you, sir," said the other authoritatively. "A young woman of Miss Reid's — ah — spirituality and worldly inexperience must always be, to a certain extent, injured by contact with such illiterate, unrefined, and, I have no doubt, morally deficient characters."

"But, look here, Professor," returned Phil, still grinning, "what do you expect me to do about it? I am not Kitty Reid's guardian. Why don't you talk to her yourself?"

"Really," returned the little man, "I — there are reasons why I do not see my way clear to such a course. I had hoped that you might keep an eye on the fellow, and, if necessary, use your authority over him to prevent any such incidents in the future."

"I'll see what I can do," answered Phil, thinking how the Dean would enjoy the joke. "But, look here; Kitty was with you when you got to the ranch. What became of Patches? Run, did he, when you appeared on the scene?"

"Oh, no; he went away with a — with a maverick."

"Went away with a maverick? What, in heaven's name, do you mean by that?"

"That's what your man Patches said the fellow was. Miss Reid told me his name was Joe — Joe something."

Phil was not laughing now. The fun of the situation had vanished.

"Was it Yavapai Joe?" he demanded.

"Yes, that was it. I am quite sure that was the name. He belongs at Tailend Mountain, I think Miss Reid said; you have such curious names in this country."

"And Patches went away with him, you say?"

"Yes, the fellow seemed to have been hiding in the bushes when we discovered him, and when Miss Reid asked what he was doing there your man said that he had come to see him about something. They went away together, I believe."

As soon as he could escape from the professor, Phil went straight to Patches, who was in his room, reading. The man looked up with a welcoming smile as Phil entered, but as he saw the foreman's face his smile vanished quickly, and he laid aside his book.

"Patches," said Phil abruptly, "what's this talk of the professor's about you and Yavapai Joe?"

"I don't know what the professor is talking," Patches replied coldly, as though he did not exactly like the tone of Phil's question.

"He says that Joe was sneaking about in the brush over on the ridge wanting to see you about something," returned Phil.

"Joe was certainly over there on the ridge, and he may have wanted to see me; at any rate, I saw him."

"Well, I've got to ask you what sort of business you have with that Tailholt Mountain thief that makes it necessary for him to sneak around in the brush for a meeting with you. If he wants to see you, why doesn't he come to the ranch, like a man?"

Honorable Patches looked the Dean's foreman straight in the eyes, as he answered in a tone that he had never used before in speaking to Phil: "And I have to answer, sir, that my business with Yavapai Joe is entirely personal; that it has no relation whatever to your business as the foreman of this ranch. As to why Joe didn't come to the house, you must ask him; I don't know."

"You refuse to explain?" demanded Phil.

"I certainly refuse to discuss Joe Dryden's private affairs — that, so far as I can see, are of no importance to anyone but himself — with you or anyone else. Just as I should refuse to discuss any of your private affairs, with which I happened, by some chance, to be, in a way, familiar. I have made all the explanation necessary when I say that my business with him has nothing to do with your business. You have no right to ask me anything further."

"I have the right to fire you," retorted Phil, angrily.

Patches smiled, as he answered gently, "You have the right, Phil, but you won't use it."

"And why not?"

"Because you are not that kind of a man, Phil Acton," answered Patches slowly. "You know perfectly well that if you discharged me because of my friendship with poor Yavapai Joe, no ranch in this part of the country would give me a job. You are too honest yourself to condemn any man on mere suspicion, and you are too much of a gentleman to damn another simply because he, too, aspires to that distinction."

"Very well, Patches," Phil returned, with less heat, "but I want you to understand one thing; I am responsible for the Cross-Triangle property and there is no friendship in the world strong enough to influence me in the slightest degree when it comes to a question of Uncle Will's interests. Do you get that?"

"I got that months ago, Phil."

Without another word, the Dean's foreman left the room.

Patches sat for some time considering the situation. And now and then his lips curled in that old, self-mocking smile; realizing that he was caught in the trap of circumstance, he found a curious humor in his predicament.

Chapter XII

FRONTIER DAY

*A*gain it was July. And, with the time of the cattlemen's celebration of the Fourth at hand, riders from every part of the great western cow country assembled in Prescott for their annual contests. From Texas and Montana, from Oklahoma and New Mexico and Wyoming, the cowboys came with their saddles and riatas to meet each other and the men of Arizona in friendly trials of strength and skill. From many a wild pasture, outlaw horses famous for their vicious, unsubdued spirits, and their fierce, untamed strength, were brought to match their wicked, unbroken wills against the cool, determined courage of the riders. From the wide ranges, the steers that were to participate in the roping and bulldogging contests were gathered and driven in. From many a ranch the fastest and best of the trained cow-horses were sent for the various cowboy races. And the little city, in its rocky, mile-high basin, upon which the higher surrounding mountains look so steadfastly down, again decked itself in gala colors, and opened wide its doors to welcome all who chose to come.

From the Cross-Triangle and the neighboring ranches the cowboys, dressed in the best of their picturesque regalia, rode into the town, to witness and take part in the sports. With them rode Honorable Patches.

And this was not the carefully groomed and immaculately attired gentleman who, in troubled spirit, had walked alone over that long, unfenced way a year before. This was not the timid, hesitating, shame-faced man at whom Phil Acton had laughed on the summit of the

Divide. This was a man among men — a cowboy of the cowboys — bronzed, and lean, and rugged; vitally alive in every inch of his long body; with self-reliant courage and daring hardihood written all over him, expressed in every tone of his voice, and ringing in every note of his laughter.

The Dean and Mrs. Baldwin and Little Billy drove in the buckboard, but the distinguished guest of the Cross-Triangle went with the Reid family in the automobile. The professor was not at all interested in the celebration, but he could not well remain at the ranch alone, and, it may be supposed, the invitation from Kitty helped to make the occasion endurable.

The celebration this year — the posters and circulars declared — was to be the biggest and best that Prescott had ever offered. In proof of the bold assertion, the program promised, in addition to the usual events, an automobile race. Shades of all those mighty heroes of the saddle, whose names may not be erased from the history of the great West, think of it! An automobile race offered as the chief event in a Frontier Day Celebration!

No wonder that Mrs. Manning said to her husband that day, "But Stan, where are the cowboys?"

Stanford Manning answered laughingly, "Oh, they are here, all right, Helen; just wait a little and you will see."

Mr. and Mrs. Manning had arrived from Cleveland, Ohio, the evening before, and Helen was eager and excited with the prospect of meeting the people, and witnessing the scenes of which her husband had told her with so much enthusiasm.

As the Dean had told Patches that day when the cattleman had advanced the money for the stranger's outfit, the young mining engineer had won a place for himself amid the scenes and among the people of that western country. He had first come to the land of this story, fresh from his technical training in the East. His employers, quick to recognize not only his ability in his profession but his character and manhood, as well, had advanced him rapidly and, less than a month before Patches asked for work at the Cross-Triangle, had sent him on an important mission to their mines in the North. They were sending him, now, again to Arizona, this time as the resident manager of their properties in the Prescott district. This new advance in his profession, together with the substantial increase in salary which it brought, meant much to the engineer. Most of all, it meant his marriage to Helen Wakefield. A stop-over of two weeks at Cleveland, on way West, from the main offices of his Company in New York, had changed his return to Prescott from a simple business trip to a wedding journey.

At the home of the Yavapai Club, on top of the hill, a clock above the plaza, a number of Prescott's citizens, with their guests, had gathered to watch the beginning of the automobile race. The course, from the corner in front of the St. Michael hotel, followed the street along one side of the plaza, climbed straight up the hill, passed the clubhouse, and so away into the open country. From the clubhouse veranda, from the lawn and walks in front, or from their seats in convenient automobiles standing near, the company enjoyed, thus, an unobstructed view of the starting point of the race, and could look down as well upon the crowds that pressed against the ropes which were stretched along either side of the street. Prom a friendly automobile, Helen Manning, with her husband's field glasses, was an eager and excited observer of the interesting scene, while Stanford near by was busy greeting old friends, presenting them to his wife and receiving their congratulations. And often, he turned with a fond look and a merry word to the young woman, as though reassuring himself that she was really there. There was no doubt about it, Stamford Manning, strong and steady and forceful, was very much in love with this girl who looked down into his face with such an air of sweet confidence and companionship. And Helen, as she turned from the scene that so interested her, to greet her husband's friends, to ask him some question, or to answer some laughing remark, could not hide the love light in her soft brown eyes. One could not fail to see that her woman heart was glad — glad and proud that this stalwart, broad-shouldered leader of men had chosen her for his mate.

"But, Stan," she said, with a pretty air of disappointment, "I thought it was all going to be so different. Why, except for the mountains, and those poor Indians over there, this might all be in some little town back home. I thought there would be cowboys riding about everywhere, with long hair and big hats, and guns and things."

Stanford and his friends who were standing near laughed.

"I fear, Mrs. Manning," remarked Mr. Richards, one of Prescott's bank presidents, "that Stanford has been telling you wild west stories. The West moves as well as the East, you know. We are becoming civilized."

"Indeed you are, Mr. Richards," Helen returned. "And I don't think I like it a bit. It's not fair to your poor eastern sight-seers, like myself."

"If you are really so anxious to see a sure enough cowboy, look over there," said Stanford, and pointed across the street.

"Where?" demanded Helen eagerly.

"There," smiled Stanford, "the dark-faced chap near that automobile standing by the curb; the machine with the pretty girl at the wheel. See! he is stopping to talk with the girl."

"What! That nice looking man, dressed just like thousands of men that we might see any day on the streets of Cleveland?" cried Helen.

"Exactly," chuckled her husband, while the others laughed at her incredulous surprise. "But, just the same, that's Phil Acton; 'Wild Horse Phil,' if you please. He is the cowboy foreman of the Cross-Triangle Ranch, and won the championship in the bronco riding last year."

"I don't believe it — you are making fun of me, Stanford Manning."

Then, before he could answer, she cried, with quick excitement, "But, Stan, look! Look at the girl in the automobile! She looks like — it is, Stan, it is!" And to the amazement of her husband and her friends Mrs. Manning sprang to her feet and, waving her handkerchief, called, "Kitty! Oh, Kitty — Kitty Reid!"

As her clear call rang out, many people turned to look, and then to smile at the picture, as she stood there in the bright Arizona day, so animated and wholesomely alive in the grace and charm of her beautiful young womanhood, above the little group of men who were looking up at her with laughing admiration.

On the other side of the street, where she sat with her parents and Professor Parkhill, talking to Phil, Kitty heard the call, and looked. A moment later she was across the street, and the two young women were greeting each other with old-time schoolgirl enthusiasm. Introductions and explanations followed, with frequent feminine exclamations of surprise and delight. Then the men drew a little away, talking, laughing, as men will on such occasions, leaving the two women to themselves.

In that eastern school, which, for those three years, had been Kitty's home, Helen Wakefield and the girl from Arizona had been close and intimate friends. Indeed, Helen, with her strong womanly character and that rare gift of helpful sympathy and understanding, had been to the girl fresh from the cattle ranges more than a friend; she had been counselor and companion, and, in many ways, a wise guardian and teacher.

"But why in the world didn't you write me about it?" demanded Kitty a little later. "Why didn't you tell me that you had become Mrs. Stanford Manning, and that you were coming to Prescott?"

Helen laughed and blushed happily. "Why, you see, Kitty, it all happened so quickly that there was no time to write. You remember when I wrote you about Stan, I told you how poor he was, and how we didn't expect to be married for several years?"

"Yes."

"Well, then, you see, Stan's company, all unexpectedly to him, called him to New York and gave him this position out here. He had to start at once, and wired me from New York. Just think, I had only a week for the wedding and everything! I knew, of course, that I could find you after I got here."

"And now that you are here," said Kitty decisively, "you and Mr. Manning are coming right out to Williamson Valley to spend your honeymoon on the ranch."

But Helen shook her head. "Stan has it all planned, Kitty, and he won't listen to anything else. There is a place around here somewhere that he calls Granite Basin, and he has it all arranged that we are to camp out there for three weeks. His company has given him that much time, and we are going just as soon as this celebration is over. After that, while Stan gets started with his work, and fixes some place for us to live, I will make you a little visit."

"I suppose there is no use trying to contend against the rights of a brand-new husband," returned Kitty, "but it's a promise, that you will come to me as soon as your camping trip is over?"

"It's a promise," agreed Helen. "You see, that's really part of Stanford's plan; I was so sure you would want me, you know."

"Want you? I should say I do want you," cried Kitty, "and I need you, too."

Something in her voice made Helen look at her questioningly, but Kitty only smiled.

"I'll tell you all about it when there is more time."

"Let me see," said Helen. "There used to be — why, of course, that nice looking man you were talking to when I recognized you — Phil Acton." She looked across the street as she spoke, but Phil had gone.

"Please don't, Helen dear," said Kitty, "that was only my schoolgirl nonsense. When I came back home I found how impossible it all was. But I must run back to the folks now. Won't you come and meet them?"

Before Helen could answer someone shouted, "They're getting ready for the start," and everybody looked down the hill toward the place where the racing machines were sputtering and roaring in their clouds of blue smoke.

Helen caught up the field glasses to look, saying, "We can't go now, Kitty. You stay here with us until after the race is started; then we'll go."

As Helen lowered the glasses Stanford, who had come to stand beside the automobile, reached out his hand. "Let me have a look, Helen. They say my old friend, Judge Morris, is the official starter." He put the field glasses to his eyes. "There he is all right, as big as life; finest man that ever lived. Look, Helen." He returned the glasses to his wife "If you want to see a genuine western lawyer, a scholar and a gentleman, take a look at that six-foot-three or four down there in the grey clothes."

"I see him," said Helen, "but there seems to be something the matter; there he goes back to the machines. Now he's laying down the law to the drivers."

"They won't put over anything on Morris," said Stanford admiringly.

Then a deep, kindly voice at his elbow said, "Howdy, Manning! Ain't you got time to speak to your old friends?"

Stanford whirled and, with a glad exclamation, grasped the Dean's outstretched hand. Still holding fast to the cattleman, he again turned to his wife, who was looking down at them with smiling interest. "Helen, this is Mr. Baldwin — the Dean, you know."

"Indeed, I ought to know the Dean," she cried, giving him her hand. "Stanford has told me so much about you that I am in love with you already."

"And I" — retorted the Dean, looking up at her with his blue eyes twinkling approval — "I reckon I've always been in love with you. I'm sure glad to see that this young man has justified his reputation for good judgment. Have they got anymore girls like you back East? 'Cause if they have, I'll sure be obliged to take a trip to that part of the world before I get too old."

"You are just as Stan said you were," retorted Helen.

"Uncle Will!" cried Kitty. "I am ashamed of you! I didn't think you would turn down your own home folks like that!"

The Dean lifted his hat and rumpled his grizzly hair as though fairly caught. Then: "Why, Kitty, you know that I couldn't love any girl more than I do you. Why, you belong to me most as much as you belong to your own father and mother. But, you see — honey — well, you see, we've just naturally got to be nice to strangers, you know." When they had laughed at this, Kitty explained to that Dean how Mrs. Manning was the Helen Wakefield with whom she had been such friends at school, and that, after the Mannings' outing in Granite Basin, Helen was to visit Williamson Valley.

"Campin' out in Granite Basin, heh?" said the Dean to Stanford. "I reckon you'll be seein' some o' my boys. They're goin' up into that country after outlaw steers next week."

"I hope so," returned Stanford. "Helen has been complaining that there are no cowboys to be seen. I pointed out Phil Acton, but he didn't seem to fill the bill; she doesn't believe that he is a cowboy at all."

The Dean chuckled. "He's never been anything else. They don't make 'em any better anywhere." Then he added soberly, "Phil's not ridin' in the contest this year, though."

"What's the matter?"

"I don't know. He's got some sort of a fool notion in his head that he don't want to make an exhibition of himself — that's what he said. I've got another man on the ranch now," he added, as though to change the subject, "that'll be mighty near as good as Phil in another year. His name is Patches. He's a good one, all right."

Kitty, who, had been looking away down the street while the Dean was talking, put her hand on Helen's arm. "Look down there, Helen. I believe that is Patches now — that man sitting on his horse at the cross street, at the foot of the hill, just outside the ropes."

Helen was looking through the field glasses. "I see him," she cried. "Now, that's more like it. He looks like what I expected to see. What a fine, big chap he is, isn't he?" Then, as she studied the distant horseman, a puzzled expression came over her face. "Why, Kitty!" she said in a low tone, so that the men who were talking did not hear. "Do you know, that man somehow reminds me" — she hesitated and lowered the glasses to look at her companion with half-amused, half-embarrassed eyes — "he reminds me of Lawrence Knight."

Kitty's brown, fun-loving eyes glowed with mischief. "Really, Mrs. Manning, I am ashamed of you. Before the honeymoon has waned, your thoughts, with no better excuse than the appearance of a poor cow-puncher, go back to the captivating charms of your old millionaire lover. I —"

"Kitty! Do hush," pleaded Helen.

She lifted her glasses for another look at the cowboy.

"I don't wonder that your conscience reproves you," teased Kitty, in a low tone. "But tell me, poor child, how did it happen that you lost your millionaire?"

"I didn't lose him," retorted Helen, still watching Patches. "He lost me."

Kitty persisted with a playful mockery. "What! the great, the wonderful Knight of so many millions, failed, with all his glittering charms, to captivate the fair but simple Helen! Really, I can't believe it."

"Look at that man right there," flashed Helen proudly, indicating her husband, "and you can believe it."

Kitty laughed so gaily that Stanford turned to look at them with smiling inquiry.

"Never mind, Mr. Manning," said Kitty, "we are just reminiscing, that's all."

"Don't miss the race," he answered; "they're getting ready again to start. It looks like a go this time."

"And to think," murmured Kitty, "that I never so much as saw your Knight's picture! But you used to like Lawrence Knight, didn't you,

Helen?" she added, as Helen lifted her field glasses again. And now, Mrs. Manning caught a note of earnest inquiry in her companion's voice. It was as though the girl were seeking confirmation of some purpose or decision of her own.

"Why, yes, Kitty, I liked Larry Knight very much," she answered frankly. "He was a fine fellow in many ways — a dear, good friend. Stanford and I are both very fond of him; they were college mates, you know. But, my dear girl, no one could ever consider poor old Larry seriously — as a man, you know — he is so — so utterly and hopelessly worthless."

"Worthless! With — how many millions is it?"

"Oh, Kitty, you know what I mean. But, really dear, we have talked enough about Mr. Lawrence Knight. I'm going to have another look at the cowboy. He looks like a real man, doesn't he? What is it the Dean called him?"

"Patches."

"Oh, yes; what a funny name — Patches."

"Honorable Patches," said Kitty.

"How odd!" mused Helen. "Oh, Stan, come here a minute. Take the glasses and look at that cowboy down there."

Stanford trained the field glasses as she directed.

"Doesn't he remind you of Larry Knight?"

"Larry Knight!" Stanford looked at her in amazement. "That cowpuncher? Larry Knight? I should say not. Lord! but wouldn't fastidious, cultured and correct old Larry feel complimented to know that you found anything in a common cow-puncher to remind you of him!"

"But, here, take your glasses, quick; they are going to start at last."

Even as Helen looked, Judge Morris gave the signal and the first racing car, with a mighty roar, leaped away from the starting point, and thundered up the street between the lines of the crowding, cheering people. An instant more, and Helen Manning witnessed a scene that thrilled the hearts of every man, woman and child in that great crowd.

As the big racing car, gathering speed at every throb of its powerful motor, swept toward the hill, a small boy, but little more than a toddling baby, escaped from his mother, who, with the excited throng, was crowding against the rope barrier, and before those whose eyes were fixed on the automobile noticed, the child was in the street, fairly in the path of the approaching machine. A sudden hush fell on the shouting multitude. Helen, through the field glasses, could see even the child's face, as, laughing gleefully, he looked back when his mother screamed. Stricken with horror, the young woman could not lower her glasses. Fascinated, she watched. The people seemed, for an instant, paralyzed.

Not a soul moved or uttered a sound. Would the driver of the racing car swerve aside from his course in time? If he did, would the baby, in sudden fright, dodge in front of the machine? Then Helen saw the cowboy who had so interested her lean forward in his saddle and strike his spurs deep in the flanks of his already restless horse. With a tremendous bound the animal cleared the rope barrier, and in an instant was leaping toward the child and the approaching car. The people gasped at the daring of the man who had not waited to think. It was over in a second. As Patches swept by the child, he leaned low from the saddle; and, as the next leap of his horse carried him barely clear of the machine, they saw his tall, lithe body straighten, as he swung the baby up into his arms.

Then, indeed, the crowd went wild. Men yelled and cheered; women laughed and cried; and, as the cowboy returned the frightened baby to the distressed mother, a hundred eager hands were stretched forth to greet him. But the excited horse backed away; someone raised the rope barrier, and Patches disappeared down the side street.

Helen's eyes were wet, but she was smiling. "No," she said softly to Kitty and Stanford, "that was *not* Lawrence Knight. Poor old Larry never could have done that."

It was a little after the noon hour when Kitty, who, with her father, mother and brothers, had been for dinner at the home of one of their Prescott friends, was crossing the plaza on her way to join Mr. and Mrs. Manning, with whom she was to spend the afternoon. In a less frequented corner of the little park, back of the courthouse, she saw Patches. The cowboy, who had changed from his ranch costume to a less picturesque business garb, was seated alone on one of the benches that are placed along the walks, reading a letter. With his attention fixed upon the letter, he did not notice Kitty as she approached. And the girl, when she first caught sight of him, paused for an instant; then she went toward him slowly, studying him with a new interest.

She was quite near when, looking up, he saw her. Instantly he rose to his feet, slipped the letter into his pocket, and stood before her, hat in hand, to greet her with genuine pleasure and with that gentle courtesy which always marked his bearing. And Kitty, as she looked up at him, felt, more convincingly than ever, that this man would be perfectly at ease in the most exacting social company.

"I fear I interrupted you," said the young woman. "I was just passing."

"Not at all," he protested. "Surely you can give me a moment of your busy gala day. I know you have a host of friends, of course, but — well, I am lonely. Curly and Bob and the boys are all having the time of their lives; the Dean and mother are lunching with friends; and I don't know where Phil has hidden himself."

It was like him to mention Phil in almost his first words to her. And Kitty, as Patches spoke Phil's name, instantly, as she had so often done during the past few months, mentally placed the two men side by side.

"I just wanted to tell you" — she hesitated — "Mr. Patches —"

"I beg your pardon," he interrupted smiling.

"Well, Patches then; but you seem so different somehow, dressed like this. I just wanted to tell you that I saw what happened this morning. It was splendid!"

"Why, Miss Reid, you know that was nothing. The driver of the car would probably have dodged the youngster anyway. I acted on the impulse of the moment, without thinking. I'm always doing something unnecessarily foolish, you know."

"The driver of the car would more likely have dodged into the child," she returned warmly. "And it was fortunate that someone in all that stupid crowd could act without taking time to think. Everybody says so. The dear old Dean is as pleased and proud as though you were one of his own sons."

"Really, you make too much of it," he returned, clearly embarrassed by her praise. "Tell me, you are enjoying the celebration? And what's the matter with Phil? Can't you persuade him to ride in the contest? We don't want the championship to go out of Yavapai County, do we?"

Why must he always bring Phil into their talk? Kitty asked herself.

"I am sure that Phil knows how all his friends feel about his riding," she said coolly. "If he does not wish to gratify them, it is really a small matter, is it not?"

Patches saw that he had made a mistake and changed easily to a safer topic.

"You saw the beginning of the automobile race, of course? I suppose you will be on hand this afternoon for the finish?"

"Oh, yes, I'm on my way now to join my friends, Mr. and Mrs. Stanford Manning. We are going to see the finish of the race together."

She watched his face closely, as she spoke of her friends, but he gave no sign that he had ever heard the name before.

"It will be worth seeing, I fancy," he returned. "At least everybody seems to feel that way."

"I am sure to have a good time, anyway," she returned, "because, you see, Mrs. Manning is one of my very dearest girl friends, whom I have not seen for a long time."

"Indeed! You *will* enjoy the afternoon, then."

Was there a shade too much enthusiasm in the tone of his reply? Kitty wondered. Could it be that his plea of loneliness was merely a conventional courtesy and that he was really relieved to find that she was engaged for the afternoon?

"Yes, and I must hurry on to them, or they will think I am not coming," she said. "Have a good time, Patches; you surely have earned it. Good-bye!"

He stood for a moment watching her cross the park. Then, with a quick look around, as though he did not wish to be observed, he hurried across the street to the Western Union office. A few moments later he made his way, by little-frequented side streets, to the stable where he had left his horse; and while Kitty and her friends were watching the first of the racing cars cross the line, Patches was several miles away, riding as though pursued by the sheriff, straight for the Cross-Triangle Ranch.

Several times that day, while she was with her eastern friends, Kitty saw Phil near by. But she gave him no signal to join them, and the cowboy, shy always, and hurt by Kitty's indifference, would not approach the little party without her invitation. But that evening, while Kitty was waiting in the hotel lobby for Mr. and Mrs. Manning, Phil, finding her alone, went to her.

"I have been trying to speak to you all day," he said reproachfully. "Haven't you any time for me at all, Kitty?"

"Don't be foolish, Phil," she returned; "you have seen me a dozen times."

"I have *seen* you, yes," he answered bitterly.

"But, Phil, you could have come to me, if you had wanted to."

"I have no desire to go where I am not wanted," he answered.

"Phil!"

"Well, you gave no sign that you wanted me."

"There was no reason why I should," she retorted. "You are not a child. I was with my friends from the East. You could have joined us if you had cared to. I should be very glad, indeed, to present you to Mr. and Mrs. Manning."

"Thank you, but I don't care to be exhibited as an interesting specimen to people who have no use for me except when I do a few fool stunts to amuse them."

"Very well, Phil," she returned coldly. "If that is your feeling, I do not care to present you to my friends. They are every bit as sincere and genuine as you are; and I certainly shall not trouble them with anyone who cannot appreciate them."

Kitty was angry, as she had good reason for being. But beneath her anger she was sorry for the man whose bitterness, she knew, was born of his love for her. And Phil saw only that Kitty was lost to him — saw in the girl's eastern friends those who, he felt, had robbed him of his dream.

"I suppose," he said, after a moment's painful silence, "that I had better go back to the range where I belong. I'm out of place here."

The girl was touched by the hopelessness in his voice, but she felt that it would be no kindness to offer him the relief of an encouraging word. Her day with her eastern friends, and the memories that her meeting with Mrs. Manning had aroused, convinced her more than ever that her old love for Phil, and the life of which he was a part, were for her impossible.

When she did not speak, the cowboy said bitterly, "I noticed that your fine friends did not take quite all your time. You found an opportunity for a quiet little visit with Honorable Patches."

Kitty was angry now in earnest. "You are forgetting yourself, Phil," she answered with cold dignity. "And I think that as long as you feel as you do toward my friends, and can speak to me like this about Mr. Patches, you are right in saying that you belong on the range. Mr. and Mrs. Manning are here, I see. I am going to dine with them. Good-bye!" She turned away, leaving him standing there.

A moment he waited, as though stunned; then he turned to make his way blindly out of the hotel.

It was nearly morning when Patches was awakened by the sound of someone moving about the kitchen. A moment he listened, then, rising, went quickly to the kitchen door, thinking to surprise some chance night visitor.

When Phil saw him standing there the foreman for a moment said nothing, but, with the bread knife in one hand and one of Stella's good loaves in the other, stared at him in blank surprise. Then the look of surprise changed to an expression of questioning suspicion, and he demanded harshly, "What in hell are *you* doing here?"

Patches saw that the man was laboring under some great trouble. Indeed, Phil's voice and manner were not unlike one under the influence of strong drink. But Patches knew that Phil never drank.

"I was sleeping," he answered calmly. "You woke me, I suppose. I heard you, and came to see who was prowling around the kitchen at this time of the night; that is all."

"Oh, that's all, is it? But what are you here for? Why aren't you in Prescott where you are supposed to be?"

Patches, because he saw Phil's painful state of mind, exercised admirable self-control. "I supposed I had a perfect right to come here if I wished. I did not dream that my presence in this house would be questioned."

"That depends," Phil retorted. "Why did you leave Prescott?"

Patches, still calm, answered gently. "My reasons for not staying in Prescott are entirely personal, Phil; I do not care to explain just now."

"Oh, you don't? Well, it seems to me, sir, that you have a devil of a lot of personal business that you can't explain."

"I am afraid I have," returned Patches, with his old self-mocking smile. "But, look here, Phil, you are disturbed and all wrought up about something, or you wouldn't attack me like this. You don't really think me a suspicious character, and you know you don't. You are not yourself, old man, and I'll be hanged if I'll take anything you say as an insult, until I know that you say it, deliberately, in cold blood. I'm sorry for your trouble, Phil — damned sorry — I would give anything if I could help you. Perhaps I may be able to prove that later, but just now I think the kindest and wisest thing that I can do for us both is to say good-night."

He turned at the last word, without waiting for Phil to speak, and went back to his room.

Chapter XIII

IN GRANITE BASIN

On the other side of Granite Mountain from where Phil and Patches watched the wild horses that day, there is a rocky hollow, set high in the hills, but surrounded on every side by still higher peaks and ridges. Lying close under the sheer, towering cliffs of the mountain, those fortresslike walls so grey and grim and old seem to overshadow the place with a somber quiet, as though the memories of the many ages that had wrought their countless years into those mighty battlements gave to the very atmosphere a feeling of solemn and sacred seclusion. It was as though nature had thrown about this spot a strong protecting guard, that here, in her very heart, she might keep unprofaned the sweetness and strength and beauty of her primitive and everlasting treasures.

In its wild and rugged setting, Granite Basin has, for the few who have the hardihood to find them, many beautiful glades and shady nooks, where the grass and wild flowers weave their lovely patterns for the earth floor, and tall pines spread their soft carpets of brown, while giant oaks and sycamores lift their cathedral arches to support the ceilings of green, and dark rock fountains set in banks of moss and fern hold water clear and cold. It was to one of these that Stanford Manning brought his bride for their honeymoon. Stanford himself pitched their tent and made their simple camp, for it was not in his plan that the sweet intimacy of these, the first weeks of their mated life, should be marred, even by servants. And Helen, wise in her love, permitted him to realize his dream in the fullness of its every detail.

As she lay in the hammock which he had hung for her under the canopy of living green, and watched him while he brought wood for their campfire, and made all ready for the night which was drawing near, she was glad that he had planned it so. But more than that, she was glad that he was the kind of a man who would care to plan it so. Then, when all was finished, he came to sit beside her, and together they watched the light of the setting sun fade from the summit of Old Granite, and saw the flaming cloud-banner that hung above the mountain's castle towers furled by the hand of night. In silence they watched those mighty towering battlements grow cold and grim, until against the sky the shadowy bulk stood mysterious and awful, as though to evidence in its grandeur and strength the omnipotent might and power of the Master Builder of the world and Giver of all life.

And when the soft darkness was fully come, and the low murmuring voices of the night whispered from forest depth and mountain side, while the stars peered through the weaving of leaf and branch, and the ruddy light of their campfire rose and fell, the man talked of the things that had gone into the making of his life. As though he wished his mate to know him more fully than anyone else could know, he spoke of those personal trials and struggles, those disappointments and failures, those plans and triumphs of which men so rarely speak; of his boyhood and his boyhood home life, of his father and mother, of those hard years of his youth, and his struggle for an education that would equip him for his chosen life work; he told her many things that she had known only in a general way.

But most of all he talked of those days when he had first met her, and of how quickly and surely the acquaintance had grown into friendship, and then into a love which he dared not yet confess. Smilingly he told how he had tried to convince himself that she was not for him. And how, believing that she loved and would wed his friend, Lawrence Knight, he had come to the far West, to his work, and, if he could, to forget.

"But I could not forget, dear girl," he said. "I could not escape the conviction that you belonged to me, as I felt that I belonged to you. I could not banish the feeling that some mysterious higher law — the law that governs the mating of the beautifully free creatures that live in these hills — had mated you and me. And so, as I worked and tried to forget, I went on dreaming just the same. It was that way when I first saw this place. I was crossing the country on my way to examine some prospects for the company, and camped at this very spot. And that evening I planned it all, just as it is tonight. I put the tent there, and built our fire, and stretched your hammock under the tree, and sat with you in the twilight; but even as I dreamed it I laughed at myself for a fool, for I could not believe that the dream would ever come true. And then, when I got back to Prescott, there was a letter from a Cleveland friend, telling me that Larry had gone abroad to be away a year or more, and another letter from the company, calling me East again. And so I stopped at Cleveland and —" He laughed happily. "I know now that dreams do come true."

"You foolish boy," said Helen softly. "To think that I did not know. Why, when you went away, I was so sure that you would come for me again, that I never even thought that it could be any other way. I thought you did not speak because you felt that you were too poor, because you felt that you had so little to offer, and because you wished to prove yourself and your work before asking me to share your life. I did not dream that you could doubt my love for you, or think for a moment that there could ever be anyone else. I felt that you *must* know; and so, you see, while I waited I had my dreams, too."

"But don't you see, girl," he answered, as though for a moment he found it hard to believe his own happiness, "don't you see? Larry is such a splendid fellow, and you two were such friends, and you always seemed so fond of him, and with his wealth he could give you so much that I knew I never could give —"

"Of course, I am fond of Larry; everyone is. He has absolutely nothing to do in the world but to make himself charming and pleasant and entertaining and amusing. Why, Stan, I don't suppose that in all his life he ever did one single thing that was necessary or useful. He even had a man to help him dress. He is cultured and intellectual, and bright and witty, and clean and good-natured, possessing, in fact, all the qualifications of a desirable lap dog, and you can't help liking him, just as you would like a pretty, useless pet."

Stanford chuckled. She had described Lawrence Knight so accurately. "Poor old Larry," he said. "What a man he might have been if he had not been so pampered and petted and envied and spoiled, all because of his father's money. His heart is right, and at the bottom he has the right sort of stuff in him. His athletic record at school showed us that. I think that was why we all liked him so in spite of his uselessness."

"I wish you could have known my father, Stan," said Helen thoughtfully, as though she, too, were moved to speak by the wish that her mate might know more of the things that had touched her deeper life.

"I wish so, too," he answered. "I know that he must have been fine."

"He was my ideal," she answered softly. "My other ideal, I mean. From the time I was a slip of a girl he made me his chum. Until he died we were always together. Mother died when I was a baby, you know. Many, many times he would take me with him when he made his professional visits to his patients, leaving me in the buggy to wait at each house — 'to be his hitching post' — he used to say. And on those long rides, sometimes out into the country, he talked to me as I suppose not many fathers talk to their daughters. And because he was my father and a physician, and because we were so much alone in our companionship, I believed him the wisest and best man in all the world, and felt that nothing he said or did could be wrong. And so, you see, dear, my ideal man, the man to whom I could give myself, came to be the kind of a man that my father placed in the highest rank among men — a man like you, Stan. And almost the last talk we had before he died father said to me — I remember his very words — 'My daughter, it will not be long now until men will seek you, until someone will ask you to share his life. Keep your ideal man safe in your heart of hearts, daughter, and remember that no matter what a suitor may have to offer of wealth or social rank, if he is not your ideal — if you cannot respect and admire him for his character and manhood alone — say no; say no, child, at any cost. But when your ideal man comes — the one who compels your respect and admiration for his strength of character, and for the usefulness of his life, the one whom you cannot help loving for his manhood alone — mate with him — no matter how light his purse or how lowly his rank in the world.' And so you see, as soon as I learned to know you, I realized what you were to me. But I wish — oh, how I wish — that father could have lived to know you, too."

For some time they watched the dancing campfire flames in silence, as though they had found in their love that true oneness that needs no spoken word.

Then Stanford said, "And to think that we expected to wait two years or more, and now — thanks to a soulless corporation — we are here in a little less than a year!"

"Thanks to no soulless corporation for that, sir," retorted Helen with spirit. "But thanks to the brains and strength and character of my husband."

Two of the three weeks' vacation granted the engineer had passed when Mrs. Manning, one afternoon, informed her husband that as the ordained provider for the household it was imperative that he provide some game for their evening meal.

"And what does Her Majesty, the cook, desire?" he asked. "Venison, perhaps?"

She shook her head with decision. "You will be obliged to go too far, and be gone too long, to get a deer."

"But you're going with me, of course."

Again she shook her head. "I have something else to do. I can't always be tagging around after you while you are providing, you know; and we may as well begin to be civilized again. Just go a little way — not so far that you can't hear me call — and bring me some nice fat quail like those we had day before yesterday."

She watched him disappear in the brush and then busied herself about the camp. Presently she heard the gun, and smiled as she pictured him hunting for their supper, much as though they were two primitive children of nature, instead of the two cultured members of a highly civilized race, that they really were. Then, presently she must go to the spring for water, that he might have a cool drink when he returned.

She was halfway to the spring, singing softly to herself, when a sound on the low ridge above the camp attracted her attention. Pausing, she looked and listened. The song died on her lips. It could not be Staford coming so noisily through the brush and from that direction. Even as the thought came, she heard the gun again, a little farther away down the narrow valley below the camp, and, in the same moment, the noise on the ridge grew louder, as though some heavy animal were crashing through the bushes. And then suddenly, as she stood there in frightened indecision, a long-horned, wild-eyed steer broke through the brush on the crest of the ridge and plunged down the steep slope toward the camp.

Weak and helpless with fear, Helen could neither scream nor run, but stood fascinated by the very danger that menaced her — powerless, even, to turn her eyes away from the frightful creature that had so rudely broken the quiet seclusion of the little glade. Behind the steer, even as the frenzied animal leaped from the brow of the hill, she saw a horseman, as wild in his appearance and in his reckless rushing haste as the creature he pursued. Curiously, as in a dream, she saw the horse's neck and shoulders dripping wet with sweat, as with ears flat, nose outstretched, and nostrils wide the animal strained every nerve in an effort to put his rider a few feet closer to the escaping quarry. She even noted the fringed leather chaps, the faded blue jumper, the broad hat of the rider, and that in his rein hand he held the coil of a riata high above the saddle horn, while in his right was the half-opened loop. The bridle reins were loose, as though he gave the horse no thought; and they took the steep, downward plunge from the summit of the ridge without an instant's pause, and apparently with all the ease and confidence that they would have felt on smooth and level ground.

The steer, catching sight of the woman, and seeing in her, perhaps, another enemy, swerved a little in his plunging course, and, with lowered head, charged straight at her.

The loop of that rawhide rope was whirling now above the cowboy's head, and his spurs drew blood from the heaving flanks of the straining horse, as every mad leap of the steer brought death a few feet nearer the helpless woman.

The situation must have broken with frightful suddenness upon the man, but he gave no sign — no startled shout, no excited movement. He even appeared, to Helen, to be as coolly deliberate as though no thought of her danger disturbed him; and she recognized, even in that awful moment, the cowboy whom she had watched through the field glasses, that day of the celebration at Prescott. She could not know that, in the same instant, as his horse plunged down from the summit of the ridge, Patches had recognized her; and that as his hand swung the riata with such cool and deliberate precision, the man was praying — praying as only a man who sees the woman he loves facing a dreadful death, with no hand but his to save her, could pray.

God help him if his training of nerve and hand should fail now! Christ pity him, if that whirling loop should miss its mark, or fall short!

His eye told him that the distance was still too great. He must — he *must* — lessen it; and again his spurs drew blood. He must be cool — cool and steady and sure — and he must act now — NOW!

Helen saw the racing horse make a desperate leap as the spurs tore his heaving sides; she saw that swiftly whirling loop leave the rider's hand, as the man leaned forward in his saddle. Curiously she watched the loop open with beautiful precision, as the coils were loosed and the long, thin line lengthened through the air. It seemed to move so slowly — those wickedly lowered horns were so near! Then she saw the rider's right hand move with flashlike quickness to the saddle horn, as he threw his weight back, and the horse, with legs braced and hoofs plowing the ground, stopped in half his own length, and set his weight against the weight of the steer. The flexible riata straightened as a rod of iron, the steer's head jerked sideways; his horns buried themselves in the ground; he fell, almost at her feet. And then, as the cowboy leaped from his horse, Helen felt herself sinking into a soft, thick darkness that, try as she might, she could not escape.

Still master of himself, but with a kind of fierce coolness, Patches ran to the fallen steer and securely tied the animal down. But when he turned to the woman who lay unconscious on the ground, a sob burst from his lips, and tears were streaming down his dust-grimed cheeks. And as he knelt beside her he called again and again that name which, a year before, he had whispered as he stood with empty, outstretched arms, alone, on the summit of the Divide.

Lifting her in his arms, he carried her to the hammock, and finding water and a towel, wet her brow and face; and all the while, in an agony of fear, he talked to her with words of love.

Overwrought by the unexpected, and, to him, almost miraculous meeting with Helen — weak and shaken by the strain of those moments of her danger, when her life depended so wholly upon his coolness and skill — unnerved by the sight of her lying so still and white, and beside himself with the strength of his passion — the man made no effort to account for her presence in that wild and lonely spot, so far from the scenes amid which he had learned to know and love her. He was conscious only that she was there — that she had been very near to death — that he had held her in his arms — and that he loved her with all the strength of his manhood.

Presently, with a low cry of joy, he saw the blood creep back into her white cheeks. Slowly her eyes opened and she looked wonderingly up into his face.

"Helen!" he breathed. "Helen!"

"Why, Larry!" she murmured, still confused and wondering. "So it *was* you, after all! But what in the world are you doing here like this? They told me your name was Patches — Honorable Patches."

Then the man spoke — impetuously, almost fiercely, his words came without thought.

"I am here because I would be anything, do anything that a man could be and do to win your love. A year ago, when I told you of my love, and asked you to be my wife, and, like the silly, pampered, petted fool that I was, thought that my wealth and the life that I offered could count for anything with a woman like you, you laughed at me. You told me that if ever you married, you would wed a man, not a fortune nor a social position. You made me see myself as I was — a useless idler, a dummy for the tailors, a superficial chatterer of pretty nothings to vain and shallow women; you told me that I possessed not one manly trait of character that could compel the genuine love of an honest woman. You let me see the truth, that my proposal to you was almost an insult. You made me understand that your very friendship for me was such a friendship as you might have with an amusing and irresponsible boy, or a spoiled child. You could not even consider my love for you seriously, as a woman like you must consider the love of a strong man. And you were right, Helen. But, dear, it was for me a bitter, bitter lesson. I went from you, ashamed to look men in the face. I felt myself guilty — a pitifully weak and cowardly thing, with no right to exist. In my humiliation, I ran from all who knew me — I came out here to escape from the life that had made me what I was — that had robbed me of my manhood. And here, by chance, in the contests at the celebration in Prescott, I saw a man — a cowboy — who possessed everything that I lacked, and for the lack of which you had laughed at me. And then alone one night I faced myself and fought it out. I knew that you were right, Helen, but it was not easy to give up the habits and luxury to which all my life I had been accustomed. It was not easy, I say, but my love for you made it a glorious thing to do; and I hoped and believed that if I proved myself a man, I could go back to you, in the strength of my manhood, and you would listen to me. And so, penniless and a stranger, under an assumed name, I sought useful, necessary work that called for the highest quality of manhood. And I have won, Helen; I know that I have won. Today Patches, the cowboy, can look any man in the face. He can take his place and hold his own among men of any class anywhere. I have regained that of which the circumstances of birth and inheritance and training robbed me. I have won the right of a man to come to you again. I claim that right now, Helen. I tell you again that I love you. I love you as —"

"Larry! Larry!" she cried, springing to her feet, and drawing away from him, as though suddenly awakened from some strange spell. "Larry, you must not! What do you mean? How can you say such things to me?"

He answered her with reckless passion. "I say such things because I am a man, and because you are the woman I love and want; because —"

She cried out again in protest. "Oh, stop, stop! Please stop! Don't you know?"

"Know what?" he demanded.

"My — my husband!" she gasped. "Stanford Manning — we are here on our honeymoon."

She saw him flinch as though from a heavy blow, and put out his hand to the trunk of a tree near which they stood, to steady himself. He did not speak, but his lips moved as though he repeated her words to himself, over and over again; and he gazed at her with a strange bewildered, doubting look, as though he could not believe his own suffering.

Impulsively Helen went a step toward him. "Larry!" she said. "Larry!"

Her voice seemed to arouse him and he stood erect as though by a conscious effort of will. Then that old self-mocking smile was on his lips. He was laughing at his hurt — making sport of himself and his cruel predicament.

But to Helen there was that in his smile which wrung her woman heart. "Oh, Larry," she said gently. "Forgive me; I am so sorry; I —"

He put out his hand with a gesture of protest, and his voice was calm and courteous. "I beg your pardon, Helen. It was stupid of me not to have understood. I forgot myself for the moment. It was all so unexpected — meeting you like this. I did not think." He looked away toward his waiting horse and to the steer lying on the ground. "So you and Stanford Manning — Good old Stan! I am glad for him. And for you, too, Helen. Why, it was I who introduced him to you; do you remember?"

He smiled again that mirthless, self-mocking smile, as he added without giving her time to speak, "If you will excuse me for a moment, I will rid your camp of the unwelcome presence of that beast yonder." Then he went toward his horse, as though turning for relief to the work that had become so familiar to him.

She watched him while he released the steer, and drove the animal away over the ridge, where he permitted it to escape into the wild haunts where it lived with its outlaw companions.

When he rode back to the little camp Stanford had returned.

For an hour they talked together as old friends. But Helen, while she offered now and then a word or a remark, or asked a question, and laughed or smiled with them, left the talk mostly to the two men. Stanford, when the first shock of learning of Helen's narrow escape was over, was gaily enthusiastic and warm in his admiration for his old friend, who had, for no apparent reason but the wish to assert his own manhood, turned his back upon the ease and luxury of his wealth to live a life of adventurous hardship. And Patches, as he insisted they should call him, with many a laughing jest and droll comment told them of his new life and work. He was only serious when he made them promise to keep his identity a secret until he himself was ready to reveal his real name.

"And what do you propose to do when your game of Patches is played out?" Stanford asked curiously.

For an instant they saw him smiling mockingly at himself; then he answered lightly, "Try some other fool experiment, I reckon."

Stanford chuckled; the reply was so like the cowboy Patches, and so unlike his old friend Larry Knight.

"As for that, Stan," Patches continued, "I don't see that the game will ever be played out, as you say. Certainly I can never now go back altogether to what I was. The fellow you used to know in Cleveland is not really I, you see. Fact is, I think that fellow is quite dead — peace be to his ashes! The world is wide and there is always work for a man to do."

The appearance of Phil Acton on the ridge, at the spot where the steer, followed by Patches, had first appeared, put an end to their further conversation with Lawrence Knight.

"My boss!" said that gentleman, in his character of Patches the cowboy, as the Cross-Triangle foreman halted his horse on the brow of the hill, and sat looking down upon the camp.

"Be careful, please, and don't let him suspect that you ever saw me before. I'll sure catch it now for loafing so long."

"I know him," said Stanford. Then he called to the man above, "Come on down, Acton, and be sociable."

Phil rode into camp, shook hands with Stanford cordially, and was presented to Mrs. Manning, to whom he spoke with a touch of embarrassment. Then he said, with a significant look at Patches, "I'm glad to meet you people, Mr. Manning, but we really haven't much time for sociability just now. Mr. Baldwin sent me with an outfit into this Granite Basin country to gather some of these outlaw steers. He expects us to be on the job." Turning to Patches, he continued, "When you didn't come back I thought you must have met with some serious trouble, and so trailed you. We've managed to lose a good deal of time, altogether. That steer you were after got away from you, did he?"

Helen spoke quickly. "Oh, Mr. Acton, you must not blame Mr. Patches for what happened. Really, you must not. No one was to blame; it just happened —" She stopped, unable to finish the explanation, for she was thinking of that part of the incident which was known only to herself and Patches.

Stanford told in a few words of his wife's danger and how the cowboy had saved her.

"That was mighty good work, Patches," said Phil heartily, "mighty good work. I'm sorry, Mr. Manning, that our coming up here after these outlaws happened at just this time. It is too bad to so disturb you and

Mrs. Manning. We are going home Friday, however, and I'll tell the boys to keep clear of your neighborhood in the meantime."

As the two Cross-Triangle men walked toward their horses, Helen and Stanford heard Phil ask, "But where is that steer, Patches?"

"I let him go," returned Patches.

"You let him go!" exclaimed the foreman. "After you had him roped and tied? What did you do that for?"

Patches was confused. "Really, I don't know."

"I'd like to know what you figure we're up here for," said Phil, sharply. "You not only waste two or three hours visiting with these people, but you take my time trailing you up; and then you turn loose a steer after you get him. It looks like you'd lost your head mighty bad, after all."

"I'm afraid you're right, Phil," Patches answered quietly.

Helen looked at her husband indignantly but Stanford was grinning with delight.

"To think," he murmured, "of Larry Knight taking a dressing-down like that from a mere cowboy foreman!"

But Patches was by no means so meek in spirit as he appeared in his outward manner. He had been driven almost to the verge of desperation by the trying situation, and was fighting for self-control. To take his foreman's rebuke in the presence of his friends was not easy.

"I reckon I'd better send you to the home ranch tonight, instead of Bob," continued Phil, as the two men mounted their horses and sat for a moment facing each other. "It looks like we could spare you best. Tell Uncle Will to send the chuck wagon and three more punchers, and that we'll start for the home ranch Friday. And be sure that you get back here tomorrow."

"Shall I go now?"

"Yes, you can go now."

Patches wheeled his horse and rode away, while Phil disappeared over the ridge in the direction from which he had come.

When the two cowboys were out of sight, Helen went straight to her husband, and to Stanford's consternation, when he took her in his arms, she was crying.

"Why, girl, what is it?" he asked, holding her close.

But she only answered between sobs as she clung to him, "It — it's nothing — never mind, Stan. I'm just upset."

And Stanford quite naturally thought it was only a case of nerves caused by the danger through which she had passed.

For nearly an hour, Patches rode toward the home ranch, taking only such notice of his surroundings as was necessary in order for him to keep his direction. Through the brush and timber, over the ridges down into valleys and washes, and along the rock-strewn mountain sides he allowed his horse to pick the way, and take his own gait, with scarcely a touch of rein or spur.

The twilight hour was beginning when he reached a point from which he could see, in the distance, the red roofs of the Cross-Triangle buildings. Checking his horse, he sat for a long time, motionless, looking away over the broad land that had come to mean so much to him, as though watching the passing of the day.

But the man did not note the changing colors in the western sky; he did not see the shadows deepening; he was not thinking of the coming of the night. The sight of the distant spot that, a year before, had held such possibilities for him, when, on the summit of the Divide, he had chosen between two widely separated ways of life, brought to him, now, a keener realization of the fact that he was again placed where he must choose. The sun was down upon those hopes and dreams that in the first hard weeks of his testing had inspired and strengthened him. The night of despairing, reckless abandonment of the very ideals of manhood for which he had so bravely struggled was upon him; while the spirit and strength of that manhood which he had so hardly attained fought against its surrender.

When Stanford Manning had asked, "What will you do when your game of Patches is played out?" he had said that the man whom they had known in the old days was dead. Would this new man also die? Deliberately the man turned about and started back the way he had come.

In their honeymoon camp, that evening, when the only light in the sky was the light of the stars, and the campfire's ruddy flames made weird shadows come and go in the little glade, Helen, lying in the hammock, and Stanford, sitting near, talked of their old friend Lawrence Knight. But as they talked they did not know that a lonely horseman had stopped on the other side of the low ridge, and leaving his horse, had crept carefully through the brush, to a point on the brow of the hill, from which he could look down into the camp.

From where he lay in the darkness, the man could see against the campfire's light the two, where the hammock was swung under the trees. He could hear the low murmur of their voices, with now and then a laugh. But it was always the man who laughed, for there was little mirth in Helen's heart that night. Then he saw Stanford go into the tent and return again to the hammock; and soon there came floating up to him the sweet, plaintive music of Helen's guitar, and then her voice, full and low, with a wealth of womanhood in every tone, as she sang a love song to her mate. Later, when the dancing flames of the campfire had fallen to a dull red glow, he saw them go arm in arm into their tent. Then all was still. The red glow of the fire dimmed to a spark, and darkness drew close about the scene. But even in the darkness the man could still see, under the wide, sheltering arms of the trees, a lighter spot — the white tent.

"Gethsemane," said the Dean to me once, when our talk had ranged wide and touched upon many things, "Gethsemane ain't no place; it's somethin' that happens. Whenever a man goes up against himself, right there is where Gethsemane is. And right there, too, is sure to be a fight. A man may not always know about it at the time; he may be too busy fightin' to understand just what it all means; but he'll know about it afterwards — No matter which side of him wins, he'll know afterwards that it was the one big fight of his life."

Chapter XIV
AT MINT SPRING

*W*hen those days at Prescott were over, and Mr. and Mrs. Manning had left for their camp in Granite Basin, Kitty Reid returned to Williamson Valley reluctantly. She felt that with Phil definitely out of her life the last interest that bound her to the scenes of her girlhood was broken. Before many weeks the ranch would be sold. A Prescott agent had opened negotiations for an eastern client who would soon be out to look over the property; and Mr. Reid felt, from all that the agent had said, that the sale was assured. In the meantime Kitty would wait as patiently as she could. To help her, there would be Helen's visit, and there was her friendship with Professor Parkhill. It was not strange, considering all the circumstances, that the young woman should give her time more generously than ever to the only person in the neighborhood, except Patches, perhaps, who she felt could understand and appreciate her desires for that higher life of which even her own parents were ignorant.

And the professor did understand her fully. He told her so many times each day. Had he not given all the years of his little life to the study of those refining and spiritualizing truths that are so far above the comprehension of the base and ignoble common herd? Indeed, he understood her language; he understood fully, why the sordid, brutal materialism of her crude and uncultured environment so repulsed and disgusted her. He understood, more fully than Kitty herself, in fact, and explained to her clearly, that her desires for the higher intellectual and spiritual life were born of her own rare gifts, and evidenced beyond all question the fineness and delicacy of her nature. He rejoiced with her – with a pure and holy joy – that she was so soon to be set free to live amid the surroundings that would afford her those opportunities for the higher development of her intellectual and spiritual powers which her soul craved. All this he told her from day to day; and then, one afternoon, he told her more.

It was the same afternoon that Patches had so unexpectedly found Helen and Stanford in their Granite Basin camp. Kitty and the professor had driven in the buckboard to Simmons for the mail, and were coming back by the road to the Cross-Triangle, when the man asked, "Must we return to the ranch so soon? It is so delightful out here where there is no one to intrude with vulgar commonplaces, to mar our companionship."

"Why, no," returned Kitty. "There is no need for us to hurry home." She glanced around. "We might sit over there, under those cedars on the hill, where you found me with Mr. Patches that day – the day we saw Yavapai Joe, you remember."

"If you think it quite safe to leave the vehicle," he said, "I should be delighted."

Kitty tied the horses to a convenient bush at the foot of the low hill, and soon they were in the welcome shade of the cedars.

"Miss Reid," the professor began, with portentous gravity, "I must confess that I have been rather puzzled to account for your presence here that day with such a man as that fellow Patches. You will pardon my saying so, I am sure, but you must have observed my very deep interest in you. I also chanced to see you with him one day in Prescott, in the park. You don't mind my speaking of it?"

"Not at all, Professor Parkhill," Kitty returned, smiling as she thought how ignorant the professor was of the cowboy's real character. "I like Patches. He interests me very much; and there is really no reason why I should not be friendly with him. Don't you think that I should be kind to our cowboys?"

"I suppose so," the professor sighed. "But it hurts me to see you have anything whatever in common with such a man. It shocks me to know that you must, in any degree, come in touch with such fellows. I shall be very glad, indeed, when you are free from any such kindly obligations, and safe among those of your own class."

Kitty found it very hard to reply. She did not wish to be disloyal to Patches and her many Williamson Valley friends; nor did she like to explain how Patches had played a part for the professor's benefit, for she felt that by not exposing the deception she had, in a way, been a party to it. So she said nothing, but seemed to be silently weighing the value of her learned companion's observations. At least, it so appeared to the professor, and in her ready acceptance of his implied criticism of her conduct he found the encouragement he needed for that which followed.

"You must understand, Miss Reid, that I have become exceedingly zealous for your welfare. In these months that we have been so much together your companionship — your spiritual and intellectual companionship, I should say — has come to be very dear to me. As our souls have communed, I have felt myself uplifted and inspired. I have been strengthened and encouraged, as never before, to climb on toward the mountain peaks of pure intellectuality. If I am not mistaken, you, too, have felt a degree of uplift as a result of our fellowship, have you not?"

"Yes, indeed, Professor Parkhill," Kitty answered sincerely. "Our talks together have meant much more to me than I can tell. I shall never forget this summer. Your friendship has been a wonderful influence in my life."

The little man moved uneasily and glanced timidly around. "I am truly glad to know that our companionship has not been altogether distasteful to you; I felt sure that it was not, but I — ahem! — I am glad to hear your confirmation of my opinion. It — ah — it enables me to say that which for several weeks past has been weighing heavily on my mind."

Kitty looked at him with the manner of a trusting disciple waiting for the gems of truth that were about to fall from the lips of a venerable teacher.

"Miss Reid — ah — why need our beautiful and mutually profitable companionship cease?"

"I fear that I do not understand, Professor Parkhill," she answered, puzzled by his question.

He looked at her with just a shade of mild — very mild — rebuke, as he returned, "Why, I think that I have stated my thought clearly. I mean that I am very desirous that our relation — the relation which we both have found so helpful — should continue. I am sure that we have, in these months which we have spent together, sufficient evidence that our souls vibrate in perfect harmony. I need you, dear friend; your understanding of my soul's desires is so sympathetic; I feel that you so complement and fill out, as it were, my spiritual self. I need you to encourage, to inspire, to assist me in the noble work to which I am devoting all my strength."

She looked at him, now, with an expression of amazement. "Do you mean —" she faltered in confusion while the red blood colored her cheeks.

"Yes," he answered, confidently. "I am asking you to be my wife. Not, however," he added hastily, "in the common, vulgar understanding of that relation. I am offering you, dear friend, that which is vastly higher than the union of the merely animal, which is based wholly upon the purely physical and material attraction. I am proposing marriage of our souls — a union, if you please, of our higher intellectual and spiritual selves. I feel, indeed, that by those higher laws which the vulgar, beastlike minds are incapable of recognizing, we are already one. I sense, as it were, that oneness which can exist only when two souls are mated by the great oversoul; I feel that you are already mine — that, I am — that we are already united in a spiritual union that is —"

The young woman checked him with a gesture, which, had he interpreted it rightly, was one of repulsion. "Please stop, Professor Parkhill," she gasped in a tone of disgust.

He was surprised, and not a little chagrined. "Am I to understand that you do not reciprocate my sentiment, Miss Reid? Is it possible that I have been so mistaken?"

Kitty turned her head, as though she could not bear even to look at him. "What you ask is so impossible," she said in a low tone. "Impossible!"

Strive as she might, the young woman could not altogether hide her feeling of abhorrence. And yet, she asked herself, why should this man's proposal arouse in her such antagonism and repugnance? He was a scholar, famed for his attainments in the world of the highest culture. As his wife, she would be admitted at once into the very inner circle of that life to which she aspired, and for which she was leaving her old home and friends. He had couched his proposal in the very terms of the spiritually and intellectually elect; he had declared himself in that language which she had so proudly thought she understood, and in which she had so often talked with him; and yet she was humiliated and ashamed. It was, to her, as though, in placing his offer of marriage upon the high, pure ground of a spiritual union, he had insulted her womanhood. Kitty realized wonderingly that she had not felt like this when Phil had confessed his love for her. In her woman heart, she was proud and glad to have won the love of such a man as Phil, even though she could not accept the cowboy as her mate. On that very spot which the professor had chosen for his declaration, Patches had told her that she was leaving the glorious and enduring realities of life for vain and foolish bubbles — that she was throwing aside the good grain and choosing the husks. Was this what Patches meant? she wondered.

"I regret exceedingly, Miss Reid," the professor was saying, "that the pure and lofty sentiments which I have voiced do not seem to find a like response in your soul. I —"

Again she interrupted him with that gesture of repulsion. "Please do not say anymore, Professor Parkhill. I — I fear that I am very human, after all. Come, it is time that we were returning to the house."

All through the remaining hours of that afternoon and evening Kitty was disturbed and troubled. At times she wanted to laugh at the professor's ridiculous proposal; and again, her cheeks burned with anger; and she could have cried in her shame and humiliation. And with it all her mind was distraught by the persistent question: Was not the professor's conception of an ideal mating the legitimate and logical conclusion of those very advanced ideas of culture which he represented, and which she had so much admired? If she sincerely believed the life represented by the professor and his kind so superior — so far above the life represented by Phil Acton — why should she not feel honored instead of being so humiliated and shamed by the professor's — she could not call it love? If the life which Phil had asked her to share was so low in the scale of civilization; if it were so far beneath the intellectual and spiritual ideals which she had formed, why did she feel so honored by the strong man's love? Why had she not felt humiliated and ashamed that Phil should want her to mate with him? Could it be, she asked herself again and again, that there was something, after all, superior to that culture which she had so truly thought stood for the highest ideals of the race? Could it be that, in the land of Granite Mountain, there was something, after all, that was as superior to the things she had been taught as Granite Mountain itself was superior in its primeval strength and enduring grandeur to the man-made buildings of her school?

It was not strange that Kitty's troubled thoughts should turn to Helen Manning. Clearly, Helen's education had led to no confusion. On the contrary, she had found an ideal love, and a happiness such as every true, womanly woman must, in her heart of hearts, desire.

It was far into the night when Kitty, wakeful and restless, heard the sound of a horse's feet. She could not know that it was Honorable Patches riding past on his way to the ranch on the other side of the broad valley meadows.

Weary in body, and with mind and spirit exhausted by the trials through which he had passed, Patches crept to his bed. In the morning, when he delivered his message, the Dean, seeing the man's face, urged him to stay for the day at the ranch. But Patches said no; Phil was expecting him, and he must return to the outfit in Granite Basin. As soon as breakfast was over he set out.

He had ridden as far as the head of Mint Wash, and had stopped to water his horse, and to refresh himself with a cool drink and a brief rest beside the fragrant mint-bordered spring, when he heard someone riding rapidly up the wash the way he had come. A moment later, Kitty, riding her favorite Midnight, rounded a jutting corner of the rocky wall of the bluff.

As the girl caught sight of him, there beside the spring, she waved her hand in greeting. And the man, as he waved his answer, and watched her riding toward him, felt a thrill of gladness that she had come. The strong, true friendship that began with their very first meeting, when she had been so frankly interested in the tenderfoot, and so kindly helpful, and which had developed so steadily through the year, gave him, now, a feeling of comfort and relief. Wearied and worn by his disappointment and by his struggle with himself, with the cherished hope that had enabled him to choose and endure the hard life of the range brought to a sudden end, with his life itself made so empty and futile, he welcomed his woman friend with a warmth and gladness that brought a flush of pleasure to Kitty's cheek.

For Kitty, too, had just passed through a humiliating and disappointing experience. In her troubled frame of mind, and in her perplexed and confused questioning, the young woman was as glad for the companionship of Patches as he was glad to welcome her. She felt a curious sense of relief and safety in his presence — somewhat as one, who, walking over uncertain bogs or treacherous quicksands, finds, all at once, the solid ground.

"I saw you go past the house," she said, when she reached the spring where he stood awaiting her, "and I decided right then that I would go along with you to Granite Basin and visit my friends the Mannings. They told me that I might come this week, and I think they have had quite enough honeymooning, anyway. You know where they are camped, do you?"

"Yes," he answered. "I saw them yesterday. But, come! Get down and cool off a bit. You've been riding some, haven't you?"

"I wanted to catch you as soon as I could," she laughed, as she sprang lightly to the ground. "And you see you gained a good start while I was getting Midnight saddled. What a pretty spot! I must have a drink of that water this minute."

"Sorry I have no cup," he said, and then he laughed with the pleasure of good comradeship as she answered:

"You forget that I was born to the customs of this country." And, throwing aside her broad hat, she went down on the ground to drink from the spring, even as he had done.

As the man watched her, a sudden thought flashed into his mind — a thought so startling, so unexpected, that he was for the moment bewildered.

"Talk about the nectar of the gods!" cried Kitty with a deep breath of satisfaction, as she lifted her smiling face from the bright water to look up at him. And then she drank again.

"And now, if you please, sir, you may bring me some of that water-cress; we'll sit over there in the shade, and who cares whether Granite Basin, the Mannings, and your fellow cow-punchers, are fifteen or fifty miles away?"

He brought a generous bunch of the water-cress, and stretched himself full length beside her, as she sat on the ground under a tall sycamore.

"Selah!" he laughed contentedly. "We seem to lack only the book of verses, the loaf and the jug; the wilderness is here, all right, and that's a perfectly good bough up there, and, of course, you could furnish the song; I might recite 'The Boy Stood on the Burning Deck,' but, alas! we haven't even a flask and biscuit."

"What a pity that you should be so near and yet so far from paradise!" she retorted quickly. Then she added, with a mischievous smile, "It just happens that I have a sandwich in my saddle pocket."

"Won't you sing? Please do," he returned, with an eagerness that amused her.

But she shook her head reprovingly. "We would still lack the jug of wine, you know, and, really, I don't think that paradise is for cow-punch-ers, anyway, do you?"

"Evidently not," he answered. And at her jesting words a queer feeling of rebellion possessed him. Why should he be condemned to years of loneliness? Why must he face a life without the companionship of a mate? If the paradise he had sought so hard to attain were denied him, why should he not still take what happiness he might?

He was lying flat on his back, his hands clasped beneath his head, watching an eagle that wheeled, a tiny black speck, high under the blue arch of the sky. He seemed to have forgotten his companion.

Kitty leaned toward him, and held a sprig of water-cress over his upturned face. "I haven't a penny," she said, "but I'll give you this."

He sat up quickly. "Even at that price, my thoughts might cost you too much. But you haven't told me what you have done with our dear friend the professor? Haven't you a guilty conscience, deserting him like this?"

Kitty held up both hands in a gesture of dismay. "Don't, Patches, please don't. Ugh! if you only knew how good it is to be with a *man* again!"

He laughed aloud in a spirit of reckless defiance. "And Phil is over in Granite Basin. I neglected to tell you that he knows the location of the Mannings' camp, as well as I."

Kitty was a little puzzled by the tone of his laughter, and by his words. She spoke gravely. "Perhaps I should tell you, Patches — we have been such good friends, you and I — Phil —"

"Yes!" he said.

"Phil is nothing to me, Patches. I mean —"

"You mean in the way he wanted to be?" He helped her with a touch of eager readiness.

"Yes."

"And have you told him, Kitty?" Patches asked gently.

"Yes — I have told him," she replied.

Patches was silent for a moment. Then, "Poor Phil!" he said softly. "I understand now; I thought that was it. He is a man among thousands, Kitty."

"I know — I know," she returned, as though to dismiss the subject. "But it simply couldn't be."

Patches was looking at her intently, with an expression in his dark eyes that Kitty had never before seen. The man's mind was in a whirl of quick excitement. As they had talked and laughed together, the thought that had so startled him, when her manner of familiar comradeship had brought such a feeling of comfort to his troubled spirit, had not left him. From that first moment of their meeting a year before there had been that feeling between them, of companionship, a feeling which had grown as their acquaintance had developed into the intimate friendship that had allowed him to speak to her as he had spoken that day under the cedars on the ridge. What might that friendship not grow into! He thought of her desire for the life that he knew so well, and how he could, while granting every wish of her heart, yet protect her from the shams and falseness. And with these thoughts was that feeling of rebellion against the loneliness of his life.

Kitty's words regarding Phil removed the barrier, as it were, and the man's nature, which prompted him so often to act without pausing to consider, betrayed him into saying, "Would you be greatly shocked, Kitty, if I were to tell you that I am glad? That, while I am sorry for Phil, I am glad that you have said no to him?"

"You are glad?" she said wonderingly. "Why?"

"Because, now, *I* am free to say what I could not have said had you not told me what you have. I want you, Kitty. I want to fill your life with beauty and happiness and contentment. I want you to go with me to see and know the natural wonders of the world, and the wonders that men have wrought. I want to surround you with the beauties of art and literature, with everything that your heart craves. I want you to know the people whose friendship would be a delight to you. Come with me, girl – be my wife, and together we will find – if not paradise, at least a full and useful and contented and happy life. Will you come, Kitty? Will you come with me?"

As she listened her eyes grew big with wonder and delight. It was as though some good genie had suddenly opened wide the way to an enchanted laud. Then the gladness went swiftly from her face, and she said doubtingly, "You are jesting with me, Patches."

As she spoke his cowboy name, the man laughed aloud. "I forgot that you do not even know me – I mean, that you do not know my name."

"Are you some fairy prince in disguise, Sir Patches?"

"Not a fairy, dear, and certainly not a prince; just a man, that's all. But a man, dear girl, who can offer you a clean life, an honored name, and all of which I have spoken. But I must tell you – I always knew that I would tell you some day, but I did not dream that it would be today. My name is Lawrence Knight. My home is in Cleveland, Ohio. Your father can easily satisfy himself as to my family and my own personal life and standing. It is enough for me to assure you now, dear, that I am abundantly able to give you all that I have promised."

At the mention of his name, Kitty's eyes grew bright again. Thanks to her intimate friend and schoolmate, Helen Manning, she knew much more of Lawrence Knight than that gentleman supposed.

"But, tell me," she asked curiously, trembling with suppressed excitement, "why is Mr. Lawrence Knight masquerading here as the cowboy Honorable Patches?"

He answered earnestly. "I know it must seem strange to you, dear, but the simple truth is that I became ashamed of myself and my life of idle uselessness. I determined to see if I could take my place among men, simply as a man. I wanted to be accepted by men for myself, for my manhood, if you like, and not because of my —" he hesitated, then said frankly — "my money and social position. I wanted to depend upon myself — to live as other men live, by my own strength and courage and work. If I had given my real name, when I asked for work at the Cross-Triangle — someone would have found me out before very long, and my little experiment would have failed, don't you see?"

While he spoke, Kitty's excited mind had caught at many thoughts. She believed sincerely that her girlhood love for Phil was dead. This man, even as Patches the cowboy, with a questionable shadow on his life, had compelled her respect and confidence, while in his evident education and social culture he had won her deepest admiration. She felt that he was all that Phil was, and more. There was in her feeling toward him, as he offered himself to her now, no hint of that instinctive repulsion and abhorrence with which she had received Professor Parkhill's declaration of spiritual affinity. Her recent experience with the Master of Aesthetics had so outraged her womanly instincts that the inevitable reaction from her perplexed and troubled mind led her to feel more deeply, and to be drawn more strongly, toward this man with whom any woman might be proud to mate. At the same time, the attractions of the life which she knew he could give her, and for which she longed so passionately, with the relief of the thought that her parents would not need to sacrifice themselves for her, were potent factors in the power of Lawrence Knight's appeal.

"It would be wonderful," she said musingly. "I have dreamed and dreamed about such things."

"You will come with me, dear? You will let me give you your heart's wish — you will go with me into the life for which you are so fitted?"

"Do you really want me, Patches?" she asked timidly, as though in her mind there was still a shadow of doubt.

"More than anything in the world," he urged. "Say yes. Kitty. Say that you will be my wife."

The answer came softly, with a hint of questioning, still.

"Yes."

Kitty did not notice that the man had not spoken of his love for her. There were so many other things for her to consider, so many other things to distract her mind. Nor did the man notice that Kitty herself had failed to speak in any way that little word, which, rightly understood, holds in its fullest, deepest meaning, all of life's happiness — of labor and accomplishment – of success and triumph – of sacrifice and sorrow; holds, in its fullest, deepest meaning, indeed, all of life itself.

Chapter XV
ON CEDAR RIDGE

*K*itty's friends were very glad to welcome her at their camp in Granite Basin. The incident which had so rudely broken the seclusion of their honeymoon had been too nearly a tragedy to be easily forgotten. The charm of the place was, in some degree, for them, lost, and Kitty's coming helped to dispel the cloud that had a little overshadowed those last days of their outing.

It was not at all difficult for them to persuade Kitty to remain longer than the one night that she had planned, and to accompany them to Prescott. Prom Prescott, Stanford must go to the mines, to take up his work, and to arrange for Helen's coming later, and Helen would go home with Kitty for the visit she had promised. The cowboys, who were returning to the Cross-Triangle Ranch, would take Kitty's horse to her home, and would carry a message explaining the young woman's absence, and asking that someone be sent to Prescott with the clothing she would need in town, and that the Reid automobile might be in Prescott in readiness to take the two young women back to the ranch on the appointed day.

Kitty could not bring herself to tell even Helen about her engagement to Lawrence Knight, or Patches, as she would continue to call him until the time came for the cowboy himself to make his true name and character known. It had all happened so suddenly; the promises of the future were so wonderful – so far beyond the young woman's fondest dreams – that she herself could scarcely realize the truth. There would be time enough to tell Helen when they were together at the ranch. And she was insistent, too, that Patches must not interview her father until she herself had returned home.

Phil and his cowboys with the cattle reached the Cross-Triangle corrals the evening before the day set for Kitty and Helen to arrive at the ranch on the other side of the valley meadows. The Cross-Triangle men were greeted by the news that Professor Parkhill had said good-bye to Williamson Valley, and that the Pot-Hook-S Ranch had been sold. The eastern purchaser expected by Reid had arrived on the day that Kitty had gone to Granite Basin, and the deal had been closed without delay. But Reid was not to give possession of the property until after the fall rodeo.

As the men sat under the walnut trees with the Dean that evening, discussing the incidents of the Granite Basin work, and speculating about the new owner of the neighboring ranch, Phil sat with Little Billy apart from the circle, and contributed to the conversation only now and then a word or a brief answer to some question. When Mrs. Baldwin persuaded the child that it was bedtime, Phil slipped quietly away in the darkness, and they did not see him again until breakfast the next morning. When breakfast was over, the foreman gave a few directions to his men, and rode away alone.

The Dean, understanding the lad, whom he loved as one of his own sons, watched him go without a word or a question. To Mrs. Baldwin he said, "Just let him alone, Stella. The boy is all right. He's only gone off somewhere on the range to fight it out alone. Most likely he'll put in the day watching those wild horses over beyond Toohey. He generally goes to them when he's bothered about anything or in trouble of any sort."

Patches, who had been sent on an errand of some kind to Fair Oaks, was returning home early in the afternoon, and had reached the neighborhood of that spring where he had first encountered Nick Cambert, when he heard a calf bawling lustily somewhere in the cedar timber not far away. Familiar as he now was with the voices of the range, the cowboy knew that the calf was in trouble. The call was one of fright and pain.

Turning aside from his course, he rode, rapidly at first, then more cautiously, toward the sound. Presently he caught a whiff of smoke that came with the light breeze from somewhere ahead on the ridge along which he was riding. Instantly he rode into a thick clump of cedars, and, dismounting, tied his horse. Then he went on, carefully and silently, on foot. Soon he heard voices. Again the calf bawled in fright and pain, and the familiar odor of burning hair was carried to him on the breeze. Someone was branding a calf.

It might be all right — it might not. Patches was unarmed, but, with characteristic disregard of consequences, he crept softly forward, toward a dense growth of trees and brush, from beyond which the noise and the smoke seemed to come.

He had barely gained the cover when he heard someone on the other side ride rapidly away down the ridge. Hastily parting the bushes, he looked through to catch a glimpse of the horseman, but he was a moment too late; the rider had disappeared from sight in the timber. But, in a little open space among the cedars, the cowboy saw Yavapai Joe, standing beside a calf, fresh-branded with the Four-Bar-M iron, and earmarked with the Tailholt marks.

Patches knew instantly, as well as though he had witnessed the actual branding, what, had happened. That part of the range was seldom visited except by the Dean's cowboys, and the Tailholt Mountain men, knowing that the Cross-Triangle riders were all at Granite Basin, were making good use of their opportunities. The man who had ridden away so hurriedly, a moment too soon for Patches to see him, was, without doubt, driving the mother of the calf to a distance that would effectually separate her from her offspring.

But while he was so sure in his own mind, the Cross-Triangle man — as it had so often happened before — had arrived on the scene too late. He had no positive evidence that the animal just branded was not the lawful property of Nick Cambert.

As Patches stepped from the bushes, Yavapai Joe faced him for a moment in guilty astonishment and fear; then he ran toward his horse.

"Wait a minute, Joe!" called Patches. "What good will it do for you to run now? I'm not going to harm you."

Joe stopped, and stood hesitating in indecision, watching the intruder with that sneaking, sidewise look.

"Come on, Joe; let's have a little talk about this business," the Cross-Triangle man said in a matter-of-fact tone, as he seated himself on a large, flat-topped stone near the little fire. "You know you can't get away, so you might as well."

"I ain't tellin' nothin' to nobody," said Joe sullenly, as he came slowly toward the Dean's cowboy.

"No?" said Patches.

"No, I ain't," asserted the Tailholt Mountain man stoutly. "That there calf is a Four-Bar-M calf, all right."

"I see it is," returned the Cross-Triangle rider calmly. "But I'll just wait until Nick gets back, and ask him what it was before he worked over the iron."

Joe, excited and confused by the cool nerve of this man, fell readily into the verbal trap.

"You better go now, an' not wait to ask Nick no fool questions like that. If he finds you here talkin' with me when he gets back, hell'll be a-poppin' fer sure. Me an' you are friends, Patches, an' that's why I'm a-tellin' you you better pull your freight while the goin's good."

"Much obliged, Joe, but there's no hurry. You don't need to be so rushed. It will be an hour before Nick gets back, if he drives that cow as far as he ought."

Again poor Yavapai Joe told more than he intended. "You don't need to worry none 'bout Nick; he'll sure drive her far enough. He ain't takin' no chances, Nick ain't."

With his convictions so readily confirmed, Patches had good ground upon which to base his following remarks. He had made a long shot when he spoke so confidently of the brand on the calf being worked over. For, of course, the calf might not have been branded at all when the Tailholt Mountain men caught it. But Joe's manner, as well as his warning answer, told that the shot had gone home. The fact that the brand had been worked over established also the fact that it was the Cross-Triangle brand that had been changed, because the Cross-Triangle was the only brand in that part of the country that could be changed into the Four-Bar-M.

Patches, dropping his easy manner, and speaking straight to the point, said, "Look here, Joe, you and I might as well get down to cases. You know I am your friend, and I don't want to see you in trouble, but you can take it from me that you are in mighty serious trouble right now. I was hiding right there in those bushes, close enough to see all that happened, and I know that this is a Cross-Triangle calf, and that Nick and you worked the brand over. You know that it means the penitentiary for you, as well as for Nick, if the boys don't string you both up without any ceremony."

Patches paused to let his words sink in.

Joe's face was ashy white, and he was shaking with fright, as he stole a sneaking look toward his horse.

Patches added sharply, "You can't give me the slip, either; I can kill you before you get halfway to your horse."

Trapped and helpless, Joe looked pleadingly at his captor. "You wouldn't send me up, would you, now, Patches?" he whined. "You an' me's good friends, ain't we? Anyway he wouldn't let me go to the pen, an' the boys wouldn't dast do nothin' to me when they knew."

"Whom are you talking about?" demanded Patches. "Nick? Don't be a fool, Joe; Nick will be there right alongside of you."

"I ain't meanin' Nick; I mean *him* over there at the Cross-Triangle — Professor Parkhill. I'm a-tellin' you that *he* wouldn't let you do nothin' to me."

"Forget it, Joe," came the reply, without an instant's hesitation. "You know as well as I do how much chance Professor Parkhill, or anyone else, would have, trying to keep the boys from making you and Nick dance on nothing, once they hear of this. Besides, the professor is not in the valley now."

The poor outcast's fright was pitiful. "You ain't meanin' that he — that he's gone?" he gasped.

"Listen, Joe," said Patches quickly. "I can do more for you than he could, even if he were here. You know I am your friend, and I don't want to see a good fellow like you sent to prison for fifteen or twenty years, or, perhaps, hanged. But there's only one way that I can see for me to save you. You must go with me to the Cross-Triangle, and tell Mr. Baldwin all about it, how you were just working for Nick, and how he made you help him do this, and all that you know. If you do that, we can get you off."

"I — I reckon you're right, Patches," returned the frightened weakling sullenly. "Nick has sure treated me like a dog, anyway. You won't let Nick get at me, will you, if I go?"

"Nobody can get at you, Joe, if you go with me, and do the square thing. I'm going to take care of you myself, and help you to get out of this, and brace up and be a man. Come on; let's be moving. I'll turn this calf loose first, though."

He was bending over the calf when a noise in the brush caused him to stand suddenly erect.

Joe was whimpering with terror.

Patches said fiercely, but in a low tone, "Shut up, and follow my lead. Be a man, and I'll get you out of this yet."

"Nick will kill us sure," whined Joe.

"Not if I get my hands on him first, he won't," retorted Patches.

But it was with a feeling of relief that the cowboy saw Phil Acton ride toward them from the shelter of the timber.

Before Patches could speak, Phil's gun covered him, and the foreman's voice rang out sharply.

"Hands up!"

Joe's hands shot above his head. Patches hesitated.

"Quick!" said Phil.

And as Patches saw the man's eyes over the black barrel of the weapon he obeyed. But as he raised his hands, a dull flush of anger colored his tanned face a deeper red, and his eyes grew dark with passion. He realized his situation instantly. The mystery that surrounded his first appearance when he had sought employment at the Cross-Triangle; the persistent suspicion of many of the cowboys because of his friendship for Yavapai Joe; his meeting with Joe which the professor had reported; his refusal to explain to Phil; his return to the ranch when everyone was away and he himself was supposed to be in Prescott — all these and many other incidents had come to their legitimate climax in his presence on that spot with Yavapai Joe, the smoldering fire and the freshly branded calf. He was unarmed, but Phil could not be sure of that, for many a cowboy carries his gun inside the leg of his leather chaps, where it does not so easily catch in the brush.

But while Patches saw it all so clearly, he was enraged that this man with whom he had lived so intimately should believe him capable of such a crime, and treat him without question as a common cattle thief. Phil's coldness toward him, which had grown so gradually during the past three months, in this peremptory humiliation reached a point beyond which Patches' patient and considerate endurance could not go. The man's sense of justice was outraged; his fine feeling of honor was insulted. Trapped and helpless as he was under that menacing gun, he was possessed by a determination to defend himself against the accusation, and to teach Phil Acton that there was a limit to the insult he would endure, even in the name of friendship. To this end his only hope was to trap his foreman with words, as he had caught Yavapai Joe. At a game of words Honorable Patches was no unskilled novice. Controlling his anger, he said coolly, with biting sarcasm, while he looked at the cowboy with a mocking sneer, "You don't propose to take any chances, do you — holding up an unarmed man?"

Patches saw by the flush that swept over Phil's cheeks how his words bit.

"It doesn't pay to take chances with your kind," retorted the foreman hotly.

"No," mocked Patches, "but it will pay big, I suppose, for the great 'Wild Horse Phil' to be branded as a sneak and a coward who is afraid to face an unarmed man unless he can get the drop on him?"

Phil was goaded to madness by the cool, mocking words. With a reckless laugh, he slipped his weapon into the holster and sprang to the ground. At the same moment Patches and Joe lowered their hands, and Joe, unnoticed by either of the angry men, took a few stealthy steps toward his horse.

Phil, deliberately folding his arms, stood looking at Patches.

"I'll just call that bluff, you sneakin' calf stealer," he said coolly. "Now, unlimber that gun of yours, and get busy."

Angry as he was, Patches felt a thrill of admiration for the man, and beneath his determination to force Phil Acton to treat him with respect, he was proud of his friend who had answered his sneering insinuation with such fearlessness. But he could not now hesitate in his plan of provoking Phil into disarming himself.

"You're something of a four-flusher yourself, aren't you?" he mocked. "You know I have no gun. Your brave pose is very effective. I would congratulate you, only, you see, it doesn't impress me in the least."

With an oath Phil snatched his gun from the holster, and threw it aside.

"Have it any way you like," he retorted, and started toward Patches.

Then a curious thing happened to Honorable Patches. Angry as he was, he became suddenly dominated by something that was more potent than his rage.

"Stop!" he cried sharply, and with such ringing force that Phil involuntarily obeyed. "I can't fight you this way, Phil," he said; and the other, wondering, saw that whimsical, self-mocking smile on his lips. "You know as well as I do that you are no match for me barehanded. You couldn't even touch me; you have seen Curly and the others try it often enough. You are as helpless in my power, now, as I was in yours a moment ago. I am armed now and you are not. I can't fight you this way, Phil."

In spite of himself Phil Acton was impressed by the truth and fairness of Patches' words. He recognized that an unequal contest could satisfy neither of them, and that it made no difference which of the contestants had the advantage.

"Well," he said sarcastically, "what are you going to do about it?"

"First," returned Patches calmly, "I am going to tell you how I happened to be here with Yavapai Joe."

"I don't need any explanations from you. It's some more of your personal business, I suppose," retorted Phil.

Patches controlled himself. "You are going to hear the explanation, just the same," he returned. "You can believe it or not, just as you please."

"And what then?" demanded Phil.

"Then I'm going to get a gun, and we'll settle the rest of it, man to man, on equal terms, just as soon as you like," answered Patches deliberately.

Phil replied shortly. "Go ahead with your palaver. I'll have to hand it to you when it comes to talk. I am not educated that way myself."

For a moment Patches hesitated, as though on the point of changing his mind about the explanation. Then his sense of justice — justice both for Phil and himself — conquered.

But in telling Phil how he had come upon the scene too late for positive proof that the freshly branded calf was the Dean's property, and in explaining how, when the foreman arrived, he had just persuaded Joe to go with him and give the necessary evidence against Nick, Patches forgot the possible effect of his words upon Joe himself. The two Cross-Triangle men were so absorbed in their own affair that they had paid no attention to the Tailholt Mountain outcast. And Joe, taking advantage of the opportunity, had by this time gained a position beside his horse. As he heard Patches tell how he had no actual evidence that the calf was not Nick Cambert's property, a look of anger and cunning darkened the face of Nick's follower. He was angry at the way Patches had tricked him into betraying both himself and his evil master, and he saw a way to defeat the two cowboys and at the same time win Nick's approval. Quickly the fellow mounted his horse, and, before they could stop him, was out of sight in the timber.

"I've done it now," exclaimed Patches in dismay. "I forgot all about Joe."

"I don't think he counts for much in this game anyway," returned Phil, gruffly.

As he spoke, the foreman turned his back to Patches and walked toward his gun. He had reached the spot where the weapon lay on the ground, when, from the bushes to the right, and a little back of Patches, who stood watching his companion, a shot rang out with startling suddenness.

Patches saw Phil stumble forward, straighten for an instant, as though by sheer power of his will, and, turning, look back at him. Then, as Phil fell, the unarmed cowboy leaped forward toward that gun on the ground. Even as he moved, a second shot rang out and he felt the wind of the bullet on his cheek. With Phil's gun in his hand, he ran toward a cedar tree on the side of the open space opposite the point from which the shots came, and as he ran another bullet whistled past.

A man moving as Patches moved is not an easy mark. The same man armed, and protected by the trunk of a tree, is still more difficult. A moment after he had gained cover, the cowboy heard the clatter of a horse's feet, near the spot from which the shots had come, and by the sound knew that the unseen marksman had chosen to retire with only half his evident purpose accomplished, rather than take the risk that had arisen with Patches' success in turning the ambush into an open fight.

As the sound of the horse's swift rush down the side of the ridge grew fainter and fainter, Patches ran to Phil.

A quick examination told him that the bullet had entered just under the right shoulder, and that the man, though unconscious and, no doubt, seriously wounded, was living.

With rude bandages made by tearing his shirt into strips Patches checked the flow of blood, and bound up the wound as best he could. Then for a moment he considered. It was between three and four miles to the ranch. He could ride there and back in a few minutes. Someone must start for a doctor without an instant's loss of time. With water, proper bandages and stimulants, the wounded man could be cared for and moved in the buckboard with much greater safety than he could be carried in his present condition on a horse. The risk of leaving him for a few minutes was small, compared to the risk of taking him to the house under the only conditions possible. The next instant Patches was in Phil's saddle and riding as he had never ridden before.

Jim Reid, with Kitty and Helen, was on the way back from Prescott as Kitty had planned. They were within ten miles of the ranch when the cattleman, who sat at the wheel of the automobile, saw a horseman coming toward them. A moment he watched the approaching figure, then, over his shoulder, he said to the girls, "Look at that fellow ride. There's something doin', sure." As he spoke he turned the machine well out of the road.

A moment later he added, "It's Curly Elson from the Cross-Triangle. Somethin's happened in the valley." As he spoke, he stopped the machine, and sprang out so that the cowboy could see and recognize him.

Curly did not draw rein until he was within a few feet of Reid; then he brought his running horse up with a suddenness that threw the animal on its haunches.

Curly spoke tersely. "Phil Acton is shot. We need a doctor quick."

Without a word Jim Reid leaped into the automobile. The car backed to turn around. As it paused an instant before starting forward again, Kitty put her hand on her father's shoulder.

"Wait!" she cried. "I'm going to Phil. Curly, I want your horse; you can go with father."

The cowboy was on the ground before she had finished speaking. And before the automobile was under way Kitty was riding back the way Curly had come.

Kitty was scarcely conscious of what she had said. The cowboy's first words had struck her with the force of a physical blow, and in that first moment, she had been weak and helpless. She had felt as though a heavy weight pressed her down; a grey mist was before her eyes, and she could not see clearly. "Phil Acton is shot — Phil Acton is shot!" The cowboy's words had repeated themselves over and over. Then, with a sudden rush, her strength came again — the mist cleared; she must go to Phil; she must go fast, fast. Oh, why was this horse so slow! If only she were riding her own Midnight! She did not think as she rode. She did not wonder, nor question, nor analyze her emotions. She only felt. It was Phil who was hurt — Phil, the boy with whom she had played when she was a little girl — the lad with whom she had gone to school — the young man who had won the first love of her young woman heart. It was Phil, her Phil, who was hurt, and she must go to him — she must go fast, fast!

It seemed to Kitty that hours passed before she reached the meadow lane. She was glad that Curly had left the gates open. As she crossed the familiar ground between the old Acton home and the ranch house on the other side of the sandy wash, she saw them. They were carrying him into the house as she rode into the yard, and at sight of that still form the grey mist came again, and she caught the saddle horn to save herself from falling. But it was only a moment until she was strong again, and ready to do all that Mrs. Baldwin asked.

Phil had regained consciousness before they started home with him, but he was very weak from the loss of blood and the journey in the buckboard, though Bob drove ever so carefully, was almost more than he could bear. But with the relief that came when he was at last lying quietly in his own bed, and with the help of the stimulant, the splendid physical strength and vitality that was his because of his natural and unspoiled life again brought him back from the shadows into the light of full consciousness.

It was then that the Dean, while Mrs. Baldwin and Kitty were occupied for a few moments in another part of the house, listened to all that his foreman could tell him about the affair up to the time that he had fallen unconscious. The Dean asked but few questions. But when the details were all clearly fixed in his mind, the older man bent over Phil and looked straight into the lad's clear and steady eyes, while he asked in a low tone, "Phil, did Patches do this?"

And the young man answered, "Uncle Will, I don't know."

With this he closed his eyes wearily, as though to sleep, and the Dean, seeing Kitty in the doorway, beckoned her to come and sit beside the bed. Then he stole quietly from the room.

As in a dream Phil had seen Kitty when she rode into the yard. And he had been conscious of her presence as she moved about the house and the room where he lay. But he had given no sign that he knew she was there. As she seated herself, at the Dean's bidding, the cowboy opened his eyes for a moment, and looked up into her face. Then again the weary lids closed, and he gave no hint that he recognized her, save that the white lips set in firmer lines as though at another stab of pain.

As she watched alone beside this man who had, since she could remember, been a part of her life, and as she realized that he was on the very border line of that land from which, if he entered, he could never return to her, Kitty Reid knew the truth that is greater than any knowledge that the schools of man can give. She knew the one great truth of her womanhood; knew it not from text book or class room; not from learned professor or cultured associates; but knew it from that good Master of Life who, with infinite wisdom, teaches his many pupils who are free to learn in the school of schools, the School of Nature. In that hour when the near presence of death so overshadowed all the trivial and non-essential things of life — when the little standards and petty values of poor human endeavor were as nothing — this woman knew that by the unwritten edict of God, who decreed that in all life two should be as one, this man was her only lawful mate. Environment, circumstance, that which we call culture and education, even death, might separate them; but nothing could nullify the fact that was attested by the instinct of her womanhood. Bending over the man who lay so still, she whispered the imperative will of her heart.

"Come back to me, Phil — I want you — I need you, dear — come back to me!"

Slowly he came out of the mists of weakness and pain to look up at her — doubtfully — wonderingly. But there was a light in Kitty's face that dispelled the doubt, and changed the look of wondering uncertainty to glad conviction. He did not speak. No word was necessary. Nor did he move, for he must be very still, and hold fast with all his strength to the life that was now so good. But the woman knew without words all that he would have said, and as his eyes closed again she bowed her head in thankfulness.

Then rising she stole softly to the window. She felt that she must look out for a moment into the world that was so suddenly new and beautiful.

Under the walnut trees she saw the Dean talking with the man whom she had promised to marry.

Later Mr. Reid, with Helen and Curly, brought the doctor, and the noise of the automobile summoned every soul on the place to wait for the physician's verdict of life or death.

While the Dean was in Phil's room with the physician, and the anxious ones were gathered in a little group in front of the house, Jim Reid stood apart from the others talking in low tones with the cowboy Bob. Patches, who was standing behind the automobile, heard Bob, who had raised his voice a little, say distinctly, "I tell you, sir, there ain't a bit of doubt in the world about it. There was the calf a layin' right there fresh-branded and marked. He'd plumb forgot to turn it loose, I reckon, bein' naturally rattled; or else he figgered that it warn't no use, if Phil should be able to tell what happened. The way I make it out is that Phil jumped him right in the act, so sudden that he shot without thinkin'; you know how he acts quick that-a-way. An' then he seen what he had done, an' that it was more than an even break that Phil wouldn't live, an' so figgered that his chance was better to stay an' run a bluff by comin' for help, an' all that. If he'd tried to make his get-away, there wouldn't 'a' been no question about it; an' he's got just nerve enough to take the chance he's a-takin' by stayin' right with the game."

Patches started as though to go toward the men, but at that moment the doctor came from the house. As the physician approached the waiting group, that odd, mirthless, self-mocking smile touched Patches' lips; then he stepped forward to listen with the others to the doctor's words.

Phil had a chance, the doctor said, but he told them frankly that it was only a chance. The injured man's wonderful vitality, his clean blood and unimpaired physical strength, together with his unshaken nerve and an indomitable will, were all greatly in his favor. With careful nursing they might with reason hope for his recovery.

With expressions of relief, the group separated. Patches walked away alone. Mr. Reid, who would return to Prescott with the doctor, said to his daughter when the physician was ready, "Come, Kitty, I'll go by the house, so as to take you and Mrs. Manning home."

But Kitty shook her head. "No, father. I'm not going home. Stella needs me here. Helen understands, don't you, Helen?"

And wise Mrs. Manning, seeing in Kitty's face something that the man had not observed, answered, "Yes, dear, I do understand. You must stay, of course. I'll run over again in the morning."

"Very well," answered Mr. Reid, who seemed in somewhat of a hurry. "I know you ought to stay. Tell Stella that mother will be over for a little while this evening." And the automobile moved away.

That night, while Mrs. Baldwin and Kitty watched by Phil's bedside, and Patches, in his room, waited, sleepless, alone with his thoughts, men from the ranch on the other side of the quiet meadow were riding swiftly through the darkness. Before the new day had driven the stars from the wide sky, a little company of silent, grim-faced horsemen gathered in the Pot-Hook-S corral. In the dim, grey light of the early morning they followed Jim Reid out of the corral, and, riding fast, crossed the valley above the meadows and approached the Cross-Triangle corrals from the west. One man in the company led a horse with an empty saddle. Just beyond the little rise of ground outside the big gate they halted, while Jim Reid with two others, leaving their horses with the silent riders behind the hill, went on into the corral, where they seated themselves on the edge of the long watering trough near the tank, which hid them from the house.

Fifteen minutes later, when the Dean stepped from the kitchen porch, he saw Curly running toward the house. As the older man hurried toward him, the cowboy, pale with excitement and anger, cried, "They've got him, sir – grabbed him when he went out to the corral."

The Dean understood instantly. "My horse, quick, Curly," he said, and hurried on toward the saddle shed. "Which way did they go?" he asked, as he mounted.

"Toward the cedars on the ridge where it happened," came the answer. "Do you want me?"

"No. Don't let them know in the house," came the reply. And the Dean was gone.

The little company of horsemen, with Patches in their midst, had reached the scene of the shooting, and had made their simple preparations. From that moment when they had covered him with their guns as he stepped through the corral gate, he had not spoken.

"Well, sir," said the spokesman, "have you anything to say before we proceed?"

Patches shook his head, and wonderingly they saw that curious mocking smile on his lips.

"I don't suppose that any remarks I might make would impress you gentlemen in the least," he said coolly. "It would be useless and unkind for me to detain you longer than is necessary."

An involuntary murmur of admiration came from the circle. They were men who could appreciate such unflinching courage.

In the short pause that followed, the Dean, riding as he had not ridden for years, was in their midst. Before they could check him the veteran cowman was beside Patches. With a quick motion he snatched the riata from the cowboy's neck. An instant more, and he had cut the rope that bound Patches' hands.

"Thank you, sir," said Patches calmly.

"Don't do that, Will," called Jim Reid peremptorily. "This is our business." In the same breath he shouted to his companions, "Take him again, boys," and started forward.

"Stand where you are," roared the Dean, and as they looked upon the stern countenance of the man who was so respected and loved throughout all that country, not a man moved. Reid himself involuntarily halted at the command.

"I'll do this and more, Jim Reid," said the Dean firmly, and there was that in his voice which, in the wild days of the past, had compelled many a man to fear and obey him. "It's my business enough that you can call this meetin' off right here. I'll be responsible for this man. You boys mean well, but you're a little mite too previous this trip."

"We aim to put a stop to that thievin' Tailholt Mountain outfit, Will," returned Reid, "an' we're goin' to do it right now."

A murmur of agreement came from the group.

The Dean did not give an inch. "You'll put a stop to nothin' this way; an' you'll sure start somethin' that'll be more than stealin' a few calves. The time for stringin' men up promiscuous like, on mere suspicion, is past in Arizona. I reckon there's more Cross-Triangle stock branded with the Tailholt Mountain iron than all the rest of you put together have lost, which sure entitles me to a front seat when it comes, to the showdown."

"He's right, boys," said one of the older men.

"You know I'm right, Tom," returned the Dean quickly. "You an' me have lived neighbors for pretty near thirty years, without ever a hard word passed between us, an' we've been through some mighty serious troubles together; an' you, too, George, an' Henry an' Bill. The rest of you boys I have known since you was little kids; an' me and your daddies worked an' fought side by side for decent livin' an' law-abidin' times before you was born. We did it 'cause we didn't want our children to go through with what we had to go through, or do some of the things that we had to do. An' now you're all thinkin' that you can cut me out of this. You think you can sneak out here before I'm out of my bed in the mornin', an' hang one of my own cowboys – as good a man as ever throwed a rope, too. Without sayin' a word to me, you come crawlin' right into my own corral, an' start to raisin' hell. I'm here to tell you that you can't do it. You can't do it because I won't let you."

The men, with downcast eyes, sat on their horses, ashamed. Two or three muttered approval. Jim Reid said earnestly, "That's all right, Will. We knew how you would feel, an' we were just aimin' to save you anymore trouble. Them Tailholt Mountain thieves have gone too far this time. We can't let you turn that man loose."

"I ain't goin' to try to turn him loose," retorted the Dean.

The men looked at each other.

"What are you goin' to do, then?" asked the spokesman.

"I'm goin' to make you turn him loose," came the startling answer. "You fellows took him; you've got to let him go."

In spite of the grave situation several of the men grinned at the Dean's answer – it was so like him.

"I'll bet a steer he does it, too," whispered one.

The Dean turned to the man by his side. "Patches, tell these men all that you told me about this business."

When the cowboy had told his story in detail, up to the point where Phil came upon the scene, the Dean interrupted him, "Now, get down there an' show us exactly how it happened after Phil rode on to you an' Yavapai Joe."

Patches obeyed. As he was showing them where Phil stood when the shot was fired the Dean again interrupted with, "Wait a minute. Tom, you get down there an' stand just as Phil was standin'."

The cattleman obeyed.

When he had taken the position, the Dean continued, "Now, Patches, stand like you was when Phil was hit."

Patches obeyed.

"Now, then, where did that shot come from?" asked the Dean.

Patches pointed.

The Dean did not need to direct the next step in his demonstration. Three of the men were already off their horses, and moving around the bushes indicated by Patches.

"Here's the tracks, all right," called one. "An' here," added another, from a few feet further away, "was where he left his horse."

"An' now," continued the Dean, when the three men had come back from behind the bushes, and with Patches had remounted their horses, "I'll tell you somethin' else. I had a talk with Phil himself, an' the boy's story agrees with what Patches has just told you in every point. An', furthermore, Phil told me straight when I asked him that he didn't know himself who fired that shot."

He paused for a moment for them to grasp the full import of his words. Then he summed up the case.

"As the thing stands, we've got no evidence against anybody. It can't be proved that the calf wasn't Nick's property in the first place. It can't be proved that Nick was anywhere in the neighborhood. It can't be proved who fired that shot. It could have been Yavapai Joe, or anybody else, just as well as Nick. Phil himself, by bein' too quick to jump at conclusions, blocked this man's game, just when he was playin' the only hand that could have won out against Nick. If Phil hadn't 'a' happened on to Patches and Joe when he did, or if he had been a little slower about findin' a man guilty just because appearances were against him, we'd 'a' had the evidence from Yavapai Joe that we've been wantin', an' could 'a' called the turn on that Tailholt outfit proper. As it stands now, we're right where we was before. Now, what are you all goin' to do about it?"

The men grinned shamefacedly, but were glad that the tragedy had been averted. They were by no means convinced that Patches was not guilty, but they were quick to see the possibilities of a mistake in the situation.

"I reckon the Dean has adjourned the meetin', boys," said one.

"Come on," called another. "Let's be ridin'."

When the last man had disappeared in the timber, the Dean wiped the perspiration from his flushed face, and looked at Patches thoughtfully. Then that twinkle of approval came into the blue eyes, that a few moments before had been so cold and uncompromising.

"Come, son," he said gently, "let's go to breakfast. Stella'll be wonderin' what's keepin' us."

Chapter XVI
THE SKY LINE

*B*efore their late breakfast was over at the Cross-Triangle Ranch, Helen Manning came across the valley meadows to help with the work of the household. Jimmy brought her, but when she saw that she was really needed, and that Mrs. Baldwin would be glad of her help, she told Jimmy that she would stay for the day. Someone from the Cross-Triangle, the Dean said, would take her home when she was ready to go.

The afternoon was nearly gone when Curly returned from the lower end of the valley with a woman who would relieve Mrs. Baldwin of the housework, and, as her presence was no longer needed, Helen told the Dean that she would return to the Reid home.

"I'll just tell Patches to take you over in the buckboard," said the Dean. "It was mighty kind of you to give us a hand today; it's been a big help to Stella and Kitty."

"Please don't bother about the buckboard, Mr. Baldwin. I would enjoy the walk so much. But I would be glad if Mr. Patches could go with me — I would really feel safer, you know," she smiled.

Mrs. Baldwin was sleeping and Kitty was watching beside Phil, so the Dean himself went as far as the wash with Helen and Patches, as the two set out for their walk across the meadows. When Helen had said good-bye to the Dean, with a promise to come again on the morrow, and he had turned back toward the house, she said to her companion, "Oh, Larry, I am so glad for this opportunity; I wanted to see you alone, and I couldn't think how it was to be managed. I have something to tell you, Larry, something that I *must* tell you, and you must promise to be very patient with me."

"You know what happened this morning, do you?" he asked gravely, for he thought from her words that she had, perhaps, chanced to hear of some further action to be taken by the suspicious cattlemen.

"It was terrible — terrible, Larry. Why didn't you tell them who you are? Why did you let them —" she could not finish.

He laughed shortly. "It would have been such a sinful waste of words. Can't you imagine me trying to make those men believe such a fairy story — under such circumstances?"

For a little they walked in silence; then he asked, "Is it about Jim Reid's suspicion that you wanted to see me, Helen?"

"No, Larry, it isn't. It's about Kitty," she answered.

"Oh!"

"Kitty told me all about it, today," Helen continued. "The poor child is almost beside herself."

The man did not speak. Helen looked up at him almost as a mother might have done.

"Do you love her so very much, Larry? Tell me truly, do you?"

Patches could not — dared not — look at her.

"Tell me, Larry," she insisted gently. "I must know. Do you love Kitty as a man ought to love his wife?"

The man answered in a voice that was low and shaking with emotion. "Why should you ask me such a question? You know the answer. What right have you to force me to tell you that which you already know — that I love you — another man's wife?"

Helen's face went white. In her anxiety for Kitty she, had not foreseen this situation in which, by her question, she had placed herself.

"Larry!" she said sharply.

"Well," he retorted passionately, "you insisted that I tell you the truth."

"I insisted that you tell me the truth about Kitty," she returned.

"Well, you have it," he answered quickly.

"Oh, Larry," she cried, "how could you — how could you ask a woman you do not love to be your wife? How could you do it, Larry? And just when I was so proud of you; so glad for you that you had found yourself; that you were such a splendid man!"

"Kitty and I are the best of friends," he answered in a dull, spiritless tone, "the best of companions. In the past year I have grown very fond of her — we have much in common. I can give her the life she desires — the life she is fitted for. I will make her happy; I will be true to her; I will be to her everything that a man should be to his wife."

"No, Larry," she said gently, touched by the hopelessness in his voice, for he had spoken as though he already knew that his attempt to justify his engagement to Kitty was vain. "No, Larry, you cannot be to Kitty everything that a man should be to his wife. You cannot, without love, be a husband to her."

Again they walked in silence for a little way. Then Helen asked: "And are you sure, Larry, that Kitty cares for you — as a woman ought to care, I mean?"

"I could not have asked her to be my wife if I had not thought so," he answered, with more spirit.

"Of course," returned his companion gently, "and Kitty could not have answered, 'yes,' if she had not believed that you loved her."

"Do you mean that you think Kitty does not care for me, Helen?"

"I *know* that she loves Phil Acton, Larry. I saw it in her face when we first learned that he was hurt. And today the poor girl confessed it. She loved him all the time, Larry — has loved him ever since they were boy and girl together. She has tried to deny her heart — she has tried to put other things above her love, but she knows now that she cannot. It is fortunate for you both that she realized her love for Mr. Acton before she had spoiled not only her own life but yours as well."

"But, how could she promise to be my wife when she loved Phil?" he demanded.

"But, how could you ask her when you —" Helen retorted quickly, without thinking of herself. Then she continued bravely, putting herself aside in her effort to make him understand. "You tempted her, Larry. You did not mean it so, perhaps, but you did. You tempted her with your wealth — with all that you could give her of material luxuries and ease and refinement. You tempted her to substitute those things for love. I know, Larry — I know, because you see, dear man, I was once tempted, too."

He made a gesture of protest, but she went on, "You did not know, but I can tell you now that nothing but the memory of my dear father's teaching saved me from a terrible mistake. You are a man now, Larry. You are more to me than any man in the world, save one; and more than any man in the world, save that one, I respect and admire you for the manhood you have gained. But oh, Larry, Larry, don't you see? *'When a man's a man'* there is one thing above all others that he cannot do. He cannot take advantage of a woman's weakness; he cannot tempt her beyond her strength; he must be strong both for himself and her; he must save her always from herself."

The man lifted his head and looked away toward Granite Mountain. As once before this woman had aroused him to assert his manhood's strength, she called now to all that was finest and truest in the depth of his being.

"You are always right, Helen," he said, almost reverently.

"No, Larry," she answered quickly, "but you know that I am right in this."

"I will free Kitty from her promise at once," he said, as though to end the matter.

Helen answered quickly. "But that is exactly what you must not do."

The man was bewildered. "Why, I thought — what in the world do you mean?"

She laughed happily as she said, "Stupid Larry, don't you understand? You must make Kitty send you about your business. You must save her self-respect. Can't you see how ashamed and humiliated she would be if she imagined for a moment that you did not love her? Think what she would suffer if she knew that you had merely tried to buy her with your wealth and the things you possess!"

She disregarded his protest.

"That's exactly what your proposal meant, Larry. A girl like Kitty, if she knew the truth of what she had done, might even fancy herself unworthy to accept her happiness now that it has come. You must make her dismiss you, and all that you could give her. You must make her proud and happy to give herself to the man she loves."

"But — what can I do?" he asked in desperation.

"I don't know, Larry. But you must manage somehow — for Kitty's sake you *must.*"

"If only the Dean had not interrupted the proceedings this morning, how it would have simplified everything!" he mused, and she saw that as always he was laughing at himself.

"Don't, Larry; please don't," she cried earnestly.

He looked at her curiously. "Would you have me lie to her, Helen — deliberately lie?"

She answered quietly. "I don't think that I would raise that question, if I were you, Larry — considering all the circumstances."

On his way back to the Cross-Triangle, Patches walked as a man who, having determined upon a difficult and distasteful task, is of a mind to undertake it without delay.

After supper that evening he managed to speak to Kitty when no one was near.

"I must see you alone for a few minutes tonight," he whispered hurriedly. "As soon as possible. I will be under the trees near the bank of the wash. Come to me as soon as it is dark, and you can slip away."

The young woman wondered at his manner. He was so hurried, and appeared so nervous and unlike himself.

"But, Patches, I —"

"You must!" he interrupted with a quick look toward the Dean, who was approaching them. "I have something to tell you — something that I must tell you tonight."

He turned to speak to the Dean, and Kitty presently left them. An hour later, when the night had come, she found him waiting as he had said.

"Listen, Kitty!" he began abruptly, and she thought from his manner and the tone of his voice that he was in a state of nervous fear. "I must go; I dare not stay here another day; I am going tonight."

"Why, Patches," she said, forcing herself to speak quietly in order to calm him. "What is the matter?"

"Matter?" he returned hurriedly. "You know what they tried to do to me this morning."

Kitty was shocked. It was true that she did not — could not — care for this man as she loved Phil, but she had thought him her dearest friend, and she respected and admired him. It was not good to find him now like this — shaken and afraid. She could not understand. For the moment her own trouble was put aside by her honest concern for him.

"But, Patches," she said earnestly, "that is all past now; it cannot happen again."

"You do not know," he returned, "or you would not feel so sure. Phil might —" He checked himself as if he feared to finish the sentence.

Kitty thought now that there must be more cause for his manner than she had guessed.

"But you are not a cattle thief," she protested. "You have only to explain who you are; no one would for a moment believe that Lawrence Knight could be guilty of stealing; it's ridiculous on the face of it!"

"You do not understand," he returned desperately. "There is more in this than stealing."

Kitty started. "You don't mean, Patches — you can't mean — Phil —" she gasped.

"Yes, I mean Phil," he whispered. "I — we were quarreling — I was angry. My God! girl, don't you see why I must go? I dare not stay. Listen, Kitty! It will be all right. Once I am out of this country and living under my own name I will be safe. Later you can come to me. You will come, won't you, dear? You know how I want you; this need make no change in our plans. If you love me you —"

She stopped him with a low cry. "And you — it was you who did that?"

"But I tell you we were quarreling, Kitty," he protested weakly.

"And you think that I could go to you now?" She was trembling with indignation. "Oh, you are so mistaken. It seems that I was mistaken, too. I never dreamed that you — nothing — nothing, that you could ever do would make me forget what you have told me. You are right to go."

"You mean that you will not come to me?" he faltered.

"Could you really think that I would?" she retorted.

"But, Kitty, you will let me go? You will not betray me? You will give me a chance?"

"It is the only thing that I can do," she answered coldly. "I should die of shame, if it were ever known that I had thought of being more to you than I have been; but you must go tonight."

And with this she left him, fairly running toward the house.

Alone in the darkness, Honorable Patches smiled mockingly to himself.

When morning came there was great excitement at the Cross-Triangle Ranch. Patches was missing. And more, the best horse in the Dean's outfit — the big bay with the blazed face, had also disappeared.

Quickly the news spread throughout the valley, and to the distant ranches. And many were the wise heads that nodded understandingly; and many were the "I told you so's." The man who had appeared among them so mysteriously, and who, for a year, had been a never-failing topic of conversation, had finally established his character beyond all question. But the cattlemen felt with reason, because of the Dean's vigorous defense of the man when they would have administered justice, that the matter was now in his hands. They offered their services, and much advice; they quietly joked about the price of horses; but the Dean laughed at their jokes, listened to their advice, and said that he thought the sheriff of Yavapai County could be trusted to handle the case.

To Helen only Kitty told of her last interview with Patches. And Helen, shocked and surprised at the thoroughness with which the man had brought about Kitty's freedom and peace of mind, bade the girl forget and be happy.

When the crisis was passed, and Phil was out of danger, Kitty returned to her home, but every day she and Helen drove across the meadows to see how the patient was progressing. Then one day Helen said good-bye to her Williamson Valley friends, and went with Stanford to the home he had prepared for her. And after that Kitty spent still more of her time at the house across the wash from the old Acton homestead.

It was during those weeks of Phil's recovery, while he was slowly regaining his full measure of health and strength, that Kitty learned to know the cowboy in a way that she had never permitted herself to know him before. Little by little, as they sat together under the walnut trees, or walked slowly about the place, the young woman came to understand the mind of the man. As Phil shyly at first, then more freely, opened the doors of his inner self and talked to her as he had talked to Patches of the books he had read; of his observations and thoughts of nature, and of the great world movements and activities that by magazines and books and papers were brought to his hand, she learned to her surprise that even as he lived amid the scenes that called for the highest type of physical strength and courage, he lived an intellectual life that was as marked for its strength and manly vigor.

But while they came thus daily into more intimate and closer companionship they spoke to no one of their love. Kitty, knowing how her father would look upon her engagement to the cowboy, put off the announcement from time to time, not wishing their happy companionship to be marred during those days of Phil's recovery.

When he was strong enough to ride again, Kitty would come with Midnight, and together they would roam about the ranch and the country near by. So it happened that Sunday afternoon. Mr. and Mrs. Reid, with the three boys, were making a neighborly call on the Baldwins, and Phil and Kitty were riding in the vicinity of the spot where Kitty had first met Patches.

They were seated in the shade of a cedar on the ridge not far from the drift fence gate, when Phil saw three horsemen approaching from the further side of the fence. By the time the horsemen had reached the gate, Phil knew them to be Yavapai Joe, Nick Cambert and Honorable Patches. Kitty, too, had, by this time, recognized the riders, and with an exclamation started to rise to her feet.

But Phil said quietly, "Wait, Kitty; there's something about that outfit that looks mighty queer to me."

The men were riding in single file, with Yavapai Joe in the lead and Patches last, and their positions were not changed when they halted while Joe, without dismounting, unlatched the gate. They came through the opening, still in the same order, and as they halted again, while Patches closed the gate, Phil saw what it was that caused them to move with such apparent lack of freedom in their relative positions, and why Nick Cambert's attitude in the saddle was so stiff and unnatural. Nick's hands were secured behind his back, and his feet were tied under the horse from stirrup to stirrup, while his horse was controlled by a lead rope, one end of which was made fast to Yavapai Joe's saddle horn.

Patches caught sight of the two under the tree as he came through the gate, but he gave no sign that he had noticed them. As the little procession moved slowly nearer, Phil and Kitty looked at each other without a word, but as they turned again to watch the approaching horsemen, Kitty impulsively grasped Phil's arm. And sitting so, in such unconscious intimacy, they must have made a pleasing picture; at least the man who rode behind Nick Cambert seemed to think so, for he was trying to smile.

When the riders were almost within speaking distance of the pair under the tree, they stopped; and the watchers saw Joe turn his face toward Patches for a moment, then look in their direction. Nick Cambert did not raise his head. Patches came on toward them alone.

As they saw that it was the man's purpose to speak to them, Phil and Kitty rose and stood waiting, Kitty with her hand still on her companion's arm. And now, as they were given a closer and less obstructed view of the man who had been their friend, Kitty and Phil again exchanged wondering glances. This was not the Honorable Patches whom they had known so intimately. The man's clothing was soiled with dirt, and old from rough usage, with here and there a ragged tear. His tall form drooped with weariness, and his unshaven face, dark and deeply tanned, and grimed with sweat and dirt, was thin and drawn and old, and his tired eyes, deep set in their dark hollows, were bloodshot as though from sleepless nights. His dry lips parted in a painful smile, as he dismounted stiffly and limped courteously forward to greet them.

"I know that I am scarcely presentable," he said in a voice that was as worn and old as his face, "but I could not resist the temptation to say 'Howdy'. Perhaps I should introduce myself though," he added, as if to save them from embarrassment. "My name is Lawrence Knight; I am a deputy sheriff of this county." A slight movement as he spoke threw back his unbuttoned jumper, and they saw the badge of his office. "In my official capacity I am taking a prisoner to Prescott."

Phil recovered first, and caught the officer's hand in a grip that told more than words.

Kitty nearly betrayed her secret when she gasped, "But you — you said that you —"

With his ready skill he saved her, "That my name was Patches? I know it was wrong to deceive you as I did, and I regret that it was necessary for me to lie so deliberately, but the situation seemed to demand it. And I hoped that when you understood you would forgive the part I was forced to play for the good of everyone interested."

Kitty understood the meaning in his words that was unknown to Phil, and her eyes expressed the gratitude that she could not speak.

"By the way," Patches continued, "I am not mistaken in offering my congratulations and best wishes, am I?"

They laughed happily.

"We have made no announcement yet," Phil answered, "but you seem to know everything."

"I feel like saying from the bottom of my heart 'God bless you, my children.' You make me feel strangely old," he returned, with a touch of his old wistfulness. Then he added in his droll way, "Perhaps, though, it's from living in the open and sleeping in my clothes so long. Talk about horses, I'd give my kingdom for a bath, a shave and a clean shirt. I had begun to think that our old friend Nick never would brand another calf; that he had reformed, just to get even with me, you know. By the way, Phil, you will be interested to know that Nick is the man who is really responsible for your happiness."

"How?" demanded Phil.

"Why, it was Nick who fired the shot that brought Kitty to her senses. My partner there, Yavapai Joe, saw him do it. If you people would like to thank my prisoner, I will permit it."

When they had decided that they would deny themselves that pleasure, Patches said, "I don't blame you; he's a surly, ill-tempered beast, anyway. Which reminds me that I must be about my official business, and land him in Prescott tonight. I am going to stop at the ranch and ask the Dean for the team and buckboard, though," he added, as he climbed painfully into the saddle. "Adios! my children. Don't stay out too late."

Hand in hand they watched him rejoin his companions and ride away behind the two Tailholt Mountain men.

The Dean and Mrs. Baldwin, with their friends from the neighboring ranch, were enjoying their Sunday afternoon together as old friends will, when the three Reid boys and Little Billy came running from the corral where they had been holding an amateur bronco riding contest with a calf for the wild and wicked outlaw. As they ran toward the group under the walnut trees, the lads disturbed the peaceful conversation of their

When a Man's a Man

elders with wild shouts of "Patches has come back! Patches has come back! Nick Cambert is with him — so's Yavapai Joe!"

Jim Reid sprang to his feet. But the Dean calmly kept his seat, and glancing up at his big friend with twinkling eyes, said to the boys, with pretended gruffness, "Aw, what's the matter with you kids? Don't you know that horse thief Patches wouldn't dare show himself in Williamson Valley again? You're havin' bad dreams — that's what's the matter with you. Or else you're tryin' to scare us."

"Honest, it's Patches, Uncle Will," cried Littly Billy.

"We seen him comin' from over beyond the corral," said Jimmy.

"I saw him first," shouted Conny. "I was up in the grand stand — I mean on the fence."

"Me, too," chirped Jack.

Jim Reid stood looking toward the corral. "The boys are right, Will," he said in a low tone. "There they come now."

As the three horsemen rode into the yard, and the watchers noted the peculiarity of their companionship, Jim Reid muttered something under his breath. But the Dean, as he rose leisurely to his feet, was smiling broadly.

The little procession halted when the horses evidenced their dislike of the automobile, and Patches came stiffly forward on foot. Lifting his battered hat courteously to the company, he said to the Dean, "I have returned your horse, sir. I'm very much obliged to you. I think you will find him in fairly good condition."

Jim Reid repeated whatever it was that he had muttered to himself.

The Dean chuckled. "Jim," he said to the big cattleman, "I want to introduce my friend, Mr. Lawrence Knight, one of Sheriff Gordon's deputies. It looks like he had been busy over in the Tailholt Mountain neighborhood."

The two men shook hands silently. Mrs. Reid greeted the officer cordially, while Mrs. Baldwin, to the Dean's great delight, demonstrated her welcome in the good old-fashioned mother way.

"Will Baldwin, I could shake you," she cried, as Patches stood, a little confused by her impulsive greeting. "Here you knew all the time; and you kept pesterin' me by trying to make me believe that you thought he had run away because he was a thief!"

It was, perhaps, the proudest moment of the Dean's life when he admitted that Patches had confided in him that morning when they were so late to breakfast. And how he had understood that the man's disappearance and the pretense of stealing a horse had been only a blind. The good Dean never dreamed that there was so much more in Honorable Patches' strategy than he knew!

"Mr. Baldwin," said Patches presently, "could you let me have the team and buckboard? I want to get my prisoners to Prescott tonight, and" — he laughed shortly — "well, I certainly would appreciate those cushions."

"Sure, son, you can have the whole Cross-Triangle outfit, if you want it," answered the Dean. "But hold on a minute." He turned with twinkling eyes to his neighbor. "Here's Jim with a perfectly good automobile that don't seem to be busy."

The big man responded cordially. "Why, of course; I'll be glad to take you in."

"Thank you," returned Patches. "I'll be ready in a minute."

"But you're goin' to have something to eat first," cried Mrs. Baldwin. "I'll bet you're half starved; you sure look it."

Patches shook his head. "Don't tempt me, mother; I can't stop now."

"But you'll come back home tonight, won't you?" she asked anxiously.

"I would like to," he said. "And may I bring a friend?"

"Your friends are our friends, son," she answered.

"Of course he's comin' back," said the Dean. "Where else would he go, I'd like to know?"

They watched him as he went to his prisoner, and as, unlocking the handcuff that held Nick's right wrist, he re-locked it on his own left arm, thus linking his prisoner securely to himself. Then he spoke to Joe, and the young man, dismounting, unfastened the rope that bound Nick's feet. When Nick was on the ground the three came toward the machine.

"I am afraid I must ask you to let someone take care of the horses," called Patches to the Dean.

"I'll look after them," the Dean returned. "Don't forget now that you're comin' back tonight; Jim will bring you."

Jim Reid, as the three men reached the automobile, said to Patches, "Will you take both of your prisoners in the back seat with you, or shall I take one of them in front with me?"

Patches looked the big man straight in the eyes, and they heard him answer with significant emphasis, as he placed his free hand on Yavapai Joe's shoulder, "I have only one prisoner, Mr. Reid. This man is my friend. He will take whatever seat he prefers."

Yavapai Joe climbed into the rear seat with the officer and his prisoner.

It was after dark when Mr. Reid returned to the ranch with Patches and Joe.

"You will find your room all ready, son," said Mrs. Baldwin, "and there's plenty of hot water in the bathroom tank for you both. Joe can take the extra bed in Curly's room. You show him. I'll have your supper as soon as you are ready."

Patches almost fell asleep at the table. As soon as they had finished he went to his bed, where he remained, as Phil reported at intervals during the next forenoon, "dead to the world," until dinner time. In the afternoon they gathered under the walnut trees — the Cross-Triangle household and the friends from the neighboring ranch — and Patches told them his story; how, when he had left the ranch that night, he had ridden straight to his old friend Stanford Manning; and how Stanford had gone with him to the sheriff, where, through Manning's influence, together with the letter which Patches had brought from the Dean, he had been made an officer of the law. As he told them briefly of his days and nights alone, they needed no minute details to understand what it had meant to him.

"It wasn't the work of catching Nick in a way to ensure his conviction that I minded," he said, "but the trouble was, that while I was watching Nick day and night, and dodging him all the time, I was afraid some enthusiastic cow-puncher would run on to me and treat himself to a shot just for luck. Not that I would have minded that so much, either, after the first week," he added in his droll way, "but considering all the circumstances it would have been rather a poor sort of finish."

"And what about Yavapai Joe?" asked Phil.

Patches smiled. "Where is Joe? What's he been doing all day?"

The Dean answered. "He's just been moseyin' around. I tried to get him to talk, but all he would say was that he'd rather let Mr. Knight tell it."

"Billy," said Patches, "will you find Yavapai Joe, and tell him that I would like to see him here?"

When Little Billy, with the assistance of Jimmy and Conny and Jack, had gone proudly on his mission, Patches said to the others, "Technically, of course, Joe is my prisoner until after the trial, but please don't let him feel it. He will be the principal witness for the state."

When Yavapai Joe appeared, embarrassed and ashamed in their presence, Patches said, as courteously as he would have introduced an equal, "Joe, I want my friends to know your real name. There is no better place in the world than right here to start that job of man-making that we have talked about. You remember that I told you how I started here."

Yavapai Joe lifted his head and stood straighter by his tall friend's side, and there was a new note in his voice as he answered, "Whatever you say goes, Mr. Knight."

Patches smiled. "Friends, this is Mr. Joseph Parkhill, the only son of the distinguished Professor Parkhill, whom you all know so well."

If Patches had planned to enjoy the surprise his words caused, he could not have been disappointed.

Presently, when Joe had slipped away again, Patches told them how, because of his interest in the young man, and because of the lad's strange knowledge of Professor Parkhill, he had written east for the distinguished scholar's history.

"The professor himself was not really so much to blame," said Patches. "It seems that he was born to an intellectual life. The poor fellow never had a chance. Even as a child he was exhibited as a prodigy — a shining example of the possibilities of the race, you know. His father, who was also a professor of some sort, died when he was a baby. His mother, unfortunately, possessed an income sufficient to make it unnecessary that Everard Charles should ever do a day's real work. At the age of twenty, he was graduated from college; at the age of twenty-one he was married to — or perhaps it would be more accurate to say — he was married *by* — his landlady's daughter. Quite likely the woman was ambitious to break into that higher life to which the professor aspired, and caught her cultured opportunity in an unguarded moment. The details are not clear. But when their only child, Joe, was six years old, the mother ran away with a carpenter who had been at work on the house for some six weeks. A maiden aunt of some fifty years, who was a worshiper of the professor's cult, came to keep his house and to train Joe in the way that good boys should go.

"But the lad proved rather too great a burden, and when he was thirteen they sent him to a school out here in the West, ostensibly for the benefit of the climate. The boy, it was said, being of abnormal mentality, needed to pursue his studies under the most favorable physical conditions. The professor, unhampered by his offspring, continued to climb his aesthetic ladder to intellectual and cultured glory. The boy in due time escaped from the school, and was educated by the man Dryden and Nick Cambert."

"And what will become of him now?" asked the Dean.

Patches smiled. "Why, the lad is twenty-one now, and we have agreed that it is about time that he began to make a man of himself — I can help him a little, perhaps — I have been trying occasionally the past year. But you see the conditions have not been altogether favorable to the experiment. It should be easy from now on."

During the time that intervened before the trial of the Tailholt Mountain man, Phil and Patches re-established that intimate friendship of those first months of their work together. Then came the evening when Phil went across the meadow to ask Jim Reid for his daughter.

The big cattleman looked at his young neighbor with frowning disapproval.

"It won't do, Phil," he said at last. "I'm Kitty's father, and it's up to me to look out for her interests. You know how I've educated her for something better than this life. She may think now that she is willin' to throw it all away, but I know better. The time would come when she would be miserable. It's got to be somethin' more than a common cow-puncher for Kitty, Phil, and that's the truth."

The cowboy did not argue. "Do I understand that your only objection is based upon the business in which I am engaged?" he asked coolly.

Jim laughed. "The *business* in which you are engaged? Why, boy, you sound like a first national bank. If you had any business of your own — if you was the owner of an outfit, an' could give Kitty the — well — the things her education has taught her to need, it would be different. I know you're a fine man, all right, but you're only a poor cow-puncher just the same. I'm speakin' for your own good, Phil, as well as for Kitty's," he added, with an effort at kindliness.

"Then, if I had a good business, it would be different?"

"Yes, son, it would sure make all the difference in the world."

"Thank you," said the cowboy quietly, as he handed Mr. Reid a very legal looking envelope. "I happen to be half owner of this ranch and outfit. With my own property, it makes a fairly good start for a man of my age. My partner, Mr. Lawrence Knight, leaves the active management wholly in my hands; and he has abundant capital to increase our holdings and enlarge our operations just as fast as we can handle the business."

The big man looked from the papers to the lad, then back to the papers. Then a broad smile lighted his heavy face, as he said, "I give it up — you win. You young fellers are too swift for me. I've been wantin' to retire anyway." He raised his voice and called, "Kitty — oh, Kitty!"

The girl appeared in the doorway.

"Come and get him," said Reid. "I guess he's yours."

Helen Manning was sitting on the front porch of that little cottage on the mountain side where she and Stanford began their years of home-building. A half mile below she could see the mining buildings that were grouped about the shaft in picturesque disorder. Above, the tree-clad ridge rose against the sky. It was too far from the great world of cities, some would have said, but Helen did not find it so. With her books and her music, and the great out-of-doors; and with the companionship of her mate and the dreams they dreamed together, her woman heart was never lonely.

She lowered the book she was reading, and looked through the open window to the clock in the living room. A little while, and she would go down the hill to Stanford, for they loved to walk home together. Then, before lifting the printed page again, she looked over the wide view of rugged mountain sides and towering peaks that every day held for her some new beauty. She had resumed her reading when the sound of horses' feet attracted her attention.

Patches and Yavapai Joe were riding up the hill.

They stopped at the gate, and while Joe held Stranger's bridle rein, Patches came to Helen as she stood on the porch waiting to receive him.

"Surely you will stay for the night," she urged when they had exchanged greetings, and had talked for a little while.

"No," he answered quietly. "I just came this way to say good-bye; I stopped for a few minutes with Stan at the office. He said I would find you here."

"But where are you going?" she asked.

Smiling he waved his hand toward the mountain ridge above. "Just over the sky line, Helen."

"But, Larry, you will come again? You won't let us lose you altogether?"

"Perhaps — some day," he said.

"And who is that with you?"

"Just a friend who cares to go with me. Stan will tell you."

"Oh, Larry, Larry! What a man you are!" she cried proudly, as he stood before her holding out his hand.

"If you think so, Helen, I am glad," he answered, and turned away.

So she watched him go. Sitting there at home, she watched him ride up the winding road. Now he was in full view on some rocky shoulder of the mountain — now some turn carried him behind a rocky point — again she glimpsed him through the trees — again he was lost to her in the shadows. At last, for a moment, he stood out boldly against the wide-arched sky — and then he had passed from sight — over the sky line, as he had said.

Printed in the United States
75250LV00006B/77